HEAVEN

David Pettyfer is taking a shortcut over the dark rooftops of London's brooding houses, when he stumbles across Heaven: a strange, beautiful, distraught girl who says that bad men have stolen her heart. Yet she's still alive.

So begins David and Heaven's wild and mysterious journey – to find Heaven's heart, and to discover the incredible truth about her origins…

HEAVEN

CHRISTOPH MARZI

ORCHARD

ORCHARD BOOKS
338 Euston Road, London NW1 3BH
Orchard Books Australia
Level 17/207 Kent Street, Sydney, NSW 2000

First published in Germany in 2009 by Arena Verlag GmbH,
Würzburg under the original title *Heaven. Stadt der Feen*
English translation first published in the UK in 2012 by Orchard Books

Published by arrangement with Rights People, London

ISBN 978 1 40831 466 1

Original German text © Christoph Marzi 2009
English language translation © Helena Ragg-Kirkby 2012

A CIP catalogue record for this book is available from the British Library.

1 3 5 7 9 10 8 6 4 2

Printed in Great Britain

Orchard Books is a division of Hachette Children's Books,
an Hachette UK company.

www.hachette.co.uk

For Catharina,
who is just the right age to read it,
and for Lucia and Stella,
who still have a few years to wait.

When there's 'ardly no day nor
'ardly no night
There's things 'alf in shadow
and 'alfway in light
On the rooftops of London
coo, what a sight!

Chim Chim Cher-ee
Richard M. Sherman and Robert B. Sherman

PROLOGUE

The night that Heaven lost her heart was cold and moonless. But the blade that sliced it out was warm with her dark blood. Forlorn, bewildered and throbbing fearfully, the heart was mirrored in the curved, silvery knife. Fingers encased in gloves made of shiny black leather held the heart up before a face that wore an expression of the utmost satisfaction.

This wasn't the first heart the man had stolen. And he wasn't alone. Lurking in the shadows was a second man, a raggedy tramp of a figure who limped over when motioned to do so.

They were all on a roof. A keen wind blew around them, and wisps of smoke from the chimneys hung in the air like living creatures. This particular dark-tiled roof belonged to number 16 Phillimore Place, which lay between Holland Park and Kensington Gardens. It offered a splendid view of the city, but neither of the figures on the roof was interested in the view. Instead, they were staring at the body that lay motionless at their feet.

The girl was young, and her jet-black hair was wet from the puddles on the roof. Her dark skin shimmered in the night; tears glistened on her cheeks.

The tall man, who was known by different names in different parts of London, had that evening set off to find a heart in Chelsea. He had first spotted the girl in Wilton Crescent, and had followed her for the next two hours. His raggedy companion, who looked like a mangy dog in his shabby old clothes, had picked up the scent in Sloane Square – and there was no escape then. The girl – a young woman, in fact, who would once upon a time undoubtedly have been referred to as 'Miss' in Hampstead – had been wandering the streets alone, heading for nowhere obvious. She had walked down Brompton Road, looked in the window of Harrods, and then had a snack in the Bunch of Grapes. Then she'd headed northwards towards Kensington Gardens, but instead of entering the park, she'd set off in the direction of Notting Hill. Outside High Street Kensington station, she had run into a group of teenagers who seemed to know her. They'd exchanged a few words (words that didn't seem to interest the girl much) and one of them, a young man whose tiepin

8

bore the crest of some posh private school, had called the girl by name: Heaven.

Her nocturnal pursuer, who had sharp eyes and ears, thought that Heaven was an odd name for a young girl, but it wasn't his job to worry about things like names. Names were but sound and smoke. He just wanted her heart.

The girl had stopped outside 16 Phillimore Place and looked up at the roof. Then she'd fiddled around with the lock. She was clearly trying to get into a house that was nothing to do with her. Then she'd darted through the door.

The raggedy man and Mr Drood, as the tall man called himself when he was out and about in Kensington, had watched the whole thing. They followed her like beasts of prey in the night. Through the door, into the house, up the stairs, and onto the roof.

She had taken a long object out of the rucksack that she'd been carrying. It was a telescope, which she hurriedly set up on the roof of the house. She stood there looking at the stars. At least there were stars here.

Then Mr Drood and the raggedy man had suddenly appeared. She hadn't heard them coming. Nobody ever did. Mr Drood and the raggedy man were like cats in the night, their boots like velvet paws. If someone needed a secret service, they rang Mr Drood or one of the many other names that he went by. They whispered their problem to him, and he did their bidding. That included stealing hearts.

Mr Drood was cunning. He always worked with someone who was able to scent a trail. This particular raggedy man would soon disintegrate; he'd have to find another one then.

Whatever. The graveyards were full of them.

Life, mused Mr Drood, could be so easy. Funny that nobody else realised it.

He allowed his thin lips to twist themselves into a smile, and looked at the heart in his hands. It looked just like all the others he'd stolen. He took pleasure in slicing them from their bodies. As a child, he had sold cat skins to the traders in Whitechapel: he'd used just the same knife as he used now. His client would be pleased. All his clients were pleased with his work.

He'd already got hold of several hearts. The girl was his latest victim. Mr Drood knew that his client wouldn't be satisfied with any old heart. Even just selecting the right heart took patience. Hence the raggedy man. It had to be a healthy heart, one that wasn't unhappy. The dead quickly sense when living hearts are happy. Presumably because they are dead and long for a warm, beating heart.

This dead man had done Mr Drood's bidding. They had found the heart; Mr Drood had drawn the blade, had made a long incision, and had taken it out. It was quite straightforward, and the more often one did it, the easier it became.

Heaven's heart was no exception.

But then something happened that didn't normally happen. Something that couldn't, in fact, happen.

The young woman, who had seconds ago been lying there motionless and dying (yes, dying: Mr Drood was quite sure of it); that young woman with the odd name of Heaven and the even odder habit of clambering up onto strange roofs to look at the stars; his victim – who was no different from any of his other victims – suddenly jumped up and began to run away.

Mr Drood stood stock still. This was a completely new experience. Nobody ran off when they had had their heart cut out.

But Heaven did.

She ran for her life.

Baffled, but quite calm, Mr Drood watched her go. There was no point following her. He had got what he came for.

As for the raggedy man: he could follow a scent, but he was no hunter. He'd been dead for far too long to be able to chase the girl.

Anyway, thought Mr Drood, girls running away after they've lost their hearts isn't normally part of the deal. Just to be sure he wasn't imagining things, he looked again at the heart in his hands. Then he shook his head and put it into the big leather pouch that he'd had specially made for the purpose by a furrier in Soho.

The raggedy man emitted a noise that sounded like a dry cough.

'We've got what we need,' said Mr Drood.

The raggedy man, whose clothes had dry earth clinging to them, made no reply. They both watched the girl as she ran off into the distance, and as her silhouette vanished in the darkness they set off on their own way. For the night was still young – and Mr Drood and the raggedy man had not yet entirely carried out the task that had brought them to Kensington.

CHAPTER 1

It wasn't the first time he'd been out at night, and he knew the roofs well in this area. He quite often chose the route that took him across tiles and chimneypots: some days (or some nights) it was quicker.

That night, David Pettyfer had tied his scarf tightly round his neck, pulled up the collar of his grubby old leather jacket, and shouldered his patched bag. He'd checked one last time to make sure the valuable cargo was safely tucked inside, and then he'd set out into the night. He liked these night-time expeditions: the city seemed different when the sun wasn't out. The lights wove a mysterious magic in the streets and alleyways before dissolving in the wispy veil of fog and drizzle that was so typical of London. Everything seemed enchanted in its own dirty way: as if the fairy tales that small children believed in had somehow come of age.

David liked the smell of the city.

David liked London.

The only thing he'd never really got used to was the

completely starless sky in the centre of the city. For as long as he could remember, the night sky there had puzzled humans – but since nobody had ever worked out the answers, they'd mostly learnt to live with it. For some reason, though, he couldn't accept it. His mate Mike had taken the piss out of him often enough for it.

David pushed his mop of brown hair off his forehead so that it stood up at the front. In the distance, the dome of St Paul's was shrouded in total darkness. There wasn't the tiniest flicker of light in the blackness.

The nocturnal cacophony on Kensington High Street wafted through the air. The true music of the night, or so it seemed.

David made his way across the crenellations, gutters and narrow pathways between the roofs, taking particular care on the slippery parts that shimmered in the drizzle. As in all the parts of London that were just beyond the centre, the stars were twinkling and the moon was shining. That wasn't the only reason he liked being out here.

Before he'd started running errands, David could never have imagined how many people lived up above the city roofs. A whole new world had opened up to him, full of hidden paths, ladders and inclines; narrow passageways and bits that jutted out to make something like bridges. There were stairwells that were always open, and trees that he could use to cross the street canyons. But there were also downwinds up there, sudden gusts. One false step could send him plunging down into the nearest abyss.

Something was sticking out from the wall, and David used it to swing himself across to the next roof. As always, he was wearing red Converse. Everything else was black. Hoodie, jeans, belt: all black. Again, as always.

His customer would be getting impatient. The valuable cargo that David was carrying was the French de luxe edition of Walter Scott's *Bride of Lammermoor*, published in 1886 by Firmin-Didot and illustrated by Brown, Godefroy and a whole host of other artists. A UPS courier had brought it into the bookshop earlier that evening, complete with a mountain of paperwork for them to sign. And Miss Trodwood, the owner of The Owl and the Pussycat, had insisted that David deliver the goods to Kensington that very night. Customers who ordered this kind of book didn't want to wait any longer than absolutely necessary.

David had taken the Tube to Kensington High Street, but had decided to make the rest of the journey up here. He wasn't a great fan of the Tube. He could do without the feeling of being trapped underground. As so often, he'd decided instead to dodge the chimney sweeps out in the fresh air, where he could keep a clear head.

And that was something he particularly needed today. For days, David had been bothered by something he'd rather forget. He was of course well aware that his problems weren't exactly going to change the world or alter the course of humankind.

No: what was bothering him was utterly banal. Just the same old stuff that bothers all teenagers.

He was seventeen years old and had realised that he didn't love the woman he'd been having a rather anguished sort-of-relationship with for the past two months. David knew that the BBC could have turned his relationship into a TV drama to rival *EastEnders*, but he didn't want to allow the whole business any more space in his life than it deserved.

He'd made a mistake, and so had Kelly.

He crash-landed on a roof on Phillimore Walk, used a chimney as a swinging-post, and carried on running along the sloping paths used by the chimney sweeps.

When he was running across the rooftops, he was

very conscious of the way that people spend most of their lives hovering over an abyss that's just waiting to destroy them. David was well aware of how easy it would be to lose his footing and go plunging down, down, to where humans looked like dots, scurrying around pursuing their goals like little ants. He knew how close he had been to the edge and that it was time to land on firm ground. And that meant steering clear of Kelly Robertson.

He stopped for a moment, breathing deeply.

In summer, the trees were so green that it looked as if there were actual fields and forests growing high above the city. Now, though, skeletal branches tapped gutters down which cold rivulets of water were splashing. It was dangerous up here in heavy rain, but the risk was relatively small in drizzle or fog.

Up in the sky, a shooting star soared over towards Bloomsbury. Its shimmering tail, as delicate as fresh words quilled on parchment, glowed briefly but brightly above the rooftops and, at that moment before it completely vanished, looked like an illuminated bird flying across to Regent's Park.

Magic. It was said that there were people who believed in it, David thought with a sigh. He really was in a weird mood this evening. Mike would probably put it down to being stressed out about his relationship and would tell him to pop a couple of pills. But that was all in the past, even if he did sometimes long for the kick. Or, rather, for something that would make him forget.

David had grown up and gone to school in Cardiff. On his fifteenth birthday, he'd crept out of the house and had gone to the cinema alone to see *Logan's Run*. That film had really opened his eyes. It was about people being prisoners in a perfect world.

David had felt as if for the first time he was seeing the world as it really was. Humans were blind and selfish. Stupid. Ignorant. In the end, there had been problems lurking everywhere: at school, on the streets and, of course, at home. He knew that the problems had been there all along: nobody could have missed them. But until then, he'd just tried to ignore them and live with them like his father and little sister Geraldine did.

In the end, as the walls closed in on him ever more, he'd lapsed into more or less total silence. Barely anyone could get a word out of him: just meagre fragments, half-sentences. Even when he was having one of his frequent rows with his father, he would sometimes just stop mid-sentence and walk off. He spent less and less time with his friends who were all just like him: they wore black, read American comics, and didn't give a toss about football. They smoked whatever was going, stole in order to get more stuff, and lived a life that they couldn't care less about.

Then came the night when David packed his bag. He hadn't planned it: it was just something he had to do. He'd not written any goodbye letters or anything. He'd just left a note for his sister: the lyrics to a Divine Comedy song, which he'd hidden in the tatty booklet of one of her favourite albums.

Then he'd taken the train to London without having a clue whether he'd feel any less hemmed in there. He'd had enough money to spend a week in an ancient B&B in Ludgate Hill for ten pounds a night.

He'd started by eking out a living. He'd been an errand boy in the skyless city. He'd served in pubs in Notting Hill. He'd been a temp in a warehouse down at the docks in Rotherhithe. Gradually, he'd slid into taking on dodgy jobs to get money more quickly. Not to mention stuff. That was the time when he'd only hung out with Mike and the others. Too many months that he didn't necessarily want to relive.

Then two things had suddenly happened that would change David's life forever.

Firstly, he'd come across The Owl and the Pussycat.

In London, he'd become accustomed to running around the city, carried along by the tumult of the traffic. He would just set off to nowhere in particular, as if he were running away from something that he couldn't quite name. And so it happened that one day he was wandering around the Seven Dials area, near Charing Cross Road. Just a bit further on, in Earlham Street, he found himself outside a bookshop called The Owl and the Pussycat, which had an advert in the window. It was just a simple little notice, squashed between piles of books. And it was straight and to the point: *Miss Trodwood seeks assistant.*

That was precisely what was handwritten on the scruffy bit of paper. She wanted a general assistant. Not an apprentice, not a bookseller, not a temp: no, an assistant. And she was offering a proper wage and accommodation.

David didn't waste a second. The wording spoke straight to his heart. He went into the shop and, after a brief chat, was offered the job. Miss Trodwood, a proper old lady like in a Jane Austen or Agatha Christie novel, showed him his room on the first floor, right above the shop. David gave notice on his bed in the hostel and moved into Earlham Street.

That was the first thing that happened.

The second thing was this:

David was just congratulating himself on the great turnaround in his life when he stole a CD from the Virgin Megastore at Piccadilly Circus – and was caught.

Even now, he couldn't say why he'd done it. Habit, stupidity, cockiness, boredom – whatever. The CD had made its way into his bag just on the spur of the moment. He'd liked the cover and, of course, the music. But that didn't matter. The only thing that mattered was that he was caught. Yes, he and Mike had spent months pushing drugs in East End clubs – and now he was going to get done for nicking a £3.99 CD.

It was the job at Miss Trodwood's that ultimately saved his neck. He had a fixed address, a proper job, and wasn't on the streets.

But he had attracted the authorities' attention. The social worker who was now supposed to be keeping an eye on him kept coming into the shop. Miss Robinson – 'Call me Kelly!' – started chatting to him, and they would sometimes go for coffee at the organic café in Cambridge Circus. She'd observe him closely and make notes in a brown book.

One evening David discovered that social

workers hang out in Clerkenwell clubs too. Kelly was twenty-eight, blonde, and liked The Clash, U2 and Leonard Cohen. He'd encountered her in Bones; they'd spotted one another through the flashing lights and had danced to Tindersticks, Glasvegas, The Cure and Muse.

David did have a feeling that a first kiss to the sound of Linkin' Park really wasn't a very good omen.

'This is probably a mistake,' she'd whispered, her perfume drowning out the music.

'Mistakes,' David had replied, 'are there to be made.' Then they'd disappeared into the loos. Blue light, muffled music through the walls, hasty movements. He pressed her up against the wall as Marilyn Manson sang 'Tainted Love'.

And so it began.

He and Kelly had become something along the lines of a secret couple and David enjoyed the feeling of not being alone, even if they didn't have much to say to one another. Kelly, though, started to be plagued by guilt, and she was anxious that someone might find out about them – which would land her in a whole load of trouble.

She was his social worker; he was still underage.

'We have to stop seeing one another,' she said.

Not over the phone, but in bed.

'Why?'

'Because it's wrong.'

'And you didn't think of that before?'

She'd turned away. 'It's always been wrong.'

'But you've enjoyed it.'

Her eyes flashed angrily. 'I'm not the only one.'

He stood up and got dressed. A cheap Kandinsky print hung above her TV: all corners and angles and cold colours. He took a glass from the table and hurled it at the picture. The frame smashed, and the fragments fell to the ground. Kelly didn't say a word. Then David left the flat and didn't return.

A gust of wind whistled through his hair and blew the drizzle, which was unusually cold for a London November, into his face. It didn't bother him. He looked down at the traffic far below on Kensington High Street. There they were, all these people scurrying about their own lives – and then it sometimes happened that two of them got to know one another. And did things that made their lives better, or that they regretted even before the night was over.

David shook his head. OK, he hadn't loved Kelly. She was just one of the few people in London who'd been kind to him. Basically, though, he didn't care about her. And staying with her really would have been asking for trouble. But nevertheless, he felt kind of – empty. Why couldn't he just get her out of his head, for God's sake?

He took a deep breath, tightened his scarf, and set off again. His customer, Mr Merryweather, who lived at 18 Phillimore Place and was an ardent fan of Walter Scott, would be smoking his pipe and scratching his sideburns, waiting for Miss Trodwood's find.

A good ten metres up above the street, David rounded the block of houses with the poplars in the courtyard and arrived at Essex Villa, one block away from his destination. The roofs here were somewhat flatter, so he could speed up. Shortly afterwards, he found himself at the narrow gap that separated numbers 16 and 18 Phillimore Place. David narrowed his eyes and jumped across. He'd often thought of replacing his perilously skiddy Converse with some more sensible shoes, but he liked his old favourites too much.

The momentum of his leap carried him forwards. He made a grab for a lightning conductor that was sticking out of the roof and held tightly on to it, which slowed him down.

Then he felt resistance where he hadn't expected it.

He stumbled and fell head over heels over a girl crouching on the roof next to an old telescope. He hadn't seen her in the twilight – and, in any case, he hadn't been expecting to bump into anyone up here.

Dark skin, long dark hair.

He took that in, but then he'd passed her. He skidded across the roof, feeling a sharp pain in his shoulder.

His hands flailed in the emptiness. He paddled with his arms, trying to get a grip on the wet tiles. His fingers scratched at the rough surface of the old roof covering, clawing desperately – every second felt like an eternity. Finally he found himself lying skewed, clinging on to something that was sticking out.

He lay there motionless for a moment. His panting broke the silence.

God, that was close! How could he have been so careless? He lifted his head and looked cautiously over the precipice. You couldn't say that the old houses in this part of Kensington, built at the turn of the century before last, were particularly tall – David was used to much higher ones – but a drop of just two or three storeys would still be enough to kill him.

Slowly, he struggled to his knees and looked around.

18 Phillimore Place had a pointy roof with several bay windows, but slightly higher up, where the girl was kneeling, was a flat bit that stuck out like a small balcony. A low wall separated it from the rest of the roof. The ground was wet with drizzle, and smoke billowed out of the neighbouring chimneys like dark fog.

The girl looked up and stared at him with her dark eyes.

'What the hell are you doing up here?' asked David.

'I…' She swallowed the words back down. Then she looked around wildly, as if she were looking for someone. She gave the impression of being caught red-handed.

'Is everything OK?' David asked mechanically. He checked his bag and was relieved to see that Walter Scott was still safely tucked inside.

'No.' She shook her head. 'Not really.'

He clambered up and knelt down beside her. 'Have you hurt yourself?'

'No, you just tripped over me. It didn't hurt.'

I'm not so sure, he thought, but bit back the remark.

'How did you get up here?' he asked instead.

'I broke in,' she replied.

'You broke in?' He raised an eyebrow disbelievingly and squatted down on the edge of the little wall. He looked at her closely for a moment as he rubbed his sore shoulder.

David was used to sizing people up, and his first impressions tended to be right.

The girl seemed tall – almost as tall as he was – and slim, like someone who didn't have to play a lot of sport to look good. When she moved, it was rather like an irresistible melody. And she was gorgeous. Not gorgeous as in 'good looking', but breathtakingly gorgeous.

She had classical features. Her olive skin shimmered in the moonlight, and her long, loose hair tumbled down her back.

She was simply dressed in clothes that weren't exactly warm for the time of year. As if she'd not given any particular thought to what she was going to wear. But they were evidently expensive. Her boots probably cost as much as he earned in six months at Miss Trodwood's.

'You broke in?' he repeated doubtfully, when she still didn't say anything.

'Yes, downstairs. Through the door, dead easy. Up the stairs and…' She gave him a tired look.

'I wanted to see the stars,' she said.

Well, that's pretty vague, thought David, looking at the telescope. It was lying there, smashed, its fragments lying all over the roof.

'Can you help me?' she asked. She seemed to be recovering her composure bit by bit.

With what? he wondered.

At the same time, though, he somehow found himself nodding.

She tried to get up, but staggered. David jumped up and helped her to her feet. She was very light.

'You're freezing,' he said as her hand touched his.

'Someone's after me,' she said. 'Up here.'

'Someone?'

'Men.'

David suppressed a groan. That's all he needed! A run-in with a bunch of guys: he could most definitely do without that. Or – he corrected himself secretly – he *should* do without it. Unless he wanted another social worker to pay him a visit.

'Which men?' he asked.

'Bad men.'

David only just managed not to roll his eyes. Oh, this was a classic!

'You mean bad men, like in a fairy story?'

She didn't bat an eyelid. 'One man with gloves, and a bloke in rags.'

Aha. Gloves and rags. 'And what did they want with you?'

'I think they stole my heart.' Her eyes were so dark that he could barely see them.

'What do you mean?'

'Exactly what I said.' She touched her chest. 'There's no heart there.' She was trying not to cry now as she fumbled anxiously with the zip of her jacket. 'He cut it out.' She swallowed. 'But there's no wound there. I…I've looked.'

David stared at her.

'Here!' She suddenly moved closer to him and grabbed his hand. Then she opened her jacket and put his hand on her chest without taking her eyes off him.

David felt himself going red. His hand clearly didn't belong where she'd put it. He looked into her dark eyes, and then he felt it beneath her thin cotton shirt.

There was her rhythmic breathing, the soft up and down of her breast, and beneath the icy cold that her skin seemed to give off, he could clearly feel it.

Or, rather: he couldn't feel it.

He jerked his hand away.

'See?' She sounded desperate now. 'I was up here. They came up behind me and grabbed me. The guy with the gloves had the knife. Afterwards I just ran away, down from the roof, into the streets, anywhere. I don't think they followed me.'

David just carried on staring at her, trying to read her eyes in the darkness. What he saw was real fear. Mortal fear.

'Why did you come back?' He couldn't think of anything better to ask. Because the whole situation was so crazy that he felt he had to offer at least something.

She stroked the broken telescope at her side. 'I didn't want to leave this behind. My father gave it to me. It means a lot to me.'

David shook his head. This was the craziest thing that had ever happened to him.

'Nobody can live without a heart,' he said, suppressing the thought that he should have been able to feel her heartbeat. His hand had been directly on her breast; he would have been able to feel it through the thin fabric. But all the same, it was impossible.

'Nobody can live without a heart,' he repeated. 'Never mind run.'

'I know,' she said, looking crushed. Tears were

dripping down her face and turning into frozen ice crystals. She wiped them away. 'But I'm here, aren't I? And I'm alive?'

David looked at her. She was wearing a dark green jacket. The zip was still open, her orange shirt visible underneath.

'I'm David.' He thought it was time to introduce himself. It might bring some kind of order to the whole business.

'Heaven,' she said.

He looked at her.

'No jokes about my name,' she pleaded.

David shrugged. 'Wouldn't have occurred to me.'

They stood there silently for a while. It felt to David as if hours had passed, although it was presumably only seconds that had fluttered by. The cold drizzle started up again, and the light mist which accompanied it turned into a curtain of dense silk.

David thought feverishly. What should he do? Something had happened to this girl, and he hadn't a clue what it was. Who knew what she was on? Or had the men really been up here with her? What if they'd assaulted her and the shock was making her say crazy things?

'I'd better take you to a hospital.' That was the best he could think of.

She nodded. 'Would you mind?'

'St Mary Abbot's is nearest.' He pointed south above the long roofs. 'It's just over there.'

She allowed herself a small smile. 'Didn't Jimi Hendrix end up there?'

David shrugged. 'That doesn't mean anything.'

She suddenly became agitated again. 'Can we go now?' she urged. She gazed across the rooftops like a frightened rabbit.

'What about the men?' he asked. 'Do you know why they were after you?'

'It looks as if they only wanted my heart.'

David sighed. He paused to choose his words carefully. 'Listen, Heaven,' he said, sounding her name particularly clearly. He shook his head. 'I don't know what kind of trip you're on, but this heart stuff isn't real. Nobody can live without a heart. Whatever those men did to you, you're standing here talking to me. You're breathing. You're alive.'

She looked at him and merely said: 'I know.'

The tone of her voice nipped all opposition in the bud.

'David?'

He realised it was the first time she'd used his name. 'Yes?'

She looked him straight in the eye. 'I'm not mad.'

He returned her gaze, but decided against replying. Finally he said: 'Where do you live?'

'What do you mean?'

'I could take you home.' All of a sudden, he wasn't sure if hospital was such a good idea. He imagined how she'd be treated by Casualty. He'd have to tell a doctor that his friend was not only called Heaven, but had lost her heart.

Yeah, right!

OK, he'd just tell the doctor that she *thought* she'd lost her heart. Which amounted to the same thing. No question of how they'd deal with that one. If she was lucky, they wouldn't believe her. If she was unlucky, they'd call the mental health team.

Whatever the case, he'd end up embroiled in the kind of trouble that he had to avoid. And anyway, Mr Merryweather was waiting for his Walter Scott.

'Marylebone,' she said. 'I live on a boat. In Little Venice.'

'On your own?'

'I'm old enough.' She sounded snappy now.

'I didn't mean it like that.'

'That's how it sounded.'

'Hey, I'm only trying to help,' said David. 'I don't bump into people up here every day, you know.'

Silence fell again.

Then David pulled himself together. 'OK, Heaven,' he said. 'I'll take you to Marylebone. To your boat. But then you're on your own. I've got stuff to do.'

She nodded and smiled.

And David Pettyfer, who didn't exactly know why he was doing any of this, set off with Heaven following him. ——

That's how it began that dark night.

CHAPTER 2

The staircase of number 16 was old and steep, and the cast-iron banisters spiralled down like the ribcage of some huge, long-forgotten animal.

David went first. He'd made up his mind. He'd take the girl back to her houseboat in Marylebone and then he could go home with a clear conscience and forget all about the whole thing. She'd be safe; someone would be there to take care of her. Girls who looked like Heaven always had someone who'd take care of them. That was an unwritten rule.

She'd put her broken telescope into her rucksack. She'd picked it up so carefully, it was almost as if she was mourning a dead pet.

'Please, slow down,' she suddenly gasped behind him. She was breathing quickly, her hands gripping the banisters.

David stopped and looked round. 'Are you OK?'

She shook her head. 'I'm all dizzy.'

He climbed the few stairs back up to her. 'You look pretty done in.'

'Thanks a lot.' She still managed to be snappy.

'I didn't mean it like that.'

'Sorry, I know you didn't.'

'To be honest, you look as if you're about to keel over.' David glanced down the stairs. People normally found it an effort to go up stairs, not down them. And Heaven looked pretty sporty.

Was it drugs after all?

'Hey, are you on anything?' he asked.

The look she gave him was so full of cold contempt that he almost recoiled.

'OK, OK,' he said. He thought for a moment. 'Do you want to sit down?'

She shook her head vigorously. 'I don't want anyone to know that we're here.'

David looked at the apartment doors on the landing. The corridor was empty, the stairs silent. 'Don't worry,' he said. 'If anyone asks what we're doing here, I'll just tell them I got the wrong house.'

She looked at him, puzzled.

'The book,' David explained, unsure whether he'd already mentioned it or not. 'I've got to deliver a book; the customer lives next door. Number 18.'

'Ah, I see.' She was silent for a moment. 'What are you staring at?' she asked. Her hands were visibly shaking.

'I'm not staring.'

This was a lie. Of course he was staring. She looked gorgeous. Incredibly beautiful. Mysterious. She was an enigma.

'Of course you're staring.'

'I'm just looking at you.'

'That's what I said.'

'No, you said I was staring at you. I wasn't staring. It would be rude to stare.'

'So you were just looking.'

He grinned slightly. 'Yes.'

'And?'

'I'm just wondering what's the matter with you.'

The silence became louder. 'I need to get outside,' Heaven finally said. 'I need fresh air. I'll be fine once I get some fresh air. Or at least I think so,' she added dubiously. 'It's just so stuffy in here,' she murmured.

'OK.' David didn't know what she was talking about, as the staircase felt pleasantly warm to him after the foul November rain outside. But whatever. 'Come on, give me your hand.' He held his out to her. 'If you fall down the stairs, you'll break every bone in your body.' He grinned more broadly. 'Promise not to stare.'

She laughed – but as she took a step towards him, her knees gave way and she clung heavily to the banister. David put his arm under her shoulders and held on to her tightly. Her hair smelled of lemon and cinnamon, and her breath was like a soft spring breeze.

She felt cold, unnaturally cold.

'Can you manage?' asked David. Perhaps she was right, and just needed some fresh air?

'I think so,' she murmured. She nodded cautiously and set off.

Step by step, slowly, carefully, they made their way down the stairs. David held her tightly and she entrusted herself to him. The front door wasn't locked, and minutes later they were slipping out into Phillimore Place.

The cold air hit them in the face, and David shivered involuntarily. The street was empty. Nothing going on around there, not at that time of night. A few cars were parked under the bare trees, but there wasn't a soul in sight.

Heaven took a deep breath and suddenly looked much better. She seemed confused and rather embarrassed. 'I've no idea what that was all about.'

'Main thing is, you're OK now.' David let go of her.

'My customer lives over there,' he said, patting his rucksack. 'Do you mind if I just go and hand Walter Scott over? Then I'll take you home.'

Heaven looked round anxiously. 'Can I come with you?' she asked.

'Course you can.' David set off. He leapt up the stairs of number 18 and rang the bell.

Heaven stood behind him, sneaking cautious glances up and down the street.

'Don't worry. Those guys have gone,' David reassured her, realising as he did so how odd his words sounded. What on earth was he doing? Was *he* starting to believe in this story of two bad men who went round stealing people's hearts?

Of course he wasn't. But he had suddenly felt the need to comfort her. Comfort seemed to be the only thing that would help her.

'Someone's coming to the door.'

She was right. Seconds later, Mr Merryweather was standing in the open doorway like a relic from *Great Expectations*. He was wearing a long, hideously patterned dressing gown and checked slippers. The meerschaum pipe in his hand was smoking away to itself.

'Ah, David Pettyfer,' he said effusively, ushering

David in. He looked warily at the girl. 'And who might this young lady be?'

'I'm David's girlfriend,' Heaven said quickly.

David didn't say a word. You had to hand it to her: she could think on her feet.

'Heaven Mirrlees.'

It was the first time he'd heard her full name. It suited her.

Mr Merryweather smiled and scratched his whiskers. 'Well, you've got good taste, boy.' He ushered Heaven in too.

'It looks less weird this way,' she whispered to David as she passed him.

David was just wondering what would be so weird about having a girl with him, but she'd already gone past and was following Mr Merryweather into the parlour.

The room was small and cosy. It smelled of warm tobacco and old books, of printing ink and long-discarded newspapers upon which were piled teacups, teapots and old bits of cake. The walls were covered with high shelves, lurid patterned wallpaper and wooden panelling. Around the table stood a wing chair and an ancient standard lamp with pompoms dangling from its shade.

David put his rucksack on the floor, opened it and rummaged inside. Then carefully, very carefully, he removed a wooden box from within. 'Here it is,' he declared solemnly as he opened the box and took the book out. 'Walter Scott: *The Bride of Lammermoor*.'

Mr Merryweather's eyes lit up, and he looked just as he might have as a little boy. 'At last. At last,' he whispered reverentially.

Heaven was watching him closely.

Mr Merryweather took up the book, opened it, and ran his finger gently across the first page. He sniffed the paper and continued to leaf through it.

'Is it as you had imagined?' David asked politely.

Mr Merryweather laughed. 'It really is the Firmin-Didot edition. Unbelievable.'

David closed his bag. Then he put the box on the table. 'So you like it, then?'

'Like it?' Mr Merryweather chortled. 'It is fabulous.' He looked at Heaven. 'Isn't it?'

'It looks vulnerable,' Heaven said solemnly.

Mr Merryweather stroked the cover. 'It reminds me of my wife,' he said softly. He went over to the window and spent a moment looking silently down into the street. Then he turned back to them. 'I met Mrs Merryweather in a theatre, over in Islington.' His voice took on a fond, familiar tone. 'It was love at first sight for me. When I went over to talk to her during the interval, it was almost quarter of an hour before I realised that she was blind. She hid it well.' He looked fixedly at the book as he spoke. 'She loved books.' He paused and sighed. 'That's a long time ago now. A long, long time ago. Mrs Merryweather died during the Thatcher era.' He paused again. 'How time flies.' He gave a wistful laugh. 'Anyway, I read this story to her countless times.'

'The whole book?' Heaven asked in surprise.

He twinkled at her. 'This is where we sat, here in this room, always in candlelight. She could sense the candles. She could actually hear them flickering. I'd read to her, and she'd touch the pictures that I'd describe. The illustrations…she said that she could see the pictures in her head.' Mr Merryweather paused again. 'But that was later,' he murmured. 'Much later.'

David glanced at Heaven. It wasn't the first time he'd been here to deliver books that Miss Trodwood had tracked down for Mr Merryweather. And every time, the old man told his stories. He started with his dead wife, and ended with the Second World War. David rather liked it in a way; it reminded him a bit of his grandfather who in the end hadn't known what day it was, but who could remember every detail of his time in a submarine during the Cold War.

But even if David was happy to be there, he wasn't quite sure what other people would make of Mr Merryweather's old stories. He wondered briefly how Kelly would have reacted. She'd probably have dismissed his tales as senile nonsense or, even worse, she'd have tried to persuade him to go to one of those degrading meetings at a so-called Over-60s Centre.

Heaven was listening, enthralled.

'When we were first married,' Mr Merryweather continued, 'my wife and I lived in a big house in Hampstead Heath. We were still so young. One night, the bombers came.' He banged his fist on the table. 'That damned Blitzkrieg – you can't begin to imagine what it was like. Then there was a real sky above the city, not these starless nights we get now.' He shook his head and drew on his pipe. 'So, the Germans came in the night and we hid ourselves away like rats in the Tube tunnels as the bombs thundered down.' He paced to and fro, staring at the book. 'Our house was bombed one night. There was a gas leak, then a fire. My father's book collection, which he'd given to me, was burnt to a cinder.' He tapped Walter Scott. 'This was one of them.'

'The book you always read out loud?' asked Heaven.

Mr Merryweather nodded. 'The very first book.'

Heaven rubbed her eyes.

'After my wife passed away, I wanted to have it back again. It will have pride of place in my library.'

Heaven swayed slightly. 'What are you going to do with it?'

David wondered if she had any idea how much the old man had paid for the book.

'I will read it to my wife again,' said Mr Merryweather. 'I'll put her picture on the chest of drawers over there and read to her, as I used to do. We'll be close to one another, as we always were.'

Heaven smiled. She was clutching the back of the wing chair, and now her legs seemed to give way.

'Are you all right, child?' Mr Merryweather said.

David rushed over to her.

She shook her head. 'I'm just feeling a bit faint,' she stammered. Her hand touched the place where her heart was. Or had been, by her reckoning. Then she sank to her knees.

David helped her up. Mr Merryweather put the book on the chest of drawers.

'She needs fresh air,' David said hastily.

Mr Merryweather hurried to the door. He was quite agitated now, tugging anxiously at his whiskers.

Outside, it was still drizzling. The air smelled strongly of grass and earth and dead leaves. Heaven leant heavily on David, but she was already looking slightly better after only a minute in the fresh air.

'I think you need a doctor, child,' Mr Merryweather said, sounding concerned.

'We're taking her to one,' promised David.

'Can I rely on you?' persisted Mr Merryweather.

'I'll take care of her.'

Heaven said faintly: 'That was a lovely story. The one you told.'

Mr Merryweather laughed. 'That's all I've got. My stories. Money doesn't matter.' He waved his hand. 'Be happy,' he said to them. 'And you,' he added, turning to David, 'pass on my very best regards to Miss Trodwood. It always amazes me, the way she finds old treasures.'

'Will do, Mr Merryweather,' David promised.

And so they left the owner of 18 Phillimore Place with his book and went out into the night. A chilly wind blew wet leaves across the asphalt.

'Are you feeling better?' asked David, before they'd even rounded the first corner.

'The fresh air's doing me good.'

They walked in silence for a while.

'So that's your life,' Heaven finally said. 'Books and Mr Merryweather.'

'Part of it.'

'Does that often happen?'

'You mean what happened just now?'

'Yes.'

'No.' He didn't have to think long. 'Customers don't normally tell me stories.'

'Do you know that book?' she asked. '*The Bride of Lammermoor*?'

David thought of the abysses that sometimes opened up, and not only on rooftops. 'It's about two hostile families. And true love that conquers all. A Scottish Romeo and Juliet, you might say.'

'Have you read it?'

He stared at his Converse. Then he changed the subject. 'We ought to do as the old man said.'

'What do you mean?'

'I don't think I should take you to Marylebone.' He looked at her insistently. 'Say what you like – I think something's wrong. Those dizzy spells...someone needs to check that out. Seriously.'

'They took my heart,' said Heaven.

David sighed. '*Heaven*. Listen. I think you need to go to hospital.'

She nodded.

'I mean, you could go to the doctor's, but Casualty is our only option at this time of night.'

'Fine.'

'But don't mention hearts,' he quickly added.

Her mood changed. 'You don't believe me.'

'That's not the point.' He rolled his eyes. 'Do you have any idea how it sounds?'

She didn't reply.

'If we go to the hospital and you go telling a doctor that story, that stuff about bad men stealing your heart, he's going to send you to the loony bin.'

'You bastard,' she hissed. She stopped walking. 'I knew it.'

'What did you know?'

'That you're just like all the others.'

'What's that supposed to mean?'

'People are so stupid.' Her eyes were blazing, and her skin had taken on an ebony hue. 'Is it so hard to believe me? Why would I lie to you? What's in it for me?'

'I dunno. But…people can't live without a heart.'

'Yes, I *know*.'

'But something's wrong with you. And you need to have it checked out.'

She turned away from him and ran off. After a few paces, though, she stopped and turned back. Tears were running down her face. 'I'm scared shitless!' she yelled at him. 'Do you think I don't know how stupid this all sounds? But it did happen to me! I've no idea what's going on. But I've told you the truth!' She was sounding hoarse now. 'I'm not lying, David.'

There was something in her voice, in the way she said his name, that rendered him helpless. 'Let's not fight,' he said. 'I'll take you to the hospital, and someone there will have a look at you. And you promise not to mention hearts. OK?'

She nodded briefly. 'OK,' she said, wiping tears away with the back of her hand.

'OK,' David repeated.

Heaven didn't move. 'But you're coming with me, aren't you?'

He sighed loudly. 'Yes. I'm coming with you.' He raised his hand by way of warning. 'But not a word about hearts.'

'Not a word.'

'Promise?'

'Promise.'

'Good.'

'Shall we go?' she asked.

They set off. Down Argyll Road, then a few metres along Phillimore Walk, then Campden Hill Road. They walked in silence until they reached Kensington High Street.

'I mean,' David suddenly burst out, 'I don't even know you. You were just sitting on the roof, telling me this story.' He buried his hands in his pockets, more out of embarrassment than cold. 'Could you tell me why I'm doing all this?'

She shook her head.

A grin flickered across his face. 'Ah well, then we've got something in common. I've not got a clue either,' he said.

Heaven smiled at him. 'Never mind. The main thing is that you're not going to leave me on my own.'

David shook his head. 'What a weird night.'

'Weird is the word.'

Then they were there.

St Mary Abbot's Hospital was in Marloes Road, south of Kensington High Street, barely five minutes' walk from the Tube station. It was a huge building that had survived the ravages of the Second World War and its aftermath. It looked intimidating, with its red-brick façade, countless spires and wide bays. David always thought it looked as if the Addams Family had decided to build a hospital. Tendrils of ivy snaked up the walls, and lights were blazing in the windows.

Casualty was in the West Wing.

David took care of the formalities. He could lie to order; he'd had plenty of practice. Mike had sent him out often enough. He always said David had the perfect poker face.

His girlfriend wasn't very well, he said. She kept having dizzy spells. Yes, she was otherwise healthy. No, she'd never had this kind of thing before. No, she wasn't taking drugs and, no, he wasn't either.

David loathed hospitals. The people who worked there always gave him the impression that dealing with sick people was the very last thing they wanted to do.

The woman on reception was no exception. Hunched over a flickering screen, she twisted her mouth into a sour smile as she shoved a form in David's direction. It was full of boxes to tick.

It was warm in there. David undid his jacket and led Heaven across to some chairs. They sat down and Heaven made as if she were filling in the form.

Casualty was no more than a long corridor with a row of chairs down both sides. Harsh neon lamps bathed everything in an unreal light and made the people waiting there look even sicker than they actually were.

There were people with gashes, people with broken bones, and junkies who were just looking for a bed. It was all happening, even at that time of night. The city never slept. A jumble of voices filled the air, and the few doctors on duty ran madly to and fro between the corridor and the treatment cubicles with their retinue of nurses and underlings. Orders were bellowed, and equipment was shifted around. It stank of despair and disinfectant.

Heaven pushed her chair closer to David's and put her cold hand on his. She was shivering.

Then she rolled her eyes and slumped to one side. Her chair tipped over and she fell to the floor, trembling from head to toe.

'Dammit!' cursed David.

A junior doctor and a nurse came running over, grabbed Heaven, and hoisted her into a nearby wheelchair. They took her blood pressure, did this and that, looked into her eyes, felt her pulse; it all happened very quickly. David didn't have the faintest idea what exactly they were doing. Then, the doctor suddenly stopped. He put the stethoscope to her chest again. The nurse felt for her pulse. They looked at one another.

'What's going on?' asked David.

They looked at him as if they'd seen a ghost.

'Why are you staring at me?'

The doctor said: 'I can't find a heartbeat.'

David felt his chest tighten. 'What?'

'Yes, that's what I said.'

Doctor and nurse exchanged looks. 'Is it possible…'

'Is what possible?' David snapped at them. Something was seriously wrong here. That meant bad news.

The junior doctor carried on staring at David as he pondered. 'I don't know.' He turned to the nurse and whispered: 'We have to call Dr Laurie. We've no choice.'

'What is it? What's the matter with her?' David took a step closer and put his hand on Heaven's lifeless shoulder. 'Hey, can't you at least have the decency to talk to me?' He was almost yelling now.

'I'm calling Dr Laurie,' said the junior doctor, running down the corridor to the phone. 'You fill in the form.'

The nurse stayed with them.

David touched Heaven's cheeks. They were icy cold.

'Where've you come from?' asked the nurse.

'What's with all the questions?' David knew how aggressive he sounded.

'Weird night, tonight.' The nurse suddenly seemed nervous. She looked across at the doctor who was further back down the corridor, on the phone. 'Half an hour ago,' she began in a whisper, 'some men from the Department of Health were here. They said they were looking for a young girl, a girl with psychological problems who'd run away from home.'

David cast a glance at Heaven.

'They said she was suffering from delusions,' the nurse continued.

David didn't know why she was telling him all this. 'So?'

'The men who were asking after her seemed odd to me,' whispered the nurse.

'In what way, odd?' David could feel his impatience mounting. *Go on, spit it out!*

'It sounds a bit silly,' said the nurse rather sheepishly. 'And they did show us some proof of identity. It was all fine. But...the men...I can't think of any other way to describe them...they seemed...bad.'

The junior doctor was talking into the phone. He nodded several times, then put the receiver down. David could feel his heart pounding beneath his hoodie. He suddenly felt hot.

Hot.

It was too hot in here.

He stared at Heaven.

Heat!

Why hadn't he realised sooner?

It was hot in here. Just like in the stairway at 16 Phillimore Place and in Mr Merryweather's apartment. But it was cold on the street. It was cold on the roof.

It was so obvious! In a cold place, Heaven was fine. But if she was in a warm place for any length of time, she started getting dizzy.

The doctor reached for the phone again.

Heaven grabbed his arm woozily. With her eyes she implored him to do something.

Damn!

It was yet another of those days when everything went wrong.

'What are you doing?' David asked the nurse. 'Why are you telling me that?'

'The men were so spooky,' she said, somewhat confused. 'I just wanted to warn you.'

David's gaze remained fixed on the junior doctor. 'Who's he calling?' he asked the nurse. Her identity badge said R. Cohen.

'The consultant. Dr Laurie.'

'And what exactly is *he* going to do?'

She shrugged. 'Dr Laurie was the one who dealt with the Department of Health men.'

Right.

The junior doctor's eyes were glittering. David knew that look. He was trying to look all casual, but you could tell he had a plan up his sleeve. He kept nodding, then pulled a face as if whatever Dr Laurie was saying didn't suit him.

The nurse – R. Cohen – turned away. 'I must get on; patients are waiting,' she murmured.

'Thanks,' said David.

She avoided his gaze.

The junior doctor was still on the phone, looking in David's direction as he spoke. He obviously wanted to make sure they didn't do a runner.

David looked round in an exaggeratedly bored manner.

Casualty was packed now. A cacophony of voices, smells, heat. It was so damn warm in there. Heaven was breathing shallowly. She was as beautiful as ever, but her lips were parched and brittle. Her dark eyes, which still wore that pleading look, had sunk into their sockets.

David's gaze fell on the fire alarm.

He'd never imagined that he'd ever think of actually doing it in real life. But now, faced with the chance, the idea was highly tempting. It was something that people only did in films. Something that the hero – who didn't yet realise that he was the hero – did to escape from the baddies.

It always worked. What was to stop it working this time?

David sprang up, sprinted to the fire alarm, and whacked the plastic cover with his elbow. Nobody paid him any attention as he pressed the button. Only the doctor worked out what was about to happen, and dropped the receiver.

The alarm shrieked, cutting shrilly through the babble of voices. David bounded back to Heaven.

Casualty erupted. Doors were flung open, nurses and patients running around madly. Nobody knew what was going on. Still the alarm blared, shrill and unpleasant, in everyone's ears. And it ended just as it always ends in the films.

In chaos.

Patients were bellowing at the doctors and nurses; some were already heading for the exits. Treatment tables were overturned; surgical instruments clattered to the ground.

David looked across at the doctor, who evidently had no idea what to do next. He was staring at the receiver which was dangling near the floor, as if he didn't know whether he should continue his conversation. But a moment later he started to make his way through the surging mob.

David grabbed Heaven's wheelchair and raced towards the nearest exit as quickly as he could. He was quite sure that Heaven would be able to walk again as soon as she got outside. He hadn't a clue why, but he was one hundred per cent convinced that a lack of fresh air was entirely to blame for the state she was in.

'Watch out!' he yelled. 'Out of the way!'

He raced down the corridor with the wheelchair, desperately hoping that Heaven wouldn't fall out. Patients, ward sisters, doctors, other people who did God-knows-what in Casualty, jumped out of the way.

They finally reached the exit. The footrests on the wheelchair slammed into the door with full force, swinging it open.

As soon as the cold air hit her face, Heaven came to. She blinked.

'What's going on?' she asked, dazed. 'Was I…'

'Fire alarm,' David replied briefly. 'Can you walk?'

He gave her his hand and helped her out of the wheelchair.

'Yes, I'm OK.' She breathed in the night air.

'Then we need to leg it.' David pulled her along with him. 'The nurse was going on about bad men.'

'Bad men?' She gulped.

'Looking for you.' He cleared his throat. 'Or, more precisely, they're looking for a girl who's psychologically disturbed and who's wandering around Kensington on her own. Sounds familiar?'

She laughed. 'Sounds like me.'

'That's what I thought,' he replied shortly.

'But you're helping me all the same?'

'I've got a weakness for pretty girls who are also nutjobs.'

'How very kind.'

He tugged her hand. 'Tube station's down here.'

Behind them, hordes of people were streaming out of Casualty; a bit further on, more people were pouring out of the other emergency exits. In the distance, they could hear the sound of approaching fire engines, and

David knew they needed to get out of there as quickly as possible. Trouble with the police was the very last thing he needed.

They ran across the car park, but then Heaven suddenly stopped. She seemed turned to stone.

'There they are!' Her voice was hard and grating, the words like splinters.

'Where?' asked David.

'Over there.'

He looked in the direction of her finger.

OK, the nurse hadn't been exaggerating. Neither had Heaven.

They were exactly as David imagined bad men to look.

They were getting out of an expensive car; a tall man wearing gloves and another man clad in rags. David couldn't see their faces, but he didn't need to. The gloved man went to the entrance of Casualty and said something to the doctor who'd come running outside. The doctor looked around and was stupid enough to point to them as he said something to the guy.

'Department of Health?' growled David. 'They didn't seriously say that!'

'Looks like it.'

A moment later, the men turned and started walking in their direction.

The raggedy man was limping slightly, but the tall man with the shiny gloves was faster, even though he wasn't particularly hurrying.

'Damn!' said David.

He and Heaven began to run. First up Marloes Road, past Iverna Court and onto Wright's Lane, and back towards Kensington High Street.

They could hear distant traffic, but these streets were empty at that time of night. Heaven was a fast runner, and David was glad that he hadn't swapped his Converse for other shoes.

They reached the Tube station. Even as David saw the entrance to the Underground, he knew that everything in him was telling him not to go down there. *We're running into a trap*, he thought suddenly.

As he knew full well, this was totally irrational. The Tube was the best way to lose their pursuers. There was normally a crush of people down there, and it would be easy to disappear.

He looked at the time. Just before midnight. The trains would still be running. And if they were lucky, they might even be overcrowded. There weren't as many night trains on the Circle and District Lines and there would be loads of people on their way home after a night out.

On the other hand, it was warm in the Underground. *Not a good idea*, his head was screaming, not a good idea at all. Just one look at Heaven told him that she was thinking the same.

'Do you think you can manage it? It's only one stop.'

She swallowed and shrugged. 'Do we have any choice?'

'OK. Let's give it a go.'

They ran down the escalator steps, followed the signs, ignored the ticket machines, and sprang over the barriers. David could smell the fuggy air blown down the winding passageways by the fans. Their footsteps clattered and their breath rattled. The posters on the tiled walls flew past, meaningless splashes of colour.

A sudden gust of wind whooshed through his hair and made Heaven's jacket fly out behind her. A train must be approaching.

David could sense that their pursuers were gaining on them, even though he couldn't see them. The gloved man didn't look like someone who'd give up readily once he'd set his mind on something. How the hell did someone like him get his hands on a Health Department identity badge? And why had the doctors believed him? David hadn't got a clue what he'd stumbled into. But one thing was for sure: he wasn't going to leave Heaven.

They could hear the rattle of the approaching train further down the station.

'That's ours!' panted David.

They shot round the next corner and met another escalator leading to the Circle Line in the direction of Aldgate.

Heaven just nodded. All the running was visibly telling on her.

They ran down the few steps to the platform. By now, David was having to support Heaven. She was trembling again. And she was still icy cold.

The train was just coming in.

Now David could see their pursuers. The gloved man appeared at the top of the escalator. He stopped briefly, appearing to weigh up the situation.

The brakes squealed.

'Stay where you are, please.' The gloved man's voice was extremely calm; he wasn't remotely out of breath or shouting. Yet it carried down to the platform, loud and clear. 'That girl is my patient.'

'That's him!' Heaven whispered anxiously.

David didn't move a muscle.

The black-gloved man didn't exactly look like a therapist. Never mind like the Health Department official that he'd claimed to be at St Mary's. 'She's my patient,' the gloved man repeated. 'I just want to help her.'

The raggedy man now appeared and shuffled alongside his gloved companion. He looked like a dog at his master's side. And there was something else wrong with him. He was limping, and his head was held at an odd angle.

'He's lying,' whispered Heaven. 'The man with the gloves – he had the knife.'

The train stopped behind them with a screech.

'Run!' David grabbed Heaven's arm and dragged her roughly along behind him. She yelped – he was probably gripping her too tightly – but there was nothing he could do about that. They had to catch that train.

Crowds of people streamed onto the platform. The last revellers, ebullient party people, tired theatre-goers.

David and Heaven ran past the windows and jumped into a carriage further down the train that wasn't quite as packed as the others. They squeezed themselves in between the people who were standing in the aisles, holding the overhead bars.

Come on! David stared fixedly at the doors. *Shut, why don't you!*

The people in the carriage were waiting. Some were staring at the platform, some were chatting, but most of them just stood there, silently crammed in.

Get a move on!

Out of the corner of his eye, David saw the gloved man calmly making his way down the escalator. He wasn't even walking: he just glided along.

For God's sake, why weren't the doors closing? Why wouldn't the bastard train just start?

David pulled Heaven further forwards, squeezing their way through the grumbling passengers.

The gloved man had reached the door. He got into the carriage and looked carefully in their direction. He still didn't seem to be in any particular hurry.

Outside, the weird raggedy man was limping his way down the platform.

They heard an electronic beeping noise.

Suddenly, David jerked Heaven to the nearest door. He counted to two. Then he jumped.

Behind them, the doors shut and the train pulled away.

The gloved man was watching them through the window. His eyes turned as big as saucers. Then he disappeared into the tunnel.

'Look!' Heaven gasped.

David saw what she meant.

The strange raggedy man was still standing on the platform, right beside them, watching them with eyes that looked somehow dead. He didn't move, but just stared at them. Then he began to stumble uncertainly towards them.

'Run!' David said again. It seemed to be becoming a habit that night.

But without his gloved companion, the raggedy man didn't seem to know what to do. He stopped again and stood still, as if someone had switched him off. David thought he looked more than strange. Not exactly evil, but incredibly...creepy. Yes, creepy was the word. Beneath his filthy old coat, which had been repeatedly patched together, he was wearing a black suit with lumps of something that looked like dried earth stuck to it. His face was waxen, and his eyes were lifeless dark pools in his deathly white face.

It reminded David of his grandfather. Of the last time he'd seen him. He'd been laid out in his grandparents' house in Cardiff. That's exactly what the raggedy man looked like. Like someone who'd been buried and had come back from the grave.

David jerked himself back to reality. Whatever the creepy guy might be, he wasn't hanging around to find out. He pulled Heaven after him, and they ran up the escalator.

Suddenly, the squeal of brakes cut through the underground labyrinth. David and Heaven stopped dead and looked back. The emergency brake. The gloved man had pulled the emergency cord.

Heaven looked at David with exhausted eyes and gasped: 'Run!' She tried to smile, but totally failed. She was frightened.

And if he was honest, so was David.

He grabbed her arm, not worrying about whether he was hurting her. 'Come on!'

She gasped desperately for air and fell over twice, but she managed to get to the next escalator. There, she collapsed on the ground. Her eyelids were flickering.

'Shit!' David glanced behind them.

He could hear footsteps. Still a long way off, but quickly gaining on them.

He bent over Heaven and lifted her up. She was very light. He stood and ran up the escalator. Her breathing was shallow. Her long hair brushed against his face. Just a few more metres, and they'd be out. Past the posters and ticket booths, past the benches and the shut kiosks, and up the steps.

At last: the cold night air.

Noise, traffic.

Relieved, David exhaled briefly. He could see London's lights again.

Heaven opened her eyes.

'We'll take a taxi,' said David. He ran into the street and hailed the first black cab that had its light on. They jumped in.

'Piccadilly Circus,' said David. He didn't have to think about it. Then he quickly wound the rear window down so the cold night air streamed into the cab. He wound his scarf more tightly around his neck. 'Is that better?'

She leant her head against his shoulder, and began to sob.

CHAPTER 3

The taxi driver didn't ask why David had wound down the window to let the icy cold wind buffet him in the face. Nor did he ask why his two passengers piled in so out of breath, then looked behind them to make sure nobody was following them. There were lots of weird passengers in London; that's just the way it was. A fast track was playing on the radio, and Heaven's fingers nervously tapped out the beat on the upholstery. David was silent, staring out of the window at the city which all of a sudden seemed as alien and cold as it had seemed when he'd first arrived there from Cardiff.

He found the music calming.

'You know who this is?' asked Heaven.

'The Divine Comedy,' David replied.

'Your kind of music?'

He nodded. 'Sometimes.'

'Now?'

He shook his head. His eyes had started to stream, and the wind was ruffling his hair.

Heaven, though, was breathing much more normally. The music seemed to be doing her good. The rucksack with the broken telescope was wedged between her legs.

David didn't want to talk. A shadowy Hyde Park flew past on his left; Wellington Arch glowed in the night like a relic of the olden days. The lights looked like disjointed fires that swam before his eyes, creating confused images. Neil Hannon was replaced on the crackling and hissing radio by Yamit Mamo who – appropriately enough – was singing about how everyone finds, once in their life, a stowaway who asks them to dance.

David sighed. He felt drained, completely exhausted, too tired to think.

They got out at Piccadilly Circus. It wasn't far from there to Seven Dials. Heaven didn't ask where they were going or what David was doing, but simply followed his lead.

They walked the rest of the way, shrouded in the great city's artificial lights that swam in the cold puddles on the pavement instead of the missing stars. The big bronze angel that balanced on one leg as it arose from the fountain in the roundabout silently regarded the traffic – still heavy even at this time of day – and all the flickering, false neon signs. High up above this glittering sea of lights and lies, there wasn't a single star. There was nothing but the very blackest blackness.

They were now in the part of London which no longer had any sky. For more than twenty-one years, there had been nothingness where there were once stars. Most Londoners blamed the comet that had made the tabloid headlines for months back then. There had been talk of spaceships and aliens; one woman even claimed to have seen her dog being carried away by a little green man. Science, of course, pooh-poohed such ideas. Astronomers had their own, increasingly complicated, explanations for the phenomenon – but ultimately they all had to admit that nobody had come up with the answer.

They reached Leceister Square. David looked behind them warily, then broke the silence.

'I don't know whoever or whatever it was that was following us,' he said, 'but we seem to have lost them.' He cast a glance at the drunken revellers who were thronging the square even at that late hour. He couldn't see the raggedy man or the guy with the gloves. All the same, he wasn't entirely certain that they'd shaken off their two pursuers.

'Why aren't you taking me home?' asked Heaven. She didn't sound in the slightest bit mistrustful.

They crossed the road. A couple of cars beeped angrily at them. 'Because we mustn't underestimate those guys who were after you,' David replied shortly. 'Just think about the fake Health Department ID. They'll have long since found out where you live.'

'I don't think so.'

'I do.'

'So where could they have got my name from? They only bumped into me by chance.'

'Are you sure?'

She didn't reply. She buried her hands in her coat pockets.

'Are you cold?' David asked.

She shook her head. 'Actually, I like it better outside.'

He blew on his hands. 'You said before that you lived on a boat.'

She nodded. 'Yeah, the houseboat is my refuge.'

'Your refuge?'

She nodded quickly. 'My sanctuary, if you like. I actually live in Richmond.' She rolled her eyes and grimaced. 'Long story.'

'We've got plenty of time.'

She shook her head, and her long hair bounced up and down. 'Not yet.' She wasn't out of breath, although they were walking quickly. 'If they really know my name and are looking for me, then they'll think I'm in Richmond. Not in Little Venice – guaranteed.'

David sighed. 'All the same,' he said. 'I'll take you to the bookshop where I live. It's safer. You can call someone from there who can help you. And you can chill out a bit before they come to pick you up.'

'Who am I supposed to ring?'

'Dunno. Parents, boyfriend, girlfriend. Whoever.'

'My parents are dead.'

David looked at her. 'I'm sorry,' he said quickly. He knew he sounded embarrassed.

'I…' She shook her head. 'There isn't anyone I could call.'

David hesitated for a fraction of a second. This time he wasn't thinking about the trouble he might get into if she stayed with him. He was thinking only of how hurt she had looked when she'd realised he didn't believe her.

He made his decision. 'Then you'll just have to stay with me,' he said firmly.

'Overnight?'

'Don't worry, you can have the bed and I'll sleep in the armchair.'

She laughed, wrinkling up her nose in a funny way as she did so. 'The armchair?'

'It's a comfy armchair,' he said quickly.

The smile reached her eyes and lit them up. 'I believe you.'

'What's so funny?' he asked, raising an eyebrow.

'Oh, nothing,' she replied hastily. 'Nothing. It's not funny. It's just…' She burst out laughing.

David had to laugh too. 'It's fine. So you're coming, then?'

She turned serious, and seemed to be weighing up her options. Then she put her head on one side. 'Do I have a choice?' It was couched as a question, but it was actually an answer.

'No one will look for you in the bookshop. Even if they know where you live, you and I really did bump into one another by chance.'

She nodded. 'Strange, eh?'

Yes, strange indeed. Strange things did happen, and he still couldn't entirely work out what sort of weird coincidences were making him stumble through the darkness now. How often did you fall over a girl like Heaven on a rooftop in Kensington?

Heaven stopped at a red man. Her breath formed a little cloud in front of her face. 'Thanks,' she said.

'S'all right,' David merely replied. He noticed that the cloud of his breath was much more pronounced than hers.

'I noticed too,' she said before he could even mention it. She held her hand in front of her mouth. 'It's not exactly warm, my breath.'

David cautiously held his hand up in front of her lips. He felt her cool breath on his skin, and shivered.

'Sorry.' Her whisper sounded choky.

He hopped from foot to foot, his hands buried in his trouser pockets. The man turned to green.

The sky above them was as dark as the girl's skin. Heaven looked up. 'When I was a child, I was afraid of this darkness,' she said.

'I can see why.' Ever since David had seen the dark patch above him, he'd felt the same. When you looked at it, it was as if you could touch the emptiness of the whole world.

'There are stars over in Richmond, you know. Maybe that's why my father bought a house in that part of town. So I could see them all.' She smiled, and fell silent once more.

They hurried on down the street. The shops were all shut. Their footsteps clattered on the paving stones as if they were doing an Irish jig.

Eventually David couldn't stand it any longer.

He stopped and exhaled heavily. 'This isn't how it works,' he said, and looked at her. 'We can't just carry on running, acting as if nothing has happened.'

'Then let's talk,' she said calmly.

'Well?'

'What do you mean, well? *You're* the one who wanted to talk.'

'I know.'

'Well, go on then.'

He stared at the garish flashing sign above an internet café. Lit up in the neon glow were hordes of people, staring at their screens. 'Heaven.' He looked her straight in the eye. 'Who are you, Heaven?'

'Is that what you wanted to ask?'

'Looks that way.'

She laughed, and as she did so, her face lit up so brightly that David had to laugh too. 'I'm Heaven,' she said. 'Well, actually, I'm called Freema. Freema Mirrlees.' She emphasised the names individually. 'But my father always called me Heaven.' The recollection flickered in her dark eyes as if she were guarding it carefully there. 'I go to Chelsea Independent College on the Fulham Road and lead a completely ordinary life. There isn't much to tell, honest. My life is just like thousands of other people's.'

'So what does your boyfriend have to say about you hanging out on the rooftops at night?'

She stopped and stared at him. 'What does your girlfriend have to say about you running across the rooftops to take books to weird old men?'

He raised his eyebrows.

'That looks funny,' she remarked.

'What?'

'Your eyebrows.'

'They're funny?'

She nodded energetically. 'They're so...small and thin.' She shook her head slightly, and her hair leapt around as if it had a life of its own. 'Like you.'

'Like me?' He knew he sounded rather offended.

More nodding. 'Suits you.'

'Thanks a lot.'

'And the sideburns.'

He grinned. 'Great.'

'I like your shoes.'

'Thanks again.'

She turned serious once more. They turned into

Charing Cross Road. Their footsteps were like cats' paws on the cobbles.

'In the hospital, they really didn't find a heart, did they?' Once spoken, the words fell in the silence like bombs.

Heaven nodded. 'It would seem that way.'

'But you're walking along next to me.'

'Yep, I can't deny it.'

'So what does that mean?'

She shrugged. 'No idea.'

'Maybe the doctor was a dead loss.'

She shook her head. 'I don't think so. I've had so many medical examinations, I can tell.'

He looked enquiringly at her.

'When I was a child, they always thought I had a heart defect. I had to go for a check-up every year. But they never found anything.' She laughed bitterly. 'Isn't fate ironic? Now they could see the problem they'd always been looking for, couldn't they?'

David thought about their two pursuers making out that they were from the Health Department. 'Maybe you shouldn't go home at all,' he said slowly. 'Not tomorrow either.'

That idea didn't appeal to her. 'I can go to the houseboat, no problem. Nobody knows exactly where it is. Not even the people in Richmond.' The way she said that was odd. She didn't say 'my family' or even 'my relatives'; just 'the people'.

'Maybe you'd better steer clear all the same. I have a bad feeling about all this.'

'Do you really think they're lying in wait for me?'

'Hey, these guys stopped the train. They're complete loons. No scruples at all.' He gave a low whistle. 'I really do have a bad feeling about all this.'

'You already said so.'

'Then I'm saying it again.'

She didn't reply. After a long pause, she murmured: 'I thought you were going to ask why I live on a boat.'

'You'll tell me if you want to.'

She smiled. 'Then ask me something else.'

He didn't have to think long. 'Did you run away from home?'

She shook her head. 'Not exactly.'

'What's that supposed to mean?'

'I just had to get away for a while. It's so big. Oppressive. Grand.' She sighed. 'It's on Twickenham Road.' She evidently didn't like talking about home. 'To be precise, it's between Richmond Green and the Old Deer Park.'

David knew the area; he'd been there a few times.

A number of wealthy customers lived in that part of town.

'Who looks after you?'

'My guardian, Mr Sims, my father's former business partner.'

'And he lives with you?'

She laughed. 'God, no! I haven't got a clue whether he lives anywhere other than his office. I see him twice a year, when he talks to me about the balance sheets. He's convinced I'm interested.' For a moment, she seemed like a completely normal girl who was enjoying taking the piss. 'Poor sod, he's quite sweet in his own way. I gather he might be in the running for a knighthood – for the business's social commitment. He and my father started the foundation.'

'So who lives with you?' David persisted. 'Who were the people you just talked about?'

'It's actually just one person. A butler.'

'Alfred?!'

She couldn't help grinning. 'No. Not Alfred. He's called Mickey.'

David stared at her. 'Mickey?'

She had to laugh. 'Dad thought he was hiring someone who was like me.'

'And what are you like?'

She stopped. Held her hands up in front of his face.

'Ah, right,' David murmured. He hadn't really noticed. Just a skin colour, like all the others.

'Children can be horrible, especially if they come from families who evidently haven't noticed that London is a kind of cultural melting pot. I used to think I was different from the others because my skin was a different colour.'

'And now?'

She smiled. 'Not a problem.' She kicked a plastic bottle that was lying on the pavement. It went scudding off into the shadows. 'When my parents got together, their families were shocked.'

'Why?'

She shrugged. 'British upper class. They had something against anyone who wasn't white. My mother—' She interrupted herself. 'But why am I telling you my life story?' Big Ben chimed the hour in the distance. 'Anyway, Mr Mickey has been looking after me ever since we were on our own.' She changed the subject abruptly. 'How about you?' She gave him a challenging look. Outside in the cold, there was no trace of weakness about her. 'You don't sound like someone born and bred in London.'

'Cardiff,' he said.

'Oh. Cardiff.'

'Yes.'

She stared at him. 'Cardiff's miles away.'

'I miss the sea.'

'And nothing else?'

'I don't miss anything else. I ran away.'

Her eyes lit up. 'Seriously?'

'Yes.'

'Why?'

David spotted a gap in the traffic and crossed Charing Cross Road. He was walking more quickly now; he always did when forced to confront unpleasant memories.

Heaven hurried along beside him. 'Hey, what's got into you all of a sudden?'

'Nothing,' he said.

'You don't have to tell me about your life.'

He stopped dead. 'No, that's not it. I just ran away. That's all.'

A cat was peeping out from between the black bin bags that were piled up against the wall of a house. Someone had sprayed graffiti on the bricks. Gloomy pictures, slogans, crazy stuff.

'Come on, we're nearly there.'

They started walking again and turned into an

alleyway. The houses here were small and narrow, mostly three storeys high with unfeasibly tall, slanting roofs.

David pointed to a little shop. The windows were dark. The sign above the door read: 'The Owl and the Pussycat'. The owl and the cat were easily recognisable. The owl was playing a guitar, and the cat was listening. They were both sitting in a pea-green boat.

'This is the home I found in London.' He knew it sounded a touch too solemn, and he felt slightly embarrassed – but that was how he actually felt about it. And she didn't laugh at him. Quite the reverse. She looked attentively up at the façade. 'Weird,' she said. 'You walk through town so many times, and you never imagine that there are people living above the shops.'

He went ahead and pulled a key from his trouser pocket. Together they went inside.

In the half-light, the little shop smelled of dust and paper, velvet sofas and wooden shelves. Oriental dreams wafted around in the gloom, soft songs of the light of distant deserts and the delights of a rest on the journey. A heater was clattering away somewhere, and a fridge was buzzing, hidden in between the rows of shelves. Yet the whole place was permeated with the scent of wanderlust.

'Joss sticks,' David said, anticipating her question. 'Miss Trodwood likes them.'

Hesitantly, Heaven followed him into the shop.

David listened. 'She's asleep,' he said unnecessarily.

Day in, day out, Miss Trodwood was to be found in her little shop full of books old and new. She knew the perfect book for every customer whom she found lurking undecided among the shelves. And even for the customers who didn't come into the shop. Like a literary Miss Marple, she searched for rare editions of antiquarian books, sometimes at the request of her customers and sometimes just for the fun of it.

And as tracking down books was exhausting (Miss Trodwood sometimes said that the older they were, the more they had a will of their own), she went to bed at eight on the dot every night.

Tonight, David was thankful for that. He knew the old lady would be only too interested in his new acquaintance, as she had a well developed radar for things that didn't concern her.

She had even brought up the subject of Kelly.

'Have you finally given her the heave-ho?' She didn't beat about the bush. 'Or did she give you the heave-ho, which amounts to pretty much the same thing?'

Although David had no desire to talk to Miss Trodwood about his relationship problems, she gave him no choice. She pestered him with a string of questions until she had, with the help of tea and cake, winkled everything out of David that he was keen to forget as quickly as possible.

'You're still so young,' she said. 'Everyone does daft things when they're young. But you need to use your head.' She had smiled kindly. 'You're not in Cardiff now. You have to look forward. It's quite easy, really. Find the girl who's right for you.'

She had said this very firmly. Just as firmly as she had once threatened to throw him out on the street again if she ever caught him doing drugs. Everything that Miss Trodwood said was firm.

'Why are you laughing?' Heaven asked curiously.

David shook his head. 'I was just thinking about something.' He switched the light on. At once, the shadows took concrete form and became shelves full of books and tables loaded with new releases. There was an extremely old-fashioned bureau with a hefty cash register sitting on top. On the wall behind it was the Edward Lear poem that gave the shop its name. Against the wall were several cardboard boxes, stuck together with parcel tape. Next to them was a precarious pile of books that had been recently delivered and were waiting to be sorted. There were no magazines; only newspapers.

'So this is where you work?'

He nodded. 'I like it.' He wondered whether Miss Trodwood would like Heaven.

She smiled. 'And you live…?'

He pointed to a curtain behind the cash register. 'Through there is the storeroom and the way up to the flat. We'll have to be quiet. Miss Trodwood lives on the next floor. And the stairs creak.'

Heaven crossed the room and stopped by a monster piece of furniture that was standing in the middle. She suddenly grinned. 'Is that the comfy armchair?'

'Bingo,' David said.

He went ahead through the curtain. He needed to take her upstairs, where he could open the window. She wasn't yet showing any signs of fainting, but he didn't want to push his luck.

Heaven followed him. Cautiously, she put one foot in front of the other. The stairs creaked regardless.

'She doesn't like me bringing people home. Miss Trodwood, I mean.'

Heaven didn't reply, but just looked around her. On the staircase walls were pictures of authors. Dylan Thomas, Edward Lear, Edith Nesbit, James Thurber, G. K. Chesterton, A. A. Milne and John Masefield. The stairs led to a corridor, and the corridor led to a door, and the door led into a room.

'My home.' David switched on the light and went across to open the window. Then he turned the heating off. 'You can use the mattress there. That's the bed.'

Heaven was taking in her surroundings. The room was small and furnished only with the bare essentials. Mattress, cupboard, shelves, armchair, an old standard lamp with tassels on its chintzy shade, Oriental patterned curtains. There was no television; instead, a big radio stood in one corner of the room. Bare boards, no carpet.

He showed her where the kitchen and bathroom were.

'And you really don't mind the cold?'

'No, I can breathe more easily when it's cold.'

'Hmm.'

For a moment they stood there without speaking; David in the doorway and Heaven by the window. The silence in the room creaked more loudly than the staircase.

'Oh yeah, you can grab some things from the cupboard. To sleep in.'

She nodded.

'And if you need anything…I'll be downstairs.'

'There's no way I'll be able to get to sleep, even though I'm shattered.'

'Me neither.'

He turned to go.

'David?'

'Yes?'

'Thanks,' she said again.

A smile. 'Try to get some sleep.'

Then he shut the door. And went downstairs.

CHAPTER 4

In his dream, he was wandering across rooftops and crenellations. Looking down into abysses and dark eyes. And there was the insistent throbbing of his heart, which was no longer where it was supposed to be. A song: 'The Stowaway'. A flashing knife, loud screams. Hands clutching one another, black and white fingers woven together.

From the distance a voice, brittle and creaky, like the stairs. 'Mr David Pettyfer,' it said, gnawing away at the rapidly disappearing dream. Something prodded him in the shoulder. A finger, old and bony. 'Get up! It's almost nine!'

David jumped. He blinked sleepily into daylight. He was completely exhausted; he felt as if he had only just gone to sleep – which was presumably the case.

'Oh, Miss Trodwood, I…'

The old lady was standing next to him, and David realised with some bemusement that the shop wasn't open yet. Gentle sunbeams fell through the dull window, and the pleasant warmth – actually due to the clattering heater – seemed to be coming from all the old books. The thick woollen blanket that David had wrapped himself in was lying on the floor.

'You slept in the armchair.' The old lady regarded him sharply. She was wearing a light brown suit made of rough fabric, and a silk shawl with an Indian clasp. 'The girl's already had her breakfast.'

All of a sudden, David was wide awake.

Heaven!

'She…'

'I met her in my kitchen, and wondered what on earth she was doing there.'

'Erm…'

'Then I wondered who on earth she was.'

David scratched his head.

The reproving look became even more reproving. 'You know what we agreed.'

David knew that visitors were a big deal, especially coming just after the business with Kelly. 'Oh, that floozy,' Miss Trodwood had never tired of saying. 'She should have picked on someone her own size. Instead, she had to go turning your head. And you so young and thin, as if you've never had a square meal in your life.'

Damn! Miss Trodwood had to go and bump into Heaven. David had forgotten to warn her more clearly about the old lady. He had shown her the kitchen, but he hadn't mentioned that it was also used by his landlady.

'Yes, the girl,' David said slowly, rubbing his eyes. 'That's a long story…' He had no idea what to tell Miss Trodwood.

'I like long stories.' She relaxed slightly and started sorting out the books on the tables.

David paused. 'Mr Merryweather was delighted with the Scott.' It was a heavy-handed attempt to distract her. 'He sent his regards.' He ran his hand through his hair, which was standing up wildly.

'The story!' She casually put Salman Rushdie next to Michael Chabon's adventure stories of swashbuckling Jews.

'She's called Heaven Mirrlees.'

The old lady growled: 'I know. She introduced herself.'

David breathed a slight sigh of relief. He knew that growl. It was a conciliatory growl. Quite different from the snappy tone that indicated genuine crossness. It looked as if things might turn out OK after all. 'I met her on a roof. She was in a bad way.'

Miss Trodwood began stacking the newspapers onto the racks. She didn't like to waste time. 'Right. You found her on a roof.'

'Yes.' David stood up to give her a hand with the papers. 'She needed my help.'

'So you brought her here?'

He nodded quickly.

'Haven't I told you how dangerous it is up there? And at this time of year.'

'I—'

'And in this weather. The BBC has forecast snow for the next few days.' She straightened her heavy steel-framed spectacles and gave him a warning look. 'You can just as easily use the streets like a normal person.' Her narrow green eyes sparkled like an old cat's.

'I'm sorry.' He knew that he sounded contrite. Miss Trodwood always managed to make him feel like a little boy. When he thought about what he'd got up to on the streets, he knew his mates from back then would be gobsmacked about how much respect he had for this little old lady in her brown suit. It sometimes felt to him as if the contrast between them was precisely why they got on so well.

Miss Trodwood raised her hand and made angry

tut-tutting noises. Then she said: 'So that's supposed to convince me?'

'She really did need help.'

'Well, how about that?' murmured Miss Trodwood, going over to the door. She shook her head as she unlocked it. 'We need to open up.' She tested the bell and seemed satisfied. 'So how long's she going to stay?' she asked.

'Not long. I hardly know her.' OK, that sounded pretty stupid. But whatever. David slowly edged his way towards the curtain.

'I'd wear a coat if I were you,' the old lady remarked. 'The girl's sitting up there in the kitchen with all the windows open.'

David was surprised to realise that Miss Trodwood had evidently agreed to let Heaven make herself at home.

'Is she OK?'

The old lady allowed herself a smile. 'She's very polite.' She took a couple of quick steps towards David, stood on her tiptoes so that she still only reached just up to his chest, and whispered conspiratorially: 'And much better looking than that floozy.'

David swallowed.

'Don't worry, I won't mention the floozy to her.'

'Thanks,' David croaked. Then he reached for his jacket, which was lying on the floor by the cash desk. 'I'll go up and see her,' he murmured, and disappeared behind the curtain.

Heaven was in the kitchen, reading a book. She snapped it shut. 'Good morning.'

David blinked. He remembered the events of the previous night and was happier to see her than he was willing to admit, even to himself.

'Hey,' he said.

It was cold in the kitchen, freezing cold.

Morning was pouring loudly through the open window. The sound of cars making their way down Charing Cross Road, bumper to bumper, the crashing and banging of lorries being unloaded in the street, an endless stream of people rushing to the Underground. London was waking up.

David looked out of the window and saw heavy clouds in the sky. He could smell snow in the air. David couldn't ever remember snow before Christmas. To be more precise, he had rarely experienced snow at all. They didn't have much snow in Cardiff, although he'd always longed for it as a child.

'How are you doing?' he said, buttoning up his coat.

Heaven was slurping tea from a cup. 'I've met Miss Trodwood.'

'I know.'

'Bad?'

He shook his head. 'She doesn't normally like visitors. She likes you, though.'

Heaven put her head on one side. 'She gave me some of her raspberry jam. I would die for raspberry jam.' She smiled. 'Though she thought I was someone else at first.'

David had guessed as much.

'Someone called Kelly.'

He sighed. 'She was...my social worker.'

'Social worker?'

'Theft. I was nicked. It was stupid.'

'And she often spent the night here?'

'Who?'

'Your social worker.'

'No, never, Miss Trodwood didn't like her.' He paused for a moment, then said, 'I don't like her any more either.'

Heaven smiled a smile that could drive away any coldness in the kitchen.

David sat down at the table with her. He pulled up his coat collar. 'So how are you doing?' he repeated.

'I didn't sleep well.' She touched her chest. All of a sudden, it was as if her smile had been wiped off her face, and she looked as despairing as the previous night. 'It all seems even more crazy this morning. And you – you must think I'm completely mad.'

'No.' He reached for her icy hand. 'I don't.' He could see himself reflected in her eyes. 'Honestly, this whole thing is so crazy that we must both be going mad.'

The corners of her mouth twitched, but a proper smile didn't materialise. 'So the question is, what are we mad people supposed to do now?'

David stood up and paced around the room. 'No idea. That's what I spent all night wondering about.'

'So you didn't sleep either?'

'Not really.'

'And you really don't think I'm mad?'

'I heard what they said at St Mary's.' Enough said.

She touched her chest again. Only then did David notice that she was wearing his things. Black jeans, black T-shirt, black shirt, black woollen socks.

She noticed him noticing. 'My clothes have got blood on them,' she explained, staring at the tabletop.

'My blood.' She looked up. 'When I woke up this morning, I tried to convince myself that it was all a dream. The kind of nightmare that gets right into your system, the kind you can't shake off. But still, just a dream. I managed to convince myself until I saw my T-shirt.'

David went over to make himself a coffee. He leant against the fridge, slurping the hot drink, desperately trying to clear his head. 'Let's go over it all again,' he began. 'What do you reckon?'

She nodded.

He took a deep breath. 'OK, so where do we start?' He stared for a moment at the steam that rose from his cup. Then he looked up. 'So: you don't have a heart. Of course, that's completely crazy, we both know that. But you've not got a heartbeat, and in the hospital they couldn't explain what was wrong with you either. The machines can't have been faulty, because he just used a stethoscope. Stethoscopes don't go wrong. And he wasn't an incompetent doctor – you said so yourself.'

'Don't forget he was in a real state, as was the nurse.'

David shrugged. 'Well, let's assume that it's possible. I mean, you're here. You're sitting in front of me. You're talking to me. You're alive.'

'Kind of.'

'Not kind of. You're breathing. You're…you're Heaven. And if they've taken your heart, then we just have to get it back again.'

Heaven held her steaming cup of tea between both hands. 'You make it sound so easy.'

He tried to grin, but failed. 'Do you have any other ideas?'

She shook her head.

'OK, then here we go,' he said. 'What about that guy? The very fact that they caught you on the roof suggests that they didn't just bump into you by accident, doesn't it? After all, people don't tend to spend cold November nights hanging out on Kensington roofs. Well, apart from us two.'

Heaven shook her head. Her hair looked even wilder today than it had done yesterday, if that was possible. 'But even if they had been following me,' she said, looking puzzled, 'why on earth would they have been doing that? I'm a complete nobody. There's nothing remotely unusual about my life.'

David shook his head. 'I haven't got a clue.' He put his cup down. 'Tell me again. What exactly do you remember?'

'The long knife.' Her expression was pained, as if

she could feel it on her skin again. 'I was thinking how unusual it looked. Long, thin, curved. Then I lost consciousness. When I woke up, I got up and ran and kept on running.' Her eyes filled with tears. 'Why does this have to happen to me?'

David resisted the impulse to go over and take her in his arms. She looked so damned vulnerable, and the thought of what she'd been through up there on the roof made his blood boil. But he stayed where he was, carried on leaning against the fridge. Something told him that it was important for Heaven to retain her pride. And he didn't want to wreck something that wasn't even really there yet.

'I...what a mess!' She wiped the tears off her face before they could freeze into little crystals. 'Shit.' She suddenly jumped up and clenched her fists angrily. She looked as if she'd have liked to hurl her cup at the wall. But then her anger subsided and she slumped back onto her chair. 'I think it'd be best if I went back to the boat,' she whispered. 'I can't stay here either.'

'Why not?'

She had a two-word reply: 'Miss Trodwood.'

David rolled his eyes. 'I'll sort that. You're safe here.'

She was silent for a long while, evidently trying to

compose herself. 'If I do stay,' she finally said, 'then I'll need some clothes.' She smiled sadly.

'I can fetch you some. You can tell me how to find your boat. And what you want me to fetch.'

She chewed her lip. 'You'd do that?'

'Yes.'

'Why?'

'What do you mean, why?'

'Well, we hardly know each other.'

'Does that matter?'

'It does normally. People don't just help one another.'

'They do in films.'

'Yes, but this isn't a film.'

'But it is London,' said David. 'Anything's possible in London.'

She sighed. 'What if someone's there?'

'I'll be careful.'

'Maybe I should come,' she said. 'I could hide somewhere and wait while you fetch my clothes. There's a café really close to the boat.'

David shook his head firmly. 'No. It's too warm, and you'll faint again.'

She sighed. 'God, that's pathetic, isn't it?'

He laughed, and she looked at him again. 'Could

you do something else for me?' Her slender fingers were wrapped round the cup handle. 'Could you give Mr Mickey a note from me? Otherwise he'll be worrying, and…' She stopped, searched for words, and finally said: 'And I don't want that.'

'Why don't you call him?'

'He'll start asking questions. I just don't want to talk to him.'

David nodded. He understood how she felt. He'd probably feel the same.

'Just chuck the note in the letter box and run.'

'Do you want me to do that first?'

'Yes.' She winked at him, slightly amused now. 'Otherwise you'd be carting my stuff halfway across town.'

David grinned. 'Good point.'

The noises of the city outside still drifted into the kitchen. And David suddenly realised that he wasn't going to leave her in the lurch, regardless of what might happen. Their paths had crossed that night, and if strange coincidences like this one meant anything, then you simply had to grab with both hands whatever opportunities they might bring.

FIRST INTERLUDE
MR QUILP

The man with the black gloves, who was now calling himself Mr Quilp, was standing on the pavement on Fulham Road, watching the pupils pouring through the entrance of a large, high-windowed building. He was calmly reading what it said in fancy lettering on the brass plate: Chelsea Independent College. The students looked tired and grumpy.

Mr Quilp's eyes were sharp. But he hadn't seen the face he was looking for. Not that he expected her to turn up here. No, he wasn't that naive. But you couldn't exclude any possibility, however absurd.

Under his arm was a copy of *The Times*. This time there wasn't an article about a corpse without a heart. No, this time it was different. More complicated? Perhaps. But one just had to regard difficulties as challenges to be overcome.

He reached for his mobile, rang Directory Enquiries, and asked for a number. He didn't ask to be connected; he just made a mental note of it. Any little test that sharpened the wits was always welcome. Then he dialled the number and waited.

He knew that the phone was ringing inside the building that he'd been watching for the past hour. He knew a secretary would answer it. And he knew he would be a piece of information better off within a couple of minutes.

Mr Quilp smiled. Anyone within the ambit of that smile felt a vague, indescribable shudder – in the same way that people sometimes have a vague feeling that something bad has happened somewhere.

Then a woman answered the phone.

Mr Quilp said a polite 'Good morning'. He introduced himself and began to ask his questions.

CHAPTER 5

Before setting off for Richmond, David took a detour. He wanted to find out more about Heaven, and as Miss Trodwood had set her face against modern things like the internet, David had to find another way to go online when he wanted to – which wasn't very often. This other way normally took the form of Michael Townson.

Mike lived in digs in Wardour Street, more or less on the way to Richmond.

They still bumped into one another in pubs and clubs every now and then, though that was happening less and less frequently. Once upon a time, they had been welded together by the bad stuff that they'd got up to. In retrospect, that sounded romantic, like some sixties film about crooks. In reality, though, it had never been like that. Theft, trafficking, drugs, everything parents warn their children about. The main thing was that it paid.

David rang the bell. He hadn't been there for weeks.

Mike opened the door sleepily. He was wearing a dressing gown and his hair was standing on end. 'Davy?'

'Mike.'

'What's up?'

'I need to use the internet.'

'You're here at this time of day to use the internet?' Mike pulled a face. 'Haven't you ever thought of getting your own internet? What time is it?'

'Almost midday,' said David. 'And I hardly ever use the internet. It's not worth getting it.'

'I know a guy who—'

'No, thanks. I've got you.'

Mike grinned sleepily and stood aside. His place smelled of stale cigarettes and beer. David could see the remains of last night's Chinese takeaway on the table: congealed noodles encrusted with cold sauce.

Mike led him across the sitting area, past the clutter of his things and through all the rubbish littering the floor.

'So you're still living like a prince,' David commented.

'You do what you can.' On the desk were several spare parts of a car engine.

'Your old Mini?' asked David.

'Knackered.'

'Bad luck.'

'I'm gonna get it going again once I've got some dosh.'

'Have you got a job?'

Mike gave him a look that David recognised. 'Yeah, over at—'

David interrupted. 'Doesn't matter.' He didn't want to know. The two of them looked at one another briefly across an abyss of time and wasted opportunity.

'All yours,' Mike finally said, switching the PC on and sloping off towards the loo.

David waited for the PC to start up, then clicked his way onto the internet.

He typed 'Freema Mirrlees' into Google. Bingo. Three cheers for the modern age.

He found several pictures of her. Just snapshots, but pictures all the same. A school photo in posh surroundings. Then Heaven in Trafalgar Square with two female friends; they were sitting on the lions' heads, laughing. Several pictures on Twitter: Heaven shopping with friends, in a café, cheerful pictures of a normal life. She was mostly laughing; even on the blurry, out-of-focus pictures that were evidently taken on a mobile, her laugh was infectious.

David went back to Google. Reluctantly, he was forced to admit to himself. Her father was mentioned: Jonathan Mirrlees. One click on his name was enough to throw up further links. Jonathan E. Mirrlees came from an old family of Richmond industrialists. He had married twenty-two years ago, and had had a daughter four years later: Freema. His wife was only briefly mentioned; she had died following the birth of their daughter. He himself had died in a plane accident in the Lake District. That was four years ago. Together with his partner Juno Sims, he had headed the Mirrlees and Sims Waist Company; Sims had managed the firm single-handedly since Mirrlees's death, and had later renamed it Sims Enterprises.

Sims. The guardian in charge of Heaven's money. What David didn't know was how much money they were actually talking about.

David clicked on the name and skimmed the Wikipedia entry: Juno Sims was head of the firm and was renowned for being a socially aware entrepreneur. He had appeared on several TV programmes and had been touted for a peerage. In the pictures, he looked like your typical businessman: highly elegant, buttoned-up, grim and filthy rich. David imagined Heaven groaning at the balance sheets. That figured.

He clicked on one of the videos. A window immediately opened. 'We aren't just a company that makes things,' Juno Sims was telling the interviewer. He was strikingly gaunt, and his blue eyes were glinting behind his gold reading glasses as if he were trying to force the viewers to agree with him. 'No: we also have to learn to accept responsibility.' He looked directly at the camera. 'We have a responsibility to humankind that we can't ignore. Sims Enterprises produces everything exclusively in Scotland and Wales. British products should be made in Britain, by our own workers.' He went on to describe his childhood in a typical working-class part of Yorkshire, emphasising that every person on the planet deserved a chance.

David rolled his eyes and clicked off the video. Yeah, he got it: Sims wasn't just Mr Moneybags, but a saint as well. He'd worked his way out of the pits and now spent his time floating around in his Armani suit, being a do-gooder. Just as fake as the people in Cardiff. Only on a different level.

David returned to the pictures of Heaven with her friends in Trafalgar Square.

He sat there quietly, looking at her. She was sitting on the lion's head by the monument, dangling her legs and laughing into the camera.

The toilet flushed, and Mike appeared behind David. 'Your latest catch?' he asked.

'No,' David replied shortly.

'What about that sexy piece I saw you with in *Train*?'

'That's over.'

'Sean said she was your social worker.'

'Sean's a moron.'

Mike grinned. 'But a moron who knows what's what.'

David turned round in the chair and glared at him. 'Every single person in London must know by now that she was my social worker. So?'

Mike shrugged and raised his hands. 'So nothing.'

'Fine.'

There was an unpleasant pause.

Mike pointed to the screen. 'Seriously, Davy, who is she?' He sounded almost abashed, conciliatory.

'I met her yesterday.'

'Looks hot.'

David found something disturbing about the way Mike said that. But he didn't reply; he knew Mike didn't mean any harm.

'Are you together?'

'Mike! We've only known each other one day.'

'You didn't waste any time with the social worker, did you?'

'She isn't Kelly.' David felt the anger rising again.

Mike nodded. 'You ought to know.'

'Yes,' David snapped. 'I ought to know.'

Mike took that in. 'Coffee?' he asked.

'Love one.'

He went into the kitchen. Two minutes later he returned with the cups.

'You look as if you're in some kind of trouble.'

'Not really.'

'You want to watch it.'

'Says who?'

Mike was still on probation, after he'd been caught selling happy pills to underage clubbers in the East End. 'Yeah, I'll watch it,' he said eventually.

They sat there for a while in silence. Mike looked as he always did: done-in from the night before.

'Are you still in touch with your sister?' he asked.

'No.'

'So you've burnt all your bridges.'

David nodded. He stood up. 'I've got to go.'

Mike punched him on the shoulder by way of farewell. 'Take care.'

'I won't do anything you wouldn't do.'

Mike said earnestly: 'That's what I mean, mate. Precisely that.'

They both laughed.

David left the digs and set off for Richmond.

Richmond was twelve and a half miles from central London. It was easily reached on the District Line but, because of his aversion to the Underground, David caught the number 415 at Victoria. It took half an hour longer, but there was no comparison with the stuffiness of the Tube.

During the journey, the houses outside changed. The town houses with their high roofs became neat rows of terrace houses until the bus was finally whizzing past plots of land with lawns and trees and detached bungalows. The journey followed the Thames upstream to the place where the Tudors had built a magnificent palace which still bore the coat of arms of Henry VII.

Here, the river was calm and meandered dreamily through Kew Gardens and the Old Deer Park. The houses that bordered the park looked grand; properties that had been built by once-wealthy families whose gnarled roots could be traced right back to the

Industrial Revolution. With their red bricks and pale basalt, they harked back to an age – a hard one for many – when factories and rumbling steam engines had brought these families wealth and prosperity. Now, though, most of the properties were let out, and Twickenham Road, Kew Road and Lower Mortlake Road had become ordinary streets.

When he got off the bus, David immediately noticed the clean air. It was colder and more pure than the air in central London. A gentle breeze was driving fat clouds across the sky.

So this was where Heaven Mirrlees had grown up. David had spent the bus journey lost in thought, concentrating on the landscape, thinking that some parts of it reminded him of picture books from his childhood, of stories of civilised badgers and toads sitting down to tea, talking about their adventures. But now his thoughts returned to what had actually happened to him.

To Heaven and the roof in Kensington.

Now everything he had experienced felt completely unreal. The further the bus took him from London, the more it all receded into the distance, and he was already feeling surprised by how ready he had been to accept the most absurd things as the truth.

He went left at the bus stop. Ahead of him was Twickenham Road; to his right, the Old Deer Park. The scraggy, twisted branches of the bare trees were waving in the wind. He could see a solitary jogger on one of the paths.

David walked down the road until he reached number 21.

High iron gates offered him a view of a long drive which led through trees and lawns to a house whose chimneys peeked out behind the trees like the antennae of some vast creature. The property seemed somehow to merge on the horizon with the park that stretched out behind it.

On earlier, occasional trips to this part of town he had already noticed the fancy metalwork on the gate. Bright stars and heavenly bodies had been worked into the iron bars and curved struts.

David looked around. The people hurrying along the pavement didn't give him a second glance.

'You don't need to talk to Mr Mickey in person – he'll just start asking questions,' Heaven had reminded him. 'Just bung the note into the letter box of number 21 and leave.'

Sounded easy enough – but it wasn't. The huge pile that loomed up at the end of the long drive might, with its gables and oriels and grey stonework and dark windows, have all the characteristics of a typical English country house – but they appeared to have overlooked the detail of a letter box, out here on the street at any rate. Presumably the kind of people who lived in a house like this expected someone to hand their post to them on a silver tray, David thought irritably.

He slowly opened the tall gate set into the wall that seemed to run all the way round the property. The curved latch felt cold, but moved easily when David pressed it down.

As he hesitantly entered the grounds, he almost expected to find himself set upon by snarling Rottweilers or Alsatians. In films, houses like this were always guarded by dogs. And they were mostly shrouded in mist.

David peered cautiously at the house. It was a good three hundred metres away in the park-like grounds. He had no desire to get embroiled in a conversation with the ominous butler. But nothing stirred behind the dark windows.

David avoided the driveway, which was all too visible from the house, and snaked his way between the trees and bushes. The further he went, the stranger the atmosphere became. The tall trees were bare skeletons, but the dense hedges were completely impenetrable to the eye.

It must be fabulously beautiful here in summer, so beautiful that you could almost touch the peace and quiet, he thought. And spring would transform this hidden world into something enchanted and magical.

He was reminded of Edith Nesbit. His mother had always read to him before she became ill. His sister Geraldine, five years younger, probably hadn't got a clue who Edith Nesbit was.

His conscience pricked him again. He gritted his teeth involuntarily and started to walk more quickly. Within a couple of minutes, he had no idea why magic and enchantment had ever occurred to him: it was mid November. It was cold and damp, and it had just started drizzling again. The lawn was muddy; foliage crunched every now and then beneath his trainers.

David tried to imagine Heaven playing here as a little girl. Once more, it crashed down on him that he was doing all this for a girl who he didn't know in the slightest.

David had always been the cautious type. He didn't trust people easily. The stuff with Kelly had just gone to show yet again how easy it was to fall flat on your face. He had trusted his sister, too, and she'd gone her own way. *Don't ever tell anybody anything. If you do, you start missing everybody.* J. D. Salinger was right.

But the business with Heaven was something different. She needed him.

He had almost reached the house. The formidable walls gleamed in the drizzle that hung over everything like a veil. The pointed turrets and gables gave the whole place a severe, harsh look, as if it were challenging the daylight.

'So this is your home,' David whispered.

He half expected to hear Heaven's smoky voice. But there was only silence and the sound of the distant traffic. A raven was squawking somewhere.

He finally saw the letter box, tucked away by the side of the drive, as if something that ordinary had to be hidden. It was small, and dark green like the hedge that surrounded it.

David rummaged in his pocket for the note that Heaven had carefully put into an envelope. He had watched as she had written her message on a piece of paper in exuberant handwriting.

Don't worry – I'm fine.

That was the entire message for Mr Mickey.

'Is that it?' David had asked.

'He'll understand.'

David cast a final glance at the house. The huge front door was decorated with a star that had been carved into the dark timber.

David saw movement out of the corner of his eye.

He instantly made out a figure.

Instinctively, he sprang behind the hedge and ducked down. He held his breath. His heart was beating loudly, and he feared its drumming alone would give him away. Silently, secretly he uttered all the swearwords he could think of.

Why hadn't he seen the guy sooner? How could he have been so stupid, for Christ's sake?

He took a deep breath, held his hands in front of his mouth, blew warm air into them, and took another breath. Then he peeped cautiously past the hedge. He immediately pulled back his head.

Damn, damn, damn.

David could have punched himself. How long was it since he'd told Heaven that these guys were bound to know where she lived? Not even ten hours. And what was he doing? Running straight into their arms!

No doubt about it: the figure by the house was the gloved man's weird sidekick who had reminded David of his dead grandfather. He was standing beneath the glistening, empty windows just as he had stood on the pavement of Kensington High Street.

Like someone who's actually dead, flashed through David's mind. Goosebumps ran down his spine.

Slowly, cautiously, David stuffed the note into his jacket.

The raggedy man still wasn't moving. He was simply staring at the path.

So where was the other man? The one with the black leather gloves?

The raggedy man started to move. He turned his head, but the rest of his body swayed oddly on the spot. It looked as if he were picking up a scent.

David felt the hairs on the back of his neck rising. What exactly did these men know? How had they got here? Did they just know that Heaven lived here? Or did they know her name too?

She had thought that she was just a random victim, someone who was unlucky enough to be in the wrong place at the wrong time. But now it was actually starting to look as if David had been right. The strange attack on the roof hadn't been a coincidence. Or had it?

David ran his fingers through his hair. His pulse was still racing.

The nurse at St Mary's. Had the guys who'd

pretended to be from the Health Department asked for Heaven by name, or had they just shown the doctor a picture of her? Described her?

Concentrate! What were the nurse's exact words? David couldn't remember.

Whatever. That could wait. What were his options? Flee into the house? But what if the black-gloved man was paying Mr Mickey a visit at that very moment?

The best thing would be for him to try to get away from there as quickly as possible. It was only a stupid old note, for Christ's sake. He could just as well call Mr Mickey from the first phone box he came across.

At the same time, he knew he wasn't going anywhere. These two men were his only clue as to what had happened to Heaven. And they might well hold the answer to how he could help her.

David was just about to press himself further into the hedge so he could wait and see what would happen next, when things started happening very quickly.

The raggedy man looked in David's direction. At almost the same moment the hedge next to him parted, and a shadowy figure threw itself at him. It grabbed him and forced him to the ground. David felt a blow and coughed; he could smell the damp earth next to his face. Then he was pulled roughly to his feet. He gasped as he felt the man's boundless strength.

'Good morning, my young friend,' the figure in front of him said. He spoke very precisely.

The reality of the situation was rapidly dawning on David.

'We need to talk.' The voice was as cutting and unruffled as a curved knife blade.

David gasped for breath as he stared into a clean-shaven, friendly, normal face. The mouth was smiling; only the eyes suggested that something was amiss. That the man had a will of iron. That he was never going to give up. They were as cold as the coldest winter.

The man, who was undoubtedly the same black-gloved guy from the Underground, was wearing dark, inconspicuous clothes. His hair was neatly parted. Carrying a briefcase, he wouldn't have warranted a second glance among a crowd of people. Here, though, the sight of him made shivers run down David's spine. He found himself wishing he still had the knuckleduster that he'd buried deep in one of the rubbish bins behind Miss Trodwood's shop when he'd moved in with her.

The man didn't waste any time. 'Where is the girl?'

David forced himself to look into those cold eyes. 'Who are you?' he retorted.

He immediately felt one of the black gloves gripping his throat. His breath was being squeezed out of him. He wheezed and began instinctively to wriggle, but couldn't escape from the man's grasp.

'It is impolite.' The gloved man's voice was calm enough to freeze blood. There wasn't the slightest trace of agitation about him. 'It is very, very impolite not to reply to a question.' He put his face close to David's. 'And you're a well brought up young man.' His breath smelled of winter, like everything else about him. 'Where is the girl? You were with her.' He smiled a predatory smile. 'Kensington High Street.' He savoured the words. 'You outsmarted us in the Underground. That was clever of you. But as you see, nobody escapes from us. We are good. And we are paid for what we do.' He loosened his grip on David's neck slightly so that David could speak. 'Where is the girl, young man?' His way of speaking seemed old-fashioned.

'Who are you?' David repeated his question.

'My name is unimportant.'

'What do you want from me?'

'I want to know where the girl is.'

David nodded weakly in the direction of the house. 'She said she lived here. I was coming to see her.'

The black-gloved man scrutinised his victim, trying to decide whether David was lying.

'The taxi brought us here yesterday. She got out. And I went home.'

'I don't believe you.' He sounded quite matter-of-fact. Calm. Composed.

'That's not my problem.'

The raggedy man had meanwhile appeared. He was shuffling past the hedge. The branches scraped his overcoat. He stopped next to the black-gloved man.

Close-up, he looked even more repulsive. He didn't smell good either. His waxen skin was covered in spots. The stench that surrounded him was that of earth, damp timber and mildewed clothes. David couldn't see his eyes – for which he was grateful.

'Who are you?' he asked for the third time. 'What do you want from me?'

'So many questions,' murmured the gloved man. He paused. 'But you are absolutely right.' His voice was friendly now. 'I really ought to introduce myself. It is also impolite to conduct such a conversation without having given you my name.'

The raggedy man hissed something that sounded nothing like words.

'My name is Scrooge,' said the man with the black

leather gloves. 'Mr Scrooge.' He did something with the fingers of the hand that wasn't around David's throat. The leather squeaked like a living thing.

David coughed again.

'And what is your name, young man?'

'Tiny Tim,' replied David.

His answer earned him an evil look.

'Good, good,' rumbled Mr Scrooge, 'so you are well read.' He smiled his snow-white smile. 'But that changes nothing about our deal, young Tiny Tim.'

'We haven't made a deal.'

'Oh yes we have.' Mr Scrooge smiled thinly. 'The reply to my question in return for your young life.' Amused, he added: 'Tiny, tiny, dying Tim.'

David was pretty sure that he wasn't joking. He tried to move, but the gloved fingers immediately tightened around his throat.

'Tiny, tiny, Tim, Tim, Tim,' crooned Mr Scrooge, using his other gloved hand to draw out a long knife. The curved silver blade traced its way across David's face and down to his chest, where the hand twisted slightly. Using his knuckles, the man tapped on David's jacket, quietly searching for his heartbeat. Then the blade crept back to his throat.

David didn't move a muscle.

'I will put this question to you one final time,' hissed the man who called himself Mr Scrooge. 'Where is Freema Heaven Mirrlees?'

'I told you – I don't know,' David hissed back. 'I didn't even know her until yesterday, for Christ's sake. Heaven, I mean. I bumped into her on the street. She was in a mess. She was rambling on about someone stealing her heart. I took her to the hospital, then we did a runner.'

Mr Scrooge seemed to be deciding whether or not to believe him. The pressure of the blade against David's throat lessened slightly.

'I had stuff on me,' David lied. 'And the guys in the hospital said someone from the Department of Health was looking for the girl.' He spoke without hesitation, trying to relax his eyes – a trick that he'd taught himself early on, and which usually worked. It was always the eyes that gave you away when you were lying. 'She was in a real state, because of the heart and stuff.' David looked from Mr Scrooge to the raggedy man. 'I gave her a bit of something to calm her down.' He spread out his hands. 'Hey, guys, I don't want any trouble.'

'And that's why you ran off?'

'I can't afford to get nabbed,' he said. 'Previous convictions.'

'Tiny, tiny Tim,' Mr Scrooge breathed. 'And I'm supposed to believe that?'

David didn't flinch. 'Why would I lie? When you're sticking a knife in my throat?'

The man paused briefly. The blade was still pointing at David's neck. 'A good story,' he murmured thoughtfully.

David returned his gaze calmly.

'A very good story.'

The gloved man looked across at the house, raised his head and shut his eyes. 'I can smell snow,' he said. His eyes opened again, and he pressed his face up to David's. 'You know what, Tiny Tim?' He didn't even blink. 'I don't believe you.' Mr Scrooge waved the knife around in front of David's face. 'Your eyes are lying. I can tell.'

The raggedy man wheezed. Only now did David notice that the skin was slowly peeling away from his face.

'Where is the girl?' Mr Scrooge asked again.

'She lives here,' David snapped. 'Go and ring the bell.'

'You don't understand anything, tiny, tiny, dying Tim.' David didn't even feel the quick slash to his throat. The knife was so sharp that he only realised he'd been cut when the warm blood started to run down his neck. 'This is just the beginning.' The friendliness had left Mr Scrooge like an old coat that had been worn as camouflage. 'I'll slit your throat if you don't tell me what I want to know.'

'What will you get by killing me?'

'Nothing,' said Mr Scrooge. 'Nothing at all. But it's fun.'

'What do you want from Heaven?' David wondered where the defiance in his voice was coming from.

Mr Scrooge thumped hard him in the stomach. David doubled up – but felt suddenly satisfied to have lured the man out of his reserve. Although the hand was still clasping his throat like a vice, it felt like something along the lines of a victory.

'Now you're going to tell me what I want to know,' snapped Mr Scrooge, his patience evidently exhausted. 'I'm going to ask you one last time, tiny, tiny Tim, and if you don't want to end up in a puddle of your own blood, you're going to give me an answer that will put me in an extremely peaceful frame of mind.' He moved the curved blade to and fro in front of David's face.

David could see the fear in his eyes reflected in the

metal, and any idea of winning suddenly seemed impossible.

The knife wandered back to his throat.

'I can read it in your eyes, young man, and this is the only question of yours that I will answer.' Mr Scrooge grinned. 'With this knife, I sliced the heart out of your new friend. Believe me, you have no idea what I can do with it.' He moved closer to David's face; so close that David could smell his wintry breath. 'Where is the girl?'

David tried to think clearly.

He could see Heaven sitting in the kitchen over in Seven Dials. He could see her smile. And he suddenly realised what all this business was about, and he felt almost cocky with relief. These two men didn't have the faintest idea where Heaven was. They were groping in the dark.

And if he kept his trap shut, it would be very difficult for them to trace her to the bookshop. David never carried any kind of ID. So it would take them a fair while to find out who he was and where he lived – if they ever managed it. And if he didn't make contact with Heaven in the next few hours, with a bit of luck she'd go and hide somewhere else.

The blade was pressing into his skin. He was

reminded of the song that had been playing on the taxi radio.

'Stowaway'. *Once I found a stowaway, upon my ship on Christmas Day.*

Then he heard a voice that was evidently not Mr Scrooge's.

'Stop there!'

The voice, deep and loud, cut through the cold air. It was as commanding and firm as the cops on a drugs raid. 'What's going on?'

Quick footsteps were approaching.

Mr Scrooge loosened his grip. 'We'll find you,' he said, and winked at David. Then he let him fall to the ground. David gasped wildly for breath. Gingerly, he felt his throat, hardly able to believe that it was over. Apart from the cut that Mr Scrooge had inflicted on him, nothing had happened.

By the time the dazed feeling had abated, Mr Scrooge and the raggedy man had vanished. Instead, two security guards were looming over him.

'Who are you, lad?' one of them asked. He was wearing a blue cap with a golden emblem bearing the name 'Gates Security'.

'What are you doing here?' the second one demanded.

'You must know this is private property?'

David just nodded. He could well imagine that he was an odd sight.

Blood was running down his neck.

'You're injured,' said the guard with the cap, helping him up.

A third man appeared. Black skin, besuited, wearing a tie. 'Who's he?'

'We've not checked his details,' replied the guard without a cap.

'There were two others with him,' the first one added. 'They've gone.'

The third man turned to David. He looked at him steadily. 'What are you doing here?'

'I...' David gasped for breath. 'I've got a note for you. From Heaven.'

The man's eyes widened. 'Where is she?'

'I can't tell you.'

The tall man took a menacing step towards David. 'What's that supposed to mean?'

The guards looked at each other uncertainly.

'Do you want me to try to catch the other two?' one of them asked.

The besuited man made an imperious gesture. 'No,' he said. 'It's fine.'

He turned to David again. 'So: you have a note?' he said firmly.

'Heaven asked me to pass it on to you.' He rummaged for the envelope in his jacket.

The man read the few lines and then looked up.

'You know who I am?'

David raised an eyebrow. 'Mr Mickey?'

For the first time, the grim expression left his face. 'That's what she said? Mr Mickey?'

David nodded.

'She's called me that ever since she was little.' He scrutinised David through different eyes. 'And you are…who *are* you?'

David looked around.

The guard tapped his cap. 'Sir, if you don't mind, I think we should check the grounds again. Just to be on the safe side. You'll have the report this afternoon.'

'Thank you.' Mr Mickey was looking very grave. Turning to David, he said: 'Come on into the house. I think you have things to tell me.'

'She warned me you'd say that if you caught me.'

'You were supposed to deliver the letter secretly?'

He nodded.

'Typical Heaven.' Then his eyes drifted to the knife wound on David's neck.

'It's nothing,' said David.

'Is she in trouble?' he asked.

'Yes.'

'In serious trouble?'

David wondered whether or not to trust him. 'Yes,' he finally said.

'We'll continue this conversation inside,' Mr Mickey replied.

They went indoors. And David Pettyfer dived into a stranger's life, suddenly so familiar.

CHAPTER 6

'The security company is well worth the money,' Mr Mickey remarked as he made his way down the hall. 'They were there within five minutes of the alarm going off.'

Not a second too soon, thought David, marvelling at the interior of the house. Every piece of furniture, every carpet, every picture looked valuable. It was as silent as a museum.

He looked around, wide-eyed. He was standing inside an imposing entrance foyer. The walls were panelled with dark wood; giant paintings stared down at him. The stone floor gleamed brightly, as if it had been polished, and ahead of him a wide, imposing staircase led upwards.

The butler closed the door behind him and glided past. 'It was the cat,' he said. His pinstriped suit looked expensive, but also as though he was wearing a disguise. Jeans and a T-shirt would have suited him better. 'We don't have any pets, but we sometimes get a cat coming in. She comes to the side door, where the kitchen is, and sits outside the door purring and washing her paws. She looks at her reflection in the glass door and waits for someone to open it.'

David stared at the man. What on earth was he talking about? Suddenly it all felt horribly unreal. This house that looked like a Hitchcock stage-set; the mortal danger he'd just found himself in; the blood on his neck; the wound that was starting to throb and sting. And now here was this butler who called himself Mr Mickey, standing there as cool as a cucumber, talking about a cat.

'The cat,' Mr Mickey chattered on: 'I call her Mrs Spoonful because she always has just a spoonful of milk – anyway, she came to the kitchen as normal today, and I was just about to put her a saucer of milk outside the door, when she ran off in a fright.' Mr Mickey raised his finger like a detective who was just about to deliver his definitive pronouncement. 'Mrs Spoonful – I call her Mrs because she regularly slips off into the bushes with a neighbouring male cat, and, let me say, always the same male cat – Mrs Spoonful is very alert.' He led the way down a corridor that had yet more oil paintings hanging in it. 'Cats will tell you when something is amiss, you know. And earlier on, Mrs Spoonful was suddenly all tense and alert. She ran off because someone was there who isn't normally there.'

That was all?

'So that's why you called security?'

Mr Mickey guffawed. 'No, they would have thought I'd gone crazy.' He stopped at another stairway, no less wide and grand than the previous one. 'I looked at the security cameras and spotted that strange man pressing himself up against the house.' He sighed. 'Homeless people sometimes loiter around the grounds. You never know what they're after. If they're pleasant, they get a hot meal; if they seem threatening and unpredictable, then I ring security.'

'As you did this time.'

'Precisely.'

David offered up silent thanks to Mrs Spoonful.

'Where are we going?' he asked.

'Up to my office. We can talk there.'

David followed Mr Mickey up the stairs. The banisters were made of stone and rested on sturdy columns. The stairs, too, were made of gleaming stone.

'How long have you known one another?' asked Mr Mickey.

'Since yesterday.'

'And she doesn't want you to tell me where she is?'

'It's better if nobody knows.'

'You still haven't told me your name.'

David shook his head. 'If I tell you my name, you'll be able to find out where she is.'

'Hmm,' said Mr Mickey.

'I'm sorry.'

Mr Mickey stopped at the top of the stairs and looked at David closely. 'And these two men who were with you just now? They were looking for Heaven, weren't they?'

David shrugged.

'By the way, my name is Michael Jones. Normally Mr Jones.' They had reached the end of the landing by now. 'Mr Mickey is just the name Heaven gave me when I started at this house.' He glanced down the corridor. 'That was twelve years ago. She was five then, and I suggested that she call me Mickey. But she always said Mr Mickey, no idea why. That's just the way Heaven is.' The man nodded at him. 'You can call me Mr Mickey too, if you like.'

David made no comment, trying instead to concentrate, to clear his head.

Think, assess the situation, then act, he was trying to tell himself.

Not the other way round.

This was, admittedly, difficult after what had just happened to him. This situation was becoming increasingly absurd. Why was the butler acting so affably? Just because David had brought the note from Heaven?

They were in a different corridor now. The whole house seemed like a labyrinth to David. There were pictures in fancy frames everywhere; up here, they were mostly photographs. They showed factory floors with weaving looms, huge contraptions with threads stretching between them like spiders' webs.

They finally arrived at a small, comfortable office with a good view of the park behind the house.

'We need to talk,' Mr Mickey said. 'Take a seat.' He gestured towards an armchair. 'I'll be back in a minute.' He glided out of the door.

David hesitated. He looked around the butler's office and went over to the window. From up there, he had a good view of the rear of the property. At that moment, everything seemed quiet; nothing was stirring between the dark trees and dense hedges. But that's what he'd thought earlier, too.

The shock of encountering the man who called himself Mr Scrooge and – above all – escaping from him, had got to David more than anything else he'd ever experienced. He was just starting to realise what a narrow escape he'd had. Mr Scrooge would have killed him. He had seen it in his eyes.

All the same – and, again, this was only dawning on him fully now – the business with the heart was much clearer. Mr Scrooge had admitted cutting Heaven's heart out of her body. He had said so loud and clear, and hadn't looked as if he was joking. Of course that still didn't explain how on earth it was possible…

In films, the protagonists were always confronted by the weirdest things – and, strangely enough, they always accepted them and were always eager to take the consequences. Whether it be strange beings or mysterious natural phenomena, illogical secrets or magic revealed – in films, all doubts were always quickly cast away. And for the first time in his life, David could suddenly see why.

Hadn't he doubted? Yes, he had. And what had he done? He'd believed Heaven's story. He'd believed what Mr Scrooge had told him. He'd believed that there was some strange man running around London with Heaven's heart.

Hadn't the black-gloved man mentioned that he was working for someone else?

Mr Mickey came back into the office. 'So, that's sorted,' he said, rubbing his hands. 'Can I offer you anything? Water? Tea?'

David shook his head and screwed up his eyes. The butler looked distinctly more friendly than before, but David still couldn't work him out. He hadn't mentioned David's wound and he hadn't called the police either – which might have been the logical thing to do with such an obvious attack. And the way he kept chattering away about nothing seemed even odder to David. He knew from experience that there was only ever one reason why someone would act so familiar from the outset. It was just a façade, either to hide something or to lull the other person into a false sense of security.

David was certain of one thing: a normal domestic employee wouldn't behave like that.

On the other hand – did it matter? Mr Mickey had known Heaven since she was a child. And if David was honest, he was burning to find out more about her.

'You're not from around here,' Mr Mickey said. He was pacing up and down by the window.

David shook his head again. He was starting to wonder whether this was going to be the question of the day.

'She needs clean clothes,' he said. 'She wants to stay with me for a couple of days.'

Mr Mickey lit a cigarette.

'She agreed to that?'

'Yes.'

He seemed suddenly amused. 'So you're out fetching her some clean clothes? From this house?'

David shook his head. 'She told me where she lives when she's not here.'

There was a flash of something in the butler's eyes, but he immediately brought himself back under control. 'I don't know,' he said casually. 'Her refuge, as she calls it, is her secret.' He didn't seem to mind unduly about her having such a secret. Or was he just saying that?

'Don't you want to know where she is?' David asked suspiciously.

'Would you tell me if I did?'

'No.'

'Fine. She trusts you. Don't tell anyone. Including me.'

David stared at him. The longer he was there, the stranger this conversation seemed to him.

'Heaven is old enough,' said the butler. 'If she needs help, I'm there for her. But I'm not looking after her. Not in that way.'

'Who are you?' David asked straight out. 'You're not really the butler, are you?'

'I have worked for the Mirrlees family for a very long time. When there were more servants than the cook and me, I was a kind of majordomo. I kept the show on the road, you might say. Now the cook and I are all that's left of the former glory.'

'Heaven mentioned her parents' deaths.'

'She told you a lot. She doesn't normally do that.'

David looked past Mr Mickey and out of the window. The garden behind the house was massive. It seemed to run seamlessly into the Old Deer Park which stretched out to the banks of the Thames.

Mr Mickey carefully extinguished his cigarette in a palm-sized ashtray made of smoked glass.

'I want to show you something,' he said. 'Then you're free to go.' Without waiting for David's response he went to the door and left the room.

David followed him. They passed quickly through long corridors which all looked so alike that David had soon lost his bearings. He wondered how a child could bear it.

Mr Mickey rounded a corner. Up a staircase, then along a passageway that smelled of the flowers that stood everywhere in tall vases. Rooms and alcoves flew past David, as the landscape had done through the bus windows.

'Here we are!' Mr Mickey finally announced.

They had reached a room right under the sloping roof.

Mr Mickey opened the door, went in, and gestured to David to follow him.

The room was empty.

Well, almost empty.

There was a mattress on the floor with a couple of books next to it. David entered the room cautiously. He took in the thick books, all of them about astronomy. A naked light bulb was hanging from the ceiling by a long cable. It almost reached the floor, dangling a couple of metres above the mattress. It was the only light in the room.

'This is her room,' said Mr Mickey. He instantly corrected himself. '*Was* her room.'

The emptiness was disconcerting. The walls were painted a soft shade of orange. Poetry quotations were written on the walls in the exuberant handwriting that David recognised from the letter. Song lyrics, too. And musical notes, next to which she had written *Music of the Spheres*.

There were no curtains, nothing. However, there was a telescope on a stand by the window, very similar to the telescope she had had on the roof.

There was no radio or TV; nothing at all. No wardrobe; just a chest that would have been far too small even for David's things.

David recalled the moment he'd met Heaven. She liked the sky and the stars; that was why she'd been on the roof. But he also recalled the photo in Trafalgar Square. Heaven amidst all her friends.

How did that all fit together?

'Why are you showing me this?' he asked.

'Heaven sent you, after all.' That was all Mr Mickey said.

David nodded slowly. The emptiness of the room appeared to be contagious.

'There are some things about her that you ought perhaps to know,' Mr Mickey began, leaving the room again. He gestured to David to follow him. Once outside, he shut the door. 'Heaven's mother – River Talbot – died after she was born. Jonathan Mirrlees's family was relieved because they had never really approved of him marrying a black woman.' He let this terrible statement hang in the air for a moment. 'She was fascinated by astronomy, by the stars, and particularly by the piece of missing night sky above central London. Heaven is very like her in that respect, even if she might not always realise it.'

'How did Heaven's parents meet?' asked David.

Mr Mickey shrugged. 'I don't exactly know,' he said.

David had a feeling that he was avoiding the question.

'All I know is servants' chitchat,' the butler continued. 'River was an incredibly beautiful woman. Calm, silent. When she laughed, people said it was infectious.' He went over to a chest of drawers on the landing and picked up a picture. 'Here she is. Looks like her daughter, doesn't she?'

David nodded.

'River came from the Fleet Street area. Jonathan didn't say much about her past, which gave rise to the most dreadful rumours. Whatever the case, he loved her very much. Idolised her, or that's how the stories made it sound.' He paused for a moment and David wondered what the relationship had been between Mr Mickey and Heaven's father. Undoubtedly not that of an employer and employee, judging by the way he spoke about him. 'Unfortunately their love ended far too soon, and left a father with a little daughter who he never really had any time for.' He gave David a meaningful look.

'Why are you telling me this?' David asked.

'Jonathan Mirrlees was rich.'

'It didn't stop him dying in a plane crash.'

Mr Mickey looked up and seemed for the first time to be losing his composure. 'You know how Jonathan died?'

'Heaven told me.' He didn't want to admit he'd googled her.

The butler was silent for a moment. 'What else did she tell you?'

'Nothing.'

Mr Mickey seemed to be wondering whether David was telling the truth. They had by now reached the main staircase above the foyer, and the butler sped up, as if he were suddenly trying to shake David off. 'Jonathan decreed very early on that the company was to be carried on by his partner in the event of his death. Heaven is to have whatever she needs and wants. But she isn't interested. She's scared of the money. And she always found the house too big.'

David could tell where the conversation was heading. 'I'm not doing this because I'm after her money.'

'So what do you want from her?' Mr Mickey eyed him suspiciously. Now he was coming to the point. And after all the chitchat that David still couldn't make out, it was almost a relief.

'I want to help her.' They reached the door. 'I've no idea what she's got herself into. But I want to help her.'

'Those men who were outside,' Mr Mickey began. He didn't finish his sentence.

David made a decision. It was time to test Mr Mickey. To test what was really behind his façade.

'Heaven said one of them had cut her heart out.'

Mr Mickey shook his head. 'That's just another of her stories.'

'What do you mean?'

'Listen,' Mr Mickey began, looking hard at David, 'she was often on her own as a child. More often than was good for her. She always invented stories, you see, in order to…in order to put herself in the spotlight.'

'So you think the story about the heart is a lie?'

'Well, I wouldn't quite call it a lie.'

David nodded.

'Let's get one thing clear,' said Mr Mickey. 'I worry about Heaven. I want her to be happy.' He moved towards David and tapped him firmly on the chest with his finger. 'If you don't treat her well, I'll find you.'

David was about to reply, but Mr Mickey raised his hand, commanding him to be silent. He smiled in a friendly way. 'Just be kind to her. I don't know where she lives. Somewhere in London, she told me that much. She comes here once a week. We drink tea and chat. But never about what she's actually doing. I know she likes clambering around on roofs, watching the night sky. When she's here, she talks about college and the things she thinks will interest and reassure me. She's a good girl. Don't you forget it.'

David nodded. 'I want to help her,' he said again. 'Really.'

'Take care out there. Those men looked dangerous.'

'Will do.'

'And whatever Heaven's told you,' he said, 'just remember, she likes stories. That's the way she's always been.'

David went outside. It felt good to breathe in the cold air.

'One more thing.'

'Yes?'

'You need to tell her something.'

'What?'

'If she's in trouble, in really serious trouble, then she needs to go to Canary Wharf.'

'Canary Wharf is huge.'

'She'll know where to go.' He leant forward and glanced around outside. 'But she'll be reluctant to ask for help.' Mr Mickey gave David a long look, perhaps trying to see if he could trust him. 'She can be very stubborn.' He sighed. 'You must make sure she does it before it's too late.'

David made no reply this time. The butler seemed to be on the point of saying something else, but then decided against it.

Outside, an icy wind was blowing. Clouds had gathered, dense and heavy. David said goodbye and then hurried back to the street.

He walked up Twickenham Road, thinking about the stranger's life that had just touched him, and the tiny, subtle lies that hide within the truth. He thought about Heaven and what he had to do, and didn't look back, even once.

SECOND INTERLUDE
MR MICKEY

The telephone rang in the big house, but nobody answered it. Michael Jones was looking out of the window, thoughtfully observing the tall, thin figure making his way down the drive towards the gate. The boy had a lithe gait, not unlike Heaven's; the long legs in the red trainers covered the ground quickly.

Mr Mickey groaned softly. Maybe he'd made a mistake, made the wrong decision. But there was nothing that could be done about it now.

The boy, who had said neither his name nor where he lived, wasn't to be underestimated. That much was immediately clear to Mr Mickey. However open and honest he might look, with those big eyes that had looked at him so innocently from under the boyishly tousled mop, as if butter wouldn't melt in his mouth – Mickey recognised a poker face when he saw one. All the more so as the boy hadn't batted an eyelid even though the cut on his neck must have hurt like anything.

Yes, it had been a real mistake. Mickey's powerful shoulders slumped. At moments like this, he cursed Jonathan Mirrlees.

Mr Jones turned away from the window and went down the long staircase. He occupied three rooms on the ground floor, right next to the sitting room where Freema had once spent her time painting pictures of the stars.

His footsteps echoed around the lonely staircase. He passed the countless oil paintings and photographs that had been his sole companions for so many months. Something brushed against his legs; it was the cat, who had emerged from the kitchen.

Michael Jones was just shutting the door to his apartment when the car turned into the drive.

CHAPTER 7

The feeling of roaming around aimlessly was one that David knew well. That had been his life in Cardiff. He'd gone bumping from one wall to the next, relentlessly, on and on. This was similar. He was moving, constantly moving, and had no idea whether it would take him anywhere. Yet he kept on moving, because there was no return.

The bus had taken him to Earl's Court. From there he had picked up the District Line and then the Bakerloo Line as the quickest way to Little Venice. Things were starting to get out of control. Too much was happening that didn't add up. So really the Tube was the last thing he needed: he hated the hustle, the loud noises, the crush of people forcing their way down passageways that were far too narrow. But the Underground was fast, and offered him some protection. He was realistic enough to see this. But he was also extremely pessimistic: the fact that nobody noticed him didn't necessarily mean that he wasn't being followed. What use was it, constantly looking round? He hadn't even noticed his pursuer in the silent garden! Better to make himself as invisible as possible. And so he dived in amongst the crowd, changed carriages twice, zigzagged his way down the tunnels and let himself be carried along in the throng of people.

He mulled over Mr Mickey's behaviour. He didn't trust the man as far as he could throw him. OK, fine: why not just let an underage heiress worth millions go off and live somewhere in the city without having a clue where she was? Sure: why not just accept that she'd moved in with a complete stranger, and simply ask him to be 'nice' to her?

Yeah, right.

David got off the train at Warwick Avenue and sprinted up the escalator, not because he'd seen someone following him, but because he wanted to get out of the Underground as quickly as possible. Moments later he saw daylight, and was soon in the open air.

Marylebone. At last.

OK, now over to the boat, grab a few clothes, on to Seven Dials, and then do nothing but stay in the bookshop.

He wondered how much he should tell Heaven of

what had gone on. The cut on his neck was hurting like mad. David cursed quietly and pulled up his collar. A cold wind was still blowing out there on the streets, but the air smelled of familiar London rain now, rather than snow. That was at least one thing that was back to normal, David thought.

It didn't take long to reach Little Venice.

The hidden area of Marylebone, which owed its name to the canal and all its brightly coloured boats, lay between old brick houses and crooked trees. Lots of bridges crossed the water, while the narrow towpaths were dotted with benches where lovers and dreamy couples sat in spring, summer and autumn to canoodle, read, or just do nothing.

Now, though, there wasn't much going on. A solitary jogger was running along one of the towpaths, and there was the occasional walker with or without a dog.

David breathed in the smell of the cold water and thought about Cardiff; about his favourite place by the coast with its surf and the cry of the seagulls, and the ships sailing in the distance. He hadn't managed to sneak off there recently.

Boats were bobbing gently on the still surface of the canal.

A lovely area. Quiet, dreamy.

Picture-postcard perfect.

David could see why Heaven had run away from the house in Richmond. He knew how it felt to have all the air forced out of you because the life someone else wants you to lead isn't the life you want to lead yourself.

Here, though, by the water, it smelled of freedom.

He found his way to the little harbour basin where the meandering Regent's Canal, the Paddington Branch and the Grand Union Canal met. It lay there between the old houses like an oasis, with ivy, trees and hedges bordering the paths.

Here, too, were anchored all kinds of brightly coloured houseboats. Lots of them were businesses and restaurants, linked together in some cases by flimsy gangplanks. Any boats leaving the basin would head off up the Grand Union Canal to Camden Lock.

Heaven had described her houseboat quite precisely. It was light blue, she'd said, with a patch of grass on the roof, not forgetting a row of brown earthenware pots filled with withered plants. A crooked chimney was poking up through the roof.

Great. That description could apply to pretty much all the boats.

Slowly David set about his search. He walked onto the iron bridge, which gave him a good view of Little Venice and the basin where the three canals met. Just a few people were wandering along the towpath. They all looked a bit lost, like extras in a Monty Python sketch.

He finally spotted Heaven's boat. Yes, that had to be it. Right next to it was another boat; they were tied together. The second boat was flatter-looking; it had round windows through which David could see only brightly coloured curtains.

David looked quickly around him once more. No Mr Scrooge, no raggedy man, no Mr Mickey.

All the same.

He left the bridge and went to the mooring where Heaven's boat was. The houseboat that he had to cross had people in it. Quiet music was coming from inside like a whisper from a thousand and one nights. Something vaguely Indian, feverishly psychedelic, childishly cheerful. Someone had painted mandalas on the side of the boat, and a stone Buddha was squatting on top of it. There were several exotic shrubs in plastic wrappers in stone tubs, and an open fireplace with ashes that were destined to be blown overboard as soon as the wind started up.

David balanced his way across the plank to the first boat, bypassed its central area, and clambered across the next plank to Heaven's boat. It was almost like being on the rooftops. Fortunately his shoes barely made a sound: he had no desire for the other boat's owners to realise he was there. He'd had his fill of conversation for that day.

Heaven had given him a key. He dug it out of his pocket and pressed his ear to the little door.

Nothing. Not a sound.

He unlocked it cautiously and went inside.

The daylight fell weakly through the little windows. Particles of dust hung in the air; shadows embraced one another. David could make out little more than silhouettes.

He fumbled for a light switch. He found one, flicked it, and gasped.

The interior of the houseboat was just one room which bore no similarity to Heaven's sparse room over in Richmond. From the low ceiling hung colourful Chinese lanterns and mobiles with little cardboard figures that looked like ragged creatures from a silhouette show. The bare floorboards were occasionally visible between the wealth of Indian rugs. The table and chairs had been screwed to the floor next to the little galley kitchen. The walls were covered with bookshelves, and David couldn't help but look at the books. They were mostly about stars and astronomy and suchlike. He also found detailed notes of observations of the sky, and a whole host of illustrated books about the strange phenomenon that plunged central London into darkness every night.

For a moment, David felt like a thief, like an intruder in a life that didn't belong to him. This here was evidently Heaven's life; that was clear to him. But discovering it without her was precisely why it felt so odd.

All the same, he took one of the books off a shelf. It was entitled *The Stolen Night of London*. He opened it up. Inside was a name, written in blue ink in beautiful handwriting, distinguished and refined: *River*.

He flicked through the book. The story was nothing new. It was about the comet that had fallen to earth on the night that the sky disappeared. Not a single observatory in the world had seen the comet coming. So when a fiery glow appeared over London people fled from their houses in sheer panic. Then, though, the fire went out and the sky became totally black. That was that. It had simply gone. No stars, no lights, nothing. Only by day did the sky look the way it had looked before. At night there was just a gaping void which nobody could begin to measure. It still looked like that now, as if someone had ripped a piece out of the firmament with all their might. It was disturbing to look up into this emptiness; that degree of emptiness was beyond anything humans could bear. That was precisely why nobody ever looked up at it any more.

David shut the book and put it back on the shelf. Then he looked around again. So many books, all on the same topic. He opened up a few more and leafed through them. Heaven's mother's name was everywhere. She had written her name meticulously in every book on the first page, immediately beneath the title. Alongside it was the date of purchase.

David glanced at the publication dates. River's books were all at least eighteen years old. Heaven must have carried on her mother's tradition. The new books were all signed by her. And they were all about the stolen night above London.

When David was still living in Cardiff, he knew about the emptiness only from the films and documentaries that he'd seen at school. Every child in Britain knew about it. The centre of the nocturnal nothingness had appeared above the city; from there, it stretched southwards to the middle of Southwark and across to the South Bank, northwards to Spitalfields and on almost as far as Soho. In the early years, the missing night even reached Kensington.

David shut this book, too, and put it back on the shelf with the others. In the cabin, which looked incredibly narrow, pictures and postcards were pinned to the timber wall. Yet more snapshots from another life: Heaven's parents in a happy embrace, a red plastic car with a proud little girl in it, a gravestone with flowers, several postcards with motifs from films and TV series: *Blackpool, The Onedin Line, Upstairs Downstairs*. Alongside were several more books: *13 Clocks* by James Thurber, *The Box of Delights* by John Masefield, *Peter Pan* by James Barrie, and *Tom's Midnight Garden* by Philippa Pearce. Then there was an extremely well-thumbed copy of J. D. Salinger's *The Catcher in the Rye* and an even more dog-eared copy of *A Trip to the Stars* by Nicholas Christopher.

For a moment, David stood there breathing in the strange life that was suddenly so tangible. He reached out to stroke the spines of the books, as if they might whisper their secrets to him if he touched them. But the books remained silent, as all good books tend to do when touched by people to whom they don't belong.

David turned and went back through the little cabin, trying to imagine a normal day in the life of Heaven Mirrlees. This was where she woke up; that bunk was where she rubbed the sleep from her eyes. She stretched, got dressed, looked at herself sleepily in the mirror. She went to college, went to classes, returned to the boat and…then what?

What did she do then?

He knew nothing about her. Who were the friends in the photo? Did she have a boyfriend? What subjects was she taking? Did she come here often, or did she spend most of her time in Richmond?

There were plants everywhere. They were growing in pots and tubs and rusty watering cans; some were even planted in drawers. Some of them reached up to the ceiling, where they touched the Chinese lanterns.

David went across to a cupboard and opened it. He found a bag, as she'd said he would, and the few other things that she'd asked him to bring. Again, he felt very close to her at that moment. He'd known her for less than twelve hours. And yet he had no choice but to admit it. He felt close to Heaven.

All of a sudden the door to the cabin was wrenched open and two dark figures came plunging towards him.

The larger of the two had thrown him to the floor

before David could see who it was. But whoever it was was strong and was shouting something at him that he couldn't make out because his ear was pressed onto the floor and his head was humming from the impact.

The other figure remained at a safe distance in the cabin doorway. It was holding something. A stick, a spade, a broom? David couldn't exactly tell what it was. It was barely more than a silhouette.

'Who are you?' the tall figure shouted at him. 'What are you doing here?' The figure's voice was, at least, young and husky and definitely not Mr Scrooge's.

'Heaven sent me.' David could barely speak, with the guy forcing him to the ground with all his might. The wound on his neck was starting to throb again.

'That has to be the most stupid excuse I've ever heard.' The voice that came from the doorway was that of a young woman, maybe two or three years older than he was.

David gasped for breath. 'Hey, it's not an excuse.'

'So you empty out her cupboard and go rummaging around in her underwear,' the woman said angrily. 'I can hardly imagine that Heaven has sent someone here to go fondling her knickers.'

'Couldn't agree more,' said the man.

David could see the sleeve of a brightly coloured

shirt. The man smelled strongly of joss sticks.

'I'll call the police,' said the woman.

David croaked.

'Did you say something?' asked the man. He didn't sound as if he was going to be very interested in the reply.

'Who are you, for God's sake?' David tried to pull free, but the man had him in a vice-like grip. 'Hey, I've got a key. How did you think I got in?'

'You crept on board like a thief,' said the woman.

'And you look like a thief,' added the man.

'Your excuses are like a thief's.'

'But I'm not a thief,' David wheezed. Couldn't anything go right, for Christ's sake?

'Shut it.'

'What should we do now?' asked the woman.

The man pondered, but only briefly. 'We'll call the police. No matter what.'

'No,' said David.

'They'll cart you off.'

David gasped for breath. He was thinking madly. Cops – absolutely not. For his own sake, but more for Heaven's. They'd register whose houseboat had been broken into. Heaven's name would crop up on some police file somewhere, and if David was right about Mr

Scrooge, then it was just a matter of time until he found out about the boat and, moreover, where David lived.

'I'm just helping Heaven,' he repeated. 'I'm a friend.'

'She doesn't have any boyfriends,' the man said. His tone said it loud and clear: *You liar!*

'We know her,' the woman added.

With some degree of relief, David realised that the man had misunderstood his croak. 'Not her *boyfriend* – just a friend.'

The pair looked at one another rather uncertainly. The man said: 'We've never seen you here before.'

'It's the first time I've been on the boat.'

'And what do you want?' His grip loosened slightly.

'I told you. I'm collecting her stuff.'

'Why?'

'She needs clean clothes. She…' Why on earth was he telling the guy all this? He didn't even know him. Quite apart from the fact that Mr Joss Sticks was still pressing his face into the floor.

'OK, listen. I met Heaven yesterday on the roof. She was looking at the stars. She goes to Chelsea Independent College and likes raspberry jam.'

It seemed to do the trick. The man loosened his

grasp a bit more. David wriggled out from under his assailant's body and managed to turn round. He found himself looking into a round face with a goatee beard and sideburns that were large and bushy, as if the guy had jumped out of a Dickens novel. The bright clothes, though, weren't Dickens. Jeans, a colourful shirt, amulets on leather thongs around his neck, and feathery earrings. Matted dreadlocks hung down to his shoulders.

'I'm Julian,' said the man. 'And this is Eve.'

The woman emerged from the shadows. She was thin and clad in black, like a young Sinead O'Connor. 'We live over there on the other boat.'

'We're Heaven's neighbours.'

The woman – Eve – said: 'People don't normally come creeping around on the boats. We all watch out for one another, you know.'

'All?'

'The boat people, the people who live in Little Venice.'

'We get suspicious if we see strangers wandering around.'

'And you sound as if you're not from…'

Oh, not again!

'Cardiff,' David said irritably. 'I'm from Cardiff.'

'Oh, Cardiff.'

'We went there once.'

'In summer.'

David rolled his eyes. 'Great. Can I get up now?'

Julian held out his hand. 'Come on.' He helped him to his feet.

'Is Heaven in trouble?' asked Eve.

David nodded.

'You're not allowed to say what's up?' Eve guessed, exchanging a long look with her dreadlocked boyfriend. 'Typical Heaven.'

'Is it? I mean, is that typical of her?' asked David.

'Yeah, absolutely.' Julian laughed. 'It really is typical of her.'

David brushed the hair out of his face. 'How well do you know her?'

'We're neighbours.' As if that explained everything.

Eve was more precise. 'We've known her since she bought the boat. That was…' She paused. 'Something like a year and a half ago. She doesn't normally have visitors, not on the boat. She comes here to be alone. She told us that she sometimes lives somewhere else. And that the people who live there have no idea that she has a houseboat.'

'So she's mostly here.'

'Exactly.'

'Yes, she is,' Julian added. 'Secretly.' He grinned broadly. 'She sometimes comes out with these long stories and you have no idea whether they're true or not. Then she goes all buttoned up again.'

Julian looked at David. 'Eve picked her up. They met at a party. Heaven heard what Eve did, and was fascinated by it.' He pointed to a kind of amulet that was dangling from one of his leather thongs. 'Eve makes these stars with a shiny stone in the middle,' he said proudly.

'They're lovely,' David said.

'Thanks.' Eve smiled for the first time. But her eyes were still full of mistrust.

'I cook,' said Julian, 'and Eve writes music and makes these stars.'

David merely nodded. 'Listen. That's all very interesting. But I've got to go. Heaven's in serious trouble.'

'And you're helping her.' The mistrust was back in Julian's eyes too. 'By nicking her clothes.'

'I'm not nicking them,' David said. 'I'm taking them to her.'

Not again, for Christ's sake.

'Look at it this way,' said Julian. 'We catch you in

Heaven's place. You're up to your elbows in her underwear. And you're not exactly very talkative.'

'I know.'

Eve came to the point. 'You just don't want us to ring the police.'

'True,' David admitted. Why deny it?

'So?' Eve stared at him.

'So what?'

'What's your name?'

Only then did David realise that he hadn't introduced himself. 'David,' he said.

'OK.'

'David,' said Eve.

'David,' repeated Julian.

'Do you have a surname?'

'Yes.'

'Hmm.' Julian tugged at his dreadlocks.

'If I tell you my surname, you'd be able to find out where I come from.'

'And what would be so bad about that?'

'Heaven's in hiding,' he explained, aware of how weird it must all sound. He told them the story of Mr Scrooge and his companion, albeit in censored form. He left out the business about the heart, and didn't precisely describe the two men either.

When he'd finished, Julian and Eve were silent.

They exchanged looks.

Their looks were like words.

'I'm all for the police,' said Eve.

Julian stepped between David and the door, blocking his potential escape.

'How about calling Heaven, for God's sake? Ask her yourself.'

'I thought you didn't want us to know where she is.'

David rolled his eyes. 'I'll dial the number.'

'You stay where you are,' Julian warned him.

Eve went over to a chest that was lying on the floor in the corner. She knelt down, opened it, and brought out a telephone. The kind of mobile that had been the latest thing twenty years ago. Huge and clunky and orange. Definitely not a mobile that could store numbers.

She came back and gave it to David. Without taking his eyes off Eve and Julian, he tapped a number into it.

It was ringing in The Owl and the Pussycat. Miss Trodwood answered.

'It's David. Can I speak to Heaven?'

Miss Trodwood went to call her.

Eve went up to David, grabbed the phone from his

hand, and withdrew to the galley. She was evidently talking to Heaven because she was murmuring something indistinct, nodding, murmuring, nodding again. Then she said: 'Yes, he's here. He's called David. So he says.' She then murmured and nodded again. She came back over to David and passed him the phone. 'She wants to talk to you.'

'What a surprise,' David retorted, glaring at Eve.

He held the phone to his ear. 'You've got lovely neighbours,' he said. 'They guard your boat as if they'd got nothing else to do.'

Julian and Eve grinned proudly.

'We have to meet,' Heaven said. 'Have you got my stuff?'

He nodded, realised that she couldn't see him, and said, 'Yes. Almost.' He could explain everything later. 'What's wrong?'

'Everything,' she said. 'Do you know the Fitzroy on Charlotte Street?'

'I'll find it.'

'Can you be there in half an hour?'

'Has something happened?'

She sounded agitated. 'Just be there. Please!'

David suppressed a groan. He wasn't sure that he really wanted to know what had happened.

'Yes, fine.'

'Thanks,' she said, then hung up.

David was left staring at the phone. Then he said to Julian and Eve, who were looking at him rather sheepishly: 'Do you know where the Fitzroy is?'

Eve took the phone from him. 'The Fitzroy Tavern,' she said. 'Over on Charlotte Street.' She went over to the chest, put the phone in it, and shut it again.

'How do I get there?'

Julian explained eagerly, as if he were trying to make amends.

David finished packing the bag and zipped it up. 'I've got to go.'

Eve grasped his wrist. 'Look after her, OK? Heaven is a special person.'

'I know,' David replied, meeting her eyes. 'Anything else I need to know?' He had a feeling that she was going to say more.

'Her mother was obsessed with the stolen sky.' Julian pointed at the books.

'I thought so.'

It was Eve who came to the point. 'Do you know when Heaven's birthday is?'

David shook his head.

'The twenty-fifth of November.' She gave the year.

David didn't know how to respond. He stared at Eve, then at Julian.

'Is that why her father called her Heaven?'

Eve shrugged. 'We don't know.'

'Her mother died shortly after her birth. That's all we know.'

David didn't ask any more questions, as no one would have been able to answer them. The twenty-fifth of November, a date that every child in London knew. What did that mean? Who was Heaven really?

Nobody seemed to know anything about her. Everyone had a couple of pieces of the jigsaw puzzle, but nobody could fit them together to make a whole picture.

'I have to go,' said David again, because he didn't know what else to say.

'If she needs help,' Eve said firmly, 'then she should get in touch.' She rolled her eyes. 'I know she won't do it. But we're here for her. Tell her that.'

'Will do.'

'And tell her we'll look after the boat.'

Julian and Eve watched him as he left the houseboat.

David went out into the gathering dusk. If there were days when you brushed against strangers' lives, in the way that dreamy images can haunt you just as you wake up, then this was one of those days. David Pettyfer set off, crossing rivers and roads to meet Heaven somewhere in the darkening city.

CHAPTER 8

On leaving Little Venice, David took a bus to St Pancras station on the Euston Road, where he put the bag of Heaven's clothes in a locker. He put the key in his trouser pocket and crossed the huge hall with its iron and steel roof that spanned the entire station in one elegant curve. A surging mass of people were pouring out of the Underground exits, the usual throng of commuters quitting London in the late afternoon to get out to the suburbs. David left the station as quickly as possible.

He ran down Euston Road, ignoring the icy cold wind that was blowing in his face. He could run faster without the bag; he didn't like carting stuff around. It made him feel tied down.

The hastening hordes of people didn't give him a second glance. The sky was darkening to become the nothingness that it always was at night. Further on, where Kensington began, the nothingness changed into a normal sky with clouds and stars.

He couldn't stop thinking about what Julian had said, about the day that Heaven was born. But he had no idea what, if anything, it might mean.

Why did she want to speak to him so urgently? Had something happened that might help them? Had she discovered something that might explain what had happened to her?

Casting a watchful glance over his shoulder had by now become second nature. But it didn't look as if anyone was following him.

It was about a mile as the crow flies from King's Cross and St Pancras station to Charlotte Street. And the direct route was the one that David planned to take. The very thought of crossing the rooftops, with no walls to block his view, made David breathe a deep sigh of relief.

He went into a house on Judd Street. It was a huge building that had been converted into offices and apartments. There were several ways to get onto the rooftops. The easiest was to find a house with an open door. These tended to be old office buildings without high-tech security systems, or buildings that housed smaller businesses. These always had unlocked doors that he could use to get onto a staircase. If this wasn't the case, you just had to ring the bells of the flats until somebody buzzed open the door. If neither of these worked, David kept a set of skeleton keys dangling from his keyring like little pocket knives. At the start, when he was still new to the rooftops of London, he had been surprised by how little it bothered people, finding strangers on the stairs. He was only very rarely asked who he was and what he was doing. Most people nodded at him in passing, and that was that. He would then sprint up the stairs and try to find an exit to the roof or a window or a balcony. Anything that would enable him to get up high.

The house in Judd Street posed no problems. He buzzed twice, and the door was immediately opened. Nobody cared who he was. At the top of the staircase he spotted a window, and went straight out onto the roof.

David enjoyed his route from Euston Road to Fitzroy Square. He went quickly but carefully. There were lots of rivulets, some of them covered in a thin layer of ice. Crossing from one house to the next tended to be the trickiest part. Sometimes he had to jump. Or there were hidden rods left behind by chimney sweeps, which he could use to cross larger gaps quite easily.

Every now and then David looked down, and it

seemed to him as if he were looking at a strange postcard of a place he'd never been to. A city in which everything looked different just because his life was in the process of fundamentally changing.

He set off again and ran along the crenellations, balanced his way across gutters, used projecting bits of wall and bays until he saw opposite him the glow of the old pub where Heaven was waiting for him.

The Fitzroy Tavern.

Warm light was shining in the windows, illuminating the classic old timber cladding. As if a soul were glowing there, born of the stories of visitors past and present.

David made his way down via a narrow staircase, a branch, and part of a fire escape. He jumped lightly down to the street, ready for anything.

He quickly crossed the junction. He knew this place; he'd walked past it several times before. It was an ancient pub with an extension housing a restaurant. It had once been a meeting place for artists and writers. Their portraits now decorated the low walls of the ground floor bar: Dylan Thomas, Augustus John, George Orwell and Michael Bentine. They had all met here to exchange ideas. The only things remaining of the romantic atmosphere of olden times were the furnishings and the pictures on the walls. Now it was full of business people killing time at the end of the day, having a last beer before setting off home on the Tube.

When David went into the pub, he was hit by the warm air and babble of voices like a carpet of brown, rough pile. Music floated above it all.

David scanned the crowd for Heaven, wondering how she would cope in this heat. He was just undoing his coat when he spotted her. She was sitting in one of the nooks at the back by the window, waving at him. She had evidently had a wary eye on the door.

David made his way through the throng of drinkers, muttering half-hearted 'excuse-me's as he pushed past them. Memories arose unbidden: lowered blinds, stuffy rooms, the walls coming in on him – but he forced them down. He hated it. Really, truly hated it.

Heaven didn't take her eyes off him. He finally reached her.

'Here I am.' He sat down on the chair opposite. She had opened the window and was sitting directly in front of it so that she could feel the fresh air without it disturbing anyone else.

'I've still got a problem with warm rooms,' she explained. 'But I've no idea why.' Her dark skin was gleaming in the red candlelight. 'Thanks for coming.'

Before her was a cup of tea; she had crumbled up the lump of sugar that had come with it.

'Your stuff's in a locker at St Pancras station. We can collect it later.'

Heaven took this in without comment.

David quickly told her what had happened in Richmond. She listened anxiously, then inspected the cut on his neck, full of concern. David brushed her away.

'What's up? Why did you want to meet me here?'

'I rang the college from a phone box at Seven Dials.'

'And?'

'The secretary said a man had phoned a quarter of an hour earlier and asked about me.' Her eyes were like the dark night. 'A Mr Quilp.'

'Mr Quilp?'

'Yes, like the guy in Dickens.'

'Why doesn't that surprise us?' he asked.

She nodded. 'Yeah, why doesn't it?' She sounded hopeless.

David didn't quite know what to say. He had a feeling that this wasn't all she wanted to tell him, but he didn't want to press her.

The waitress came to the table and David ordered a cup of tea. Earl Grey, black. Heaven waited until she had gone, then asked: 'Did you see my bedroom? I mean the one in Richmond.'

'Yes.'

'And?'

'Looks empty.'

'It's less empty than it used to be,' she replied.

'Your houseboat's more cosy,' David said. He had to grin. 'If, that is, you're not being grilled by two neo-hippies who've got nothing better to do than start yelling for the cops.'

'Julian and Eve are OK,' said Heaven. 'I trust them.'

'More than your other friends?' David thought of the photos he had seen.

She was silent for a moment, staring at him.

'Have I asked the wrong question?'

She shook her head. 'No,' she said, running her fingers through her hair. 'You haven't. It's just that Julian and Eve are the only ones who know me on the boat. My other friends, the college ones and friends from school, they're part of my life in Richmond. Even my job…'

She had a job? *Heaven had a job?*

She laughed. 'Why the disbelieving look? Mr Mickey always gets in a tizz about it, but I like doing it. I'm a waitress in a little café near the Fulham Road. We're closed for a fortnight at the moment, though. Renovations.'

David shut his eyes for a brief moment. 'Why me and not one of the others?' he finally asked.

She immediately understood what he meant.

'You were there.' She looked at the table, picking nervously at the old wax from the candle next to her cup of tea. 'And you got me out of that hospital before Mr Scrooge or Mr Quilp or bloody Oliver Twist for all I care came walking in to Casualty. You believed me.' She swallowed. 'I trust you.'

David shook his head. 'But I know nothing about you. I mean, we're up to our necks in it, and I don't even know you. Hey, I nearly fell off my chair when you told me you had a job!'

'I am Heaven,' said Heaven.

'I know.'

'And?'

'Who are you really?'

She shook her head. 'I'm complicated,' she replied.

David had to grin. 'Who isn't?'

'Yes, who isn't?'

David held Heaven's gaze, and the chattering and the music behind them turned into a curtain of sound that enveloped them, just the two of them, for one long moment.

But then the waitress brought the tea, and the moment passed.

David began mechanically poking about with his teabag and cup. 'The phone call to the college – was that all you wanted to tell me?' he asked hesitantly.

'Afterwards, I spent the whole time sitting in the kitchen, thinking,' she said. 'Miss Trodwood left me alone. She really is a very nice, discreet lady.' She sighed deeply. 'I mean, there must be something we can do, mustn't there?'

'I reckon so.'

She looked across at the bar. 'I've decided to tell you something,' she began. 'I have to, because you'll otherwise think I'm completely crazy to suggest what I want to suggest.'

'I'm all ears.' David sipped his steaming tea.

'OK. You saw inside the house in Richmond.'

'So that's why you sent me there.' He had thought as much, and she had confirmed his suspicions.

She nodded. 'Now you know where I grew up. And you might also understand why I wanted to get away.'

'Your father?'

She nodded quickly. 'He died four years ago. He

flew to Scotland because he wanted to find a new business partner.' She made a dismissive gesture. 'Work stuff. Nothing important.' She was looking into the far distance. 'On the way back, his plane crashed.' She swallowed. 'That's it. A plane crash in the middle of the Lake District, near to Scafell Pike. An accident. Sounds somehow unspectacular, doesn't it?' She didn't wait for his reply. 'They told me about it at school. They called me out of lessons, and the Head and a psychologist told me themselves. In a room with a plant and a pale wood table with a hideous tablecloth. There was a coffee machine against the wall.' Her fingers were playing with her teaspoon. 'And the chairs were plastic. It was like I was paralysed. A taxi took me home to Richmond.' She looked up. 'Mr Mickey and Mr Sims took care of everything.' She paused, took a sip of her tea. Then she said, as quietly as if it were a secret: 'They buried him in Highgate, in my mother's grave.'

David didn't know what to say. He held her gaze. It was all he could do.

'All of a sudden I was an orphan. Weird, eh? The word sounds as if there weren't any such things nowadays. Sounds more like something from a Dickens novel. But it actually happened.' She smiled, but her smile turned into a grimace. 'A poor orphan.'

The smile withered and died. 'Well, not exactly poor. More like rich.'

'Mr Mickey was afraid I might be after your money.'

'Typical Mr Mickey. He's always so mistrustful.'

'Right.'

She turned her head to one side and breathed in the cold air that was streaming through the window.

'Your father and Mr Mickey – were they actually friends?'

She looked at him for a moment, confused. 'What do you mean? Mr Mickey has always been our butler. My father left him to me when he died, so to speak.'

David recalled how familiar Mr Mickey had sounded when talking about Jonathan Mirrlees. But he didn't probe any further. 'How did you end up on the houseboat?' he asked instead.

'I met Eve at a party, in the way you just happen to bump into people. I liked what she did, and she invited me onto her houseboat. My boat belongs to them too; I rent it from them.'

'Then?'

'It was a proper new start. That was almost two years ago. Nobody knew where I'd disappeared to.' She laughed. 'I went back to Richmond every now and then, talked to Mr Mickey about this and that, and then disappeared again.'

'What about the college?'

'They've got my Richmond address. And they only ever send stuff by email.' As if she'd guessed what David's next question would be, she added: 'I don't have a computer on the boat. That's what internet cafés are for.'

'Two separate lives, that sounds very mysterious.'

Heaven shrugged. 'I didn't want to be the poor girl from the big house. The one with all the money and no parents.'

'I can understand that.'

'I wanted to be me, not someone else.'

'Looks as if you managed it.'

'It wasn't easy.' She turned the cup round and round on the table.

Then she smiled, a bit like the light of the moon before it disappears behind a cloud. 'But that's not actually what I wanted to tell you. It's something completely different. When my father was buried, I went to Highgate Cemetery for the first time in my life.'

'You'd never seen your mother's grave before?'

'No.' Her voice was stony.

'Why not?' He couldn't stop himself.

'Because,' she retorted, almost stroppily – then she pulled herself together and said: 'There was a letter that my mother wrote when she was pregnant with me.'

Thea Gilmore was coming out of the loudspeakers hidden in the corners of the ceiling.

'*Look up at the sky when you think of me*, it said.'

'A bit kitschy for my taste,' he said. Immediately he could have bitten off his tongue but it was too late. The words were already out there. 'Sorry,' he muttered shamefacedly. 'I didn't mean to hurt you.'

To his surprise, though, she smiled briefly. Her smile was like the shooting star that David had seen the previous day. 'No need to apologise. You're right.' Her fingers were tapping out the song's rhythm on the table. 'Anyway, I never wanted to go to the graveyard. I don't like graveyards. I don't like places where there's so much death. I had a photo of her grave, and that was enough.'

David remembered the photo. He'd seen it in the houseboat.

'My father,' she continued, 'was buried in the family grave, and that was the only time I ever set foot in Highgate.' She drained her cup and put it back on the table with a bang. 'It was raining. It's supposed to rain at proper funerals. It's not right, saying goodbye to someone in the sunshine. There were so many people there. Suits, people like my guardian Mr Sims. Faces I'd never seen before. They all carried dark umbrellas and some of them were wearing sunglasses.' Heaven's olive skin took on a darker hue; she seemed angry all of a sudden. 'They were all grieving, and they didn't know him at all.'

David wondered what she was getting at.

'There was a letter for me amongst his things. He'd written it years before, and it was just one sentence.' She rubbed her eyes. 'You can visit us any time!' She looked up. 'That was what was in the letter. Nothing else.'

'You can visit us any time?'

'I've spent the last few hours thinking nonstop about what's happened to me. What's wrong with me.' She fiddled with the beer mats on the table before slowly, meticulously shredding them. 'But I suddenly remembered the letter and this one sentence, which I hadn't thought about for years because it didn't make any sense.' She rubbed her eyes again. 'My parents are both dead, and there's no reason for me to visit them. They can't talk to me, because they're not here any more. But if there's anything in this sentence, then it points to Highgate.' She stopped. 'Or am I just going completely crazy?' She looked pleadingly at David and reached for his hand. Her fingers were as cold as ice-cubes, burningly cold, but it felt strangely good to be touched by her.

He shook his head. 'No,' he said. 'I don't think you are.'

'So will you come with me? Please?'

He looked at her hands, which were knotted on the table. He nodded. 'No problem.'

'I'm sorry to drag you into all this,' she whispered, glancing anxiously at the cut on his neck. Her voice was husky. 'It's probably mad and unnecessary and, what's more, I promised myself I'd never go back there, after the funeral with the men in sunglasses and the women all in hats, you know, I've never seen so many...'

David reached for her other hand and drew it close to him.

'Heaven,' he said calmly. 'We can go anywhere.'

She stopped and looked at him. Then the smile spread across her face, the smile that was Heaven, first slow, then radiant.

They sat there in silence for a while. The cold draught from outside was blowing in his face.

'I don't even know anything about you,' Heaven suddenly said.

'True,' David replied.

'You're from Cardiff.'

Nod.

'You don't like the Underground.'

Another nod.

'And I know that you don't like talking about the past.'

He looked at her silently.

'I'd love to know who you are,' she said openly. 'Why you're here.'

David sipped his tea and didn't say a word, as he never did when anyone asked about his past. Kelly was the last one; she wouldn't give up. She'd tried to say that it was for professional reasons at first; later, she had accused him of deliberately shutting her out of his life. Whatever.

'The precise medical term is agoraphobia,' he said suddenly. There was a lump in his throat which he tried to clear. 'Which means fear of public spaces. Sounds pretty banal, doesn't it? But it can be sheer hell.'

He lapsed into silence once more, and they sat there without speaking. Heaven didn't ask anything, but just looked at him closely. Her hand was on his. He finally continued: 'My mother hasn't been out of the house for seven years,' he said. 'It's crazy. I didn't notice it at first; she just didn't go out very often. Maybe I was too young to realise. Or maybe it wasn't so bad then. But in recent years it became unbearable. She was terrified that something might happen to us outside. That's what she always called it: outside. She only let us go to school, my sister and me. Sometimes we couldn't even do that.'

'What about your father?'

David shrugged. 'We had to understand. Everything would be fine. Shut up and put up so that she'd get better.' He looked at Heaven, amazed by how easy he was finding it to talk about this. 'That was the worst thing, I think. The façade of normality. My father didn't really believe that my mother was going to get better.' David remembered how often and how fiercely he had argued with his father about it. 'He knew full well that there was virtually no chance of her recovering. And yet he locked us in too – and he still does it to my sister. Plays at ideal homes in that stuffy house in Cardiff where the walls close in more every day.'

'That's why you don't like the Underground.'

'Yes.'

'Anything else?'

'Quite early on, I started thinking of going to London. All very normal, you know? Studying.'

'Studying what?' she asked, interested.

'Dunno. Literature, art, that sort of thing.'

'But they didn't let you.'

'No.' He shook his head as he remembered the last time he'd tried to talk to them. They had been sitting in the dark, narrow living room; the blinds were closed as they were every day from morning to night and from night to morning. It had been summer – a record-breaking one, so people said later on. His mates were sitting by the sea, drinking beer, smoking pot; they'd texted him to ask where he was, but he hadn't gone, just as he so often hadn't gone that summer.

His parents hadn't banned him from going. Of course they hadn't. But did he have any choice? His mother's panic attacks when he sneaked out of the front door, her shrill crying that resounded through the house for hour after hour, louder and louder, the accusing look of his father, who blamed it all on him: the endless recriminations were more effective than any ban. Before, when it had all started, his father had even lashed out at him when his wife's screaming had left him with no other outlet for his pent-up emotions.

David involuntarily moved towards the open

window and breathed in the cold air that streamed in from outside. He could still remember how unbearably stuffy it had been that afternoon in the room where the windows hadn't been opened for years. The TV was on day and night, as if it could replace the world outside. That's why David hated TVs. His sister spent her afternoons squatting close up to it.

'I need to talk to you,' David had said. But when he'd seen the crazed look in his mother's eyes and the pleading look on his father's face, he hadn't been able to say it. He simply couldn't say it. He was struck dumb. But that night, he had packed his things.

'I ran away from home,' he said. He went on to recount a few of his experiences to Heaven, very briefly. Finally he mentioned Kelly, the social worker. And the other stuff, too.

'I don't have anyone because I don't want anyone,' Heaven admitted.

'Why not?'

'You're nosey.'

'I know.'

She smiled. Then she turned serious. 'My parents loved one another like couples do in films.' She sighed. 'In photos of them, my father was always laughing. I never knew him like that. He wasn't at home much when I was a child, but when he was, he had all the time in the world for me. But he didn't laugh, and I missed it.' She brushed a strand of hair off her face. 'If you love someone, you always end up losing them, don't you? One person always loses the other at some point. That's why I'm not going to fall in love. Short-term relationships: yes.' She looked away, out of the window. 'But really loving someone...' The idea seemed to make her uncomfortable. 'That's not good.'

David thought about the old photographs that everyone carries around inside them. Dog-eared, with little tears and brown spots. Nobody looks at them very often, but everybody secretly knows that they are all postcards that will stay with them for ever.

'Let's go,' David suddenly said. He didn't let go of Heaven's hands, not even when she half-heartedly tried to pull them away. 'It isn't always good to be alone.'

A new song was coming from the loudspeakers: 'Raven Star' by Lunascape.

David looked up.

'What's the matter?' asked Heaven.

'That song,' said David.

'What about it?'

'It reminds me of something. But I don't know what.'

She smiled.

Then they left the Fitzroy Tavern. And set off for the graveyard.

CHAPTER 9

They caught the bus to Archway station, near to Swain's Lane. It was an old bus. Heaven sat by the little sliding window so that she could breathe in the fresh, cold air. The city outside was a blur of colour and movement and light.

'We need the eastern part,' Heaven said as they got off the bus.

The main gate was still open. The Victorian building looked out onto the street like a watchman with cavernous windows for eyes. It was reminiscent of the entrance to a ruined palace which might still house enchanted creatures. The stone was weathered, and wind and rain had rendered unrecognisable the shadowy figures that emerged from the walls.

'Highgate Cemetery is one of the "Magnificent Seven",' Heaven said as they followed the path inside. 'Most graveyards in London belong to a particular church. At some point, they ran out of space, and they thought it would be a good idea to set up seven really big graveyards on the outskirts.'

'How do you know so much about graveyards?'

'You mean why do I know so much about them when I avoid them like the plague?'

He nodded.

'People who don't like spiders are fascinated by them too.'

'S'pose so,' David murmured.

Heaven's footsteps were the only sound. She was still wearing David's clothes, though she had put her own shoes on, and the heels of her boots were click-clacking on the cobbles. She had tucked her hair back behind her ears, but strands kept falling forward, framing her olive face.

The path they were on now was twisty and turny, with tall trees on either side. It looked as if the graveyard had been built in the middle of a forest.

High up in the night sky the stars were twinkling though little ragged holes in the grey clouds. Here, the sky was normal. Thick foliage grew on either side of the path, which became increasingly narrow as it snaked its way through the night. It all seemed as if nature were reclaiming what had once been hers.

'Do you have any idea where your parents' grave is?'

'Don't worry, I'll find it.'

'What are we going to do when we get there?'

'I don't know.' Heaven's look meant: stop talking. No more of those kinds of questions, please, because I don't know the answer and I don't want to think about it either.

He understood.

Weather-beaten gravestones covered with moss and ivy rose up from the damp, dark earth like dead teeth. There were Egyptian-inspired mausoleums with figures and columns jutting from the walls. Crooked doors hanging from rusty hinges led the way into deep catacombs that lay beneath the rampant undergrowth and were touched by the shadows of monuments. Many of the monuments were resplendent with larger-than-life carvings of people who had died long ago: grey stone figures with serious expressions and high collars; whiskered aristocrats preserved forever in grey, speckled basalt.

The wind was blowing the bare branches against the gravestones. There were only a few lamps braving the shadows.

'We seem to be the only people here,' said David.

'The graveyard shuts at night.' Heaven was staying close to him. 'Quite apart from the fact that hanging around in here is strictly forbidden.'

'I thought so.'

She smiled at him, very briefly, and they carried on. Path after path. The further they went into the graveyard, the more silent Heaven became. Her eyes were rough seas in which darkness broke in gentle waves.

Headless angels on high pedestals kept watch over the silence which was broken only by the traffic on Swain's Lane. There were huge sculptures of lions and dying lambs preserved for eternity in stone. Gigantic eagles angrily stretched out their stony wings, and pale marble damsels were draped over the gravestones in dramatic dying poses.

They passed the Circle of Lebanon, a famous circle of tombs arranged around a huge cedar, their cavernous depths gaping open in the night, silent and accusing. Then they reached the Egyptian Avenue, which seemed like a city of its own. They passed rambling alleyways and stairs and squares. By the side of family tombs were rows of columns and sphinxes. They looked like palaces from a land in which the sun never rises.

David had a pretty good idea of the grave that Heaven was looking for. He imagined something imposing, flashy, expensive and old, rather like the house in Richmond. A grave with columns and figures and fancy adornments, covered in moss and oblivion.

Heaven, however, left all the fancy graves behind her. She was walking more and more quickly now, and soon she was on a path that led up to a little wood. The ground was covered with old, damp leaves, which had partly frozen and crackled underfoot. Walking along this path was like walking around a dark dream. Everything was so unreal, so grey, so shadowy.

They finally reached Heaven's parents' grave. It was just a simple stone sticking up from the ground. Two names: Jonathan Mirrlees and River Mirrlees.

Heaven stopped in front of the grave and stood there motionless.

There were no flowers; just undergrowth. No candle was burning in the lamp that was barely visible beneath the ivy. The weathered gravestone was grey, austere. It bore neither the dead people's dates of birth, nor the dates of their deaths.

'Hello, you two,' Heaven whispered. She looked uncertainly at David.

He moved closer to her, reached for her hand, and squeezed it.

'Here I am,' said Heaven. She smiled hesitantly, a smile that was almost a sob.

The wind was blowing in their faces. David was sure he could see the occasional star-like snowflake falling in the night.

He wondered whether coming here had been a good idea. Nothing about this grave looked as if it was going to provide any answers. It was just a dark, dead, forsaken place somewhere in a graveyard in a forest.

Heaven knelt down and picked up a clod of earth. She held it tightly, crumbling it between her fingers. Then she stood up again and took a step back. 'I don't know why I came here,' she whispered in a trembling voice, looking at the dark earth in her hand as if it was going to hold the answer. 'I've never visited you.' She swallowed hard. 'But I've thought about you. I never stop thinking about you.' Tears were running down her face. 'I miss you both so much.' She suppressed a sob. Then she stamped her foot angrily on the ground. 'What am I actually doing here, for Christ's sake?' She glared at David, then at her parents' grave; she was despairing, at a loss. Angrily she flung the earth back.

David put his hand on her shoulder and gently turned her to face him. Then he hugged her, held her tight, until she became calmer and silently wrapped her arms around him.

They stood there like that for a while.

The stone sculptures next to them stared cold-eyed into the night.

Then a voice cut into the wind.

'You came,' it said.

Alarmed, Heaven detached herself from David. He gave a start too. They both looked around.

'Did you hear that?' asked Heaven.

David peered into the shadows, nodding warily. 'There's someone here.' How about that for a stupid remark.

'I am here,' said the voice. It sounded like hoarfrost in the morning, and apparently had no desire to mask itself.

David and Heaven whirled round.

The woman was standing right behind them. She was wearing a floor-length dress. Her bare feet were peeping out beneath it. Long hair fell below her shoulders.

Heaven opened her mouth and shut it again.

'Who are you?' asked David.

The apparition looked at him with interest, and David was reminded of how scared of ghosts he had been as a child. Never could he have imagined meeting one. This woman certainly looked like one, though.

And Heaven appeared to accept that what she was seeing was what it seemed. After all, that is normally the case. So why bother thinking about it?

'Who are you?' Heaven repeated.

The apparition smiled kindly. 'Oh, that's a long story,' she said. The apparition was definitely female, albeit a bit transparent and holey. 'I am not your mother.' She came closer. 'But it's you, isn't it?' Her face was as pale as moonlight. 'You're Heaven – Heaven Mirrlees, actually Freema. And you're here because your father told you that you could visit your parents whenever you liked.'

Dazed, Heaven could only nod. David felt her hand tightening around his.

'Your father had no idea that he would die so soon. And unfortunately he isn't here to tell you himself, but that's another story.'

'Who are you?' David asked, this time more urgently.

'My name is Sarah Jane Cavendish,' said the woman.

'What are you doing here?'

'I am dead.'

'You're a ghost, aren't you?' Asking outright made David feel odd.

'This is my grave,' she replied.

'No, it's not. It's my parents' grave,' Heaven fired back. She sounded angry. Ghost or no ghost, this woman had no business hanging around here, and that was that.

The ghost nodded gently. 'I know, it's supposed to be. But the rules demand that the person who's buried in a grave has to live there.' She was attractive, David saw now. A woman in her forties with unusually long hair and a face that must have laughed a lot once upon a time. 'There's nothing I'd like more than a grave with my real name on it. But nobody knew it. There were just strangers at my funeral. They were mourning someone else, and I felt so alone. It was terrible.' She looked up at the stars, and David noticed that there was no reflection in her eyes. 'The dead don't reflect life,' she said, seeing his gaze. 'That's one of the many rules that you discover once you're dead.'

'Why can we see you?'

She laughed. 'Because I want you to.'

'So you really are a ghost?' Heaven said.

Sarah Jane laughed. Her laugh sounded like snow on fir trees. 'That's a bit of an exaggeration. I'm nothing. Just an echo that still blows on the wind if you listen carefully. But, yes, you could say that I'm a ghost.'

'And what are you doing in my parents' grave?'

'I've already told you,' she said patiently. 'I belong there. My remains were buried there.'

'I don't understand.' Heaven was clearly irritated.

'Nor can you understand.' Sarah Jane sighed. 'Your father was going to explain it to you, but then he died. I saw you at his burial. I listened in to the mourners; that's how I know what happened.' She pointed to a spot near to David, a little way from the grave. 'You were standing right there. I was very close to you.'

David tried to imagine the mourners all standing there, Heaven at the front with Mr Mickey or Mr Sims, although she'd rather have been at the back, hiding behind the bushes. The grave was a yawning chasm, and damp earth was clattering onto the coffin.

'Didn't you feel a cold breath?' Sarah Jane's eyes were like fog. 'This kind of thing?' She winked at Heaven. 'People normally feel that if they can't see us. If you felt something like that, then it was me.' She smiled sympathetically. 'But what am I thinking of? I should start at the beginning, shouldn't I? A story is only as good as its beginning.'

David raised an eyebrow. 'And the beginning is where, exactly?' he asked.

'I'm the beginning. I am Sarah Jane Cavendish,' she

introduced herself again. 'From Chiswick.' She paused and turned to Heaven. 'The last time I told this story, it was to your father.' She plucked a brown leaf, from a scrawny branch hanging above the path. 'You might perhaps be expecting some extraordinary story, but I can't give you that.' She examined the leaf, then let the wind carry it away. 'It wasn't anything spectacular; it was just one wrong moment that changed my life.' She laughed sadly. 'I'd still be alive if I hadn't been so silly.' Her dress was flapping in the cold wind. 'But that's no good to me now. I've been dead for more than seventeen years.'

'When did you die?' asked David.

'On the twenty-fourth of November.' She gave the year.

David looked up.

'It was in fact almost eighteen years ago,' said Sarah Jane, shaking her head. 'How time flies.'

Sounding astonished, Heaven said: 'That was the day before I was born.'

Sarah Jane nodded sadly. 'I was working as a cashier in the Chiswick branch of Tesco. I spent all day sitting at the till, scanning things.' She shrugged. 'It could have been far worse.' Memories of a whole life were within her sigh. 'Then I fell in love. He was called Ewan

Noble. He was from Hampstead Heath and looked as noble as his name.' She laughed, and the ice on her tongue shattered. 'He chatted me up and we went out together, and the same thing happened that always happens when you follow your heart and are as silly as I was. I still remember how it felt when we kissed for the first time. It was in a doorway over in Smithfield. He pulled me into it because it was raining, and we kissed, and the whole world lit up.' Her dead eyes blinked, full of tiredness. 'I was never particularly bright, not even as a child. But nice, I was really nice. Sweet little, nice little Sarah Jane who tried to do everything right. I'd never have imagined someone like Ewan Noble falling for me.' She shook her head again. 'How stupid I was. How stupid, stupid, stupid.' She began to walk – or, rather, float – around the grave, softly and lightly. 'I believed everything he said, all his promises, and I imagined marriage and children. But then I saw him with someone else.' Her laugh turned bitter. 'I did warn you that it's not a new story.' She used both hands to prop herself up against the gravestone. 'They were sitting in the window of Equinox, and I saw them when I just happened to be passing.' She paused. 'I don't know whether he saw me.' She quickly corrected herself. 'No, I'm sure he didn't see me. He didn't even realise I was there. I ran away.' She beat the gravestone with her fists, and the air around her hissed. 'How stupid of me. I should have made a scene. Hey, I was a girl from Chiswick – I'd have been good at that. But I didn't. Instead, I ran off. Crying, cursing, the whole works. I went into a pub and started drinking. Hard stuff that stops you thinking and kills memories, all of them if possible. I wanted to forget. Ewan. Myself. Chiswick. Tesco. And above all the life that I'd imagined for myself.' She was clutching the gravestone. 'Then I went down to the Embankment. I stood there for ages, where the ships are, looking at the tide. The river was pitch-black that night, and there wasn't a single star reflected in it.'

David looked up and across at the hole above the city, wondering what it might have looked like before. Once the emptiness had stretched out to Kensington, but he only knew that from films and photos, like everyone else his age.

'You're too young to remember,' said Sarah Jane. 'But I still remember what the night above London looked like when I was little. All the stars, the sky, the clouds. But then they vanished. Two years before my death. I never got used to it while I was still alive.' She looked at Heaven as if she were about to say something to her. But she returned to her story instead. 'Anyway,' she continued, 'I was standing at the edge of the Thames, and then I just let myself fall forwards.' Another sob that was supposed to be a laugh. 'I was drunk. I just let it happen. Just like that, I didn't care. I fell into the Thames, and immediately felt it dragging at my clothes. I was carried away by the current and carried out into the middle of the river. It was November and it had been raining heavily for the past few days, so the Thames was in flood. I was washed further and further away. I gasped for air, started to swim, past the bridges, but nobody noticed me.' The memory of it was like a wilted flower that she couldn't stop smelling. 'The city looked so beautiful with all its lights. They slid past me, and that was when I regretted what I'd done. It was so strange: I could feel life in all its glory, and I'd thrown it away because of some idiot who was seeing someone else. I saw all these pictures of the city and the beauty of it all, and finally I wanted to grasp hold of life again – but I went under, and everything went dark and black.'

David and Heaven were silent for a while. There was nothing but the wind in the branches and the shadows that were keeping their secrets.

'That's terrible,' was all that Heaven finally managed to say.

'They took me to the Chelsea and Westminster Hospital. But I was long dead by the time I got there. My handbag and everything in it had gone; the Thames had washed it all away. They called me Jane Doe and tied a note to my toe with that name on it. That's what they do with dead people whose identities are unknown.'

'What's it like?' Heaven asked solemnly.

'Dying?'

She nodded.

'Not very nice,' replied Sarah Jane. 'You feel pain and regret.' She made her way round the gravestone and came to stand on the middle of the grave, where she touched the weeds that were growing there. 'The worst thing,' she whispered, 'is the feeling of not being missed. Nobody comes to mourn for you. They all carry on with their lives, and being forgotten gnaws away at you.' She pressed her hands up to her eyes, as if she were wiping away tears. 'That's what we're afraid of. When nobody thinks about us any more, we really are dead. That's our final death.'

'But someone is still thinking about you,' said David. 'If you're here talking to us, then someone must be thinking about you.'

'You've not been forgotten,' Heaven agreed.

Sarah Jane smiled hesitantly. 'You may be right. Maybe there's someone, somewhere.' She struggled to maintain her composure, then continued. 'Anyway, they took me to the Chelsea and Westminster.'

David could sense that she was getting to the heart of her sad story. He wasn't surprised to see the first snowflakes starting to fall.

'What happened there is as hazy as drowning itself. Only once I was in the ground did I start to live again. When I opened my eyes, I was here.' She looked around, as if she could bring back the moment. 'I was standing next to the grave, and all these mourners had gathered around it. I didn't know any of them. That's my first memory of Highgate – my first memory as a ghost. My new life began when they lowered the coffin down into the ground.'

'But why my mother's grave?'

'Do you still not see, Heaven? Can't you guess? My remains were buried here.' Her eyes were like deep water. 'My remains – not your mother's.'

'But what happened to my mother?'

'Patience,' said Sarah Jane. 'You'll have to give me some time if you want to understand all this.'

Heaven nodded.

Sarah Jane continued her story. 'I met other ghosts here; the cemetery is full of them. They were kind to me, but nobody could tell me why I'd been buried under the name River Mirrlees. It was a mystery, a puzzle. And just as I was thinking that I'd never find out why, your father came to visit the grave. I can still remember him touching the damp earth and crying. I knew he was Jonathan Mirrlees. I could sense it. I decided to show myself to him.' She blinked glassily at Heaven with her dead eyes.

'My father spoke to you?'

'I spoke to him, more like,' said Sarah Jane.

'Why?'

'I wanted to know why I'd been buried in his wife's grave.'

'What did he say?'

'He was very composed.' She raised a long, shimmering finger. 'People don't normally react very calmly to meeting a ghost. But he was calmness personified.' She looked from one to the other. 'Like you two. You quickly accepted that there could be someone like me here. You don't doubt me; you believe what you see. When people act like that, they've already experienced things that others couldn't begin to guess at.'

David still didn't really understand what had happened back then, though an inkling was slowly forming in his mind.

'When I died, a London woman was brought into Chelsea and Westminster Hospital, already in labour.' She gave Heaven a long look. 'Coincidence can be such a strange thing. A little girl was born in the night of the twenty-fourth and twenty-fifth of November. The girl's mother died in childbirth.'

That was a part of the story that David already knew.

'But there was something different about this,' continued Sarah Jane. 'So different, so strange, so unusual that Jonathan Mirrlees had to bribe the doctors and midwives.'

David held his breath. 'What happened?'

'Jonathan Mirrlees bought their silence. River Mirrlees, you see, disappeared after the child was born.'

'What do you mean, disappeared?' Heaven faltered.

'River Mirrlees just vanished,' replied Sarah Jane. 'She died. And then she wasn't there. That's what Jonathan Mirrlees told me. And afterwards?' She sighed. 'Well, they were a wealthy family. They didn't want any headlines or palaver. They needed someone to officially bury, someone for whom they could have a normal death certificate. So they took me. The female corpse with the Jane Doe tag on her toe.' Her hands trembled in the way that ghostly hands do. 'It was the most straightforward solution. Nobody knew who I was. Nobody noticed I'd gone. It just needed a bit of fiddling around with the files.' Sarah Jane gave Heaven a meaningful look. 'Your father was a rich man. He paid for it all.'

'But why?' stammered Heaven. 'Why would my father do something like that?'

'Because nobody would have understood the truth,' replied Sarah Jane.

'What actually is the truth? What do you mean when you say that River disappeared?' asked David.

Sarah Jane glided over the gravestone. She looked sadly at Heaven. 'I don't know anything about that,' she said, her voice a transparent whisper. 'Your father didn't seem to want to talk about it. And I respect the wishes of the living. He just wanted you to know that your mother isn't buried here. And I promised to tell you.'

Heaven shook her head. 'No. No. It's not true.' She sounded angry now rather than confused. 'I'm not stupid.' Her words came tumbling out, her voice threatening to crack. 'Why doesn't my father show himself to me?' She went up to the gravestone and pointed at the inscription. 'He's buried here, isn't he?'

Sarah Jane shook her head. 'They buried an empty coffin. He isn't here. I'm all alone. The nearby graves are all deserted. Nobody remembers the dead lying there. And if nobody remembers them, they disappear. That's the death that ghosts fear. That really is the end.'

'I don't believe you.' Heaven was almost shouting, but it sounded more like crying to David. 'It's the biggest load of rubbish. I...'

'I don't know what happened to your father. But the coffin that they buried was empty.'

'No,' whimpered Heaven.

David glared at the ghost of the woman named Sarah Jane and went over to Heaven, trying to take her in his arms. But she lashed out, snapping at him: 'Leave me alone!' Then she turned and clung to the gravestone. 'It's rubbish, for God's sake, rubbish.'

David stood behind her and held out his hand, pulling her back. He remembered the story that Heaven had told him in the Fitzroy Tavern. He thought about the plane crash in the Lake District, and about the fact that they may have found nothing in the wreckage that could have been put in a coffin.

Jonathan Mirrlees really had managed to pose even

more questions for his daughter than she was already battling with. But he hadn't provided any answers.

David recollected Heaven's words. 'Look up at the sky when you think of me,' her mother had said. And he thought about what had happened on that twenty-fifth of November two years after the comet had appeared and the emptiness had spread across the city sky.

Tears of rage were running down Heaven's cheeks. 'What am I supposed to do now?' she yelled, staring at Sarah Jane. 'Why did you tell me this?'

The answer to this question came blowing across to her with the cold wind. It was given by a voice that belonged to a shadowy figure wearing gloves. In one of the black gloves was a long knife. Its blade was glinting in the darkness. 'You needn't worry your head about that any more,' the voice declared. It was as cutting as the knife itself. 'It will all be over soon.' And before anyone could really grasp what was happening, there they were, face to face.

CHAPTER 10

David instinctively placed himself between Heaven and the tall black-gloved man. The raggedy man who had been leaning against the wall in Richmond emerged from behind another grave.

'How nice to meet you here,' said the black-gloved man, who had still been calling himself Mr Scrooge only a couple of hours before. When he saw Sarah Jane, he hesitated briefly. Then he introduced himself again. 'I'm known as Mr Heep around here.'

Slowly, the raggedy man came towards David and Heaven. He was limping, and his movements were hesitant and unfocused.

'What do you want from me?' asked Heaven. Her eyes betrayed no fear; instead, she still looked angry about everything that was happening to her.

'Your heart.'

'But you stole it!'

Mr Heep gave a wan grin. 'I know.'

'How did you find us?' asked David.

'I'm good,' said the man, holding the knife up to his face. 'The possibility that at some point you would turn up at her mother's grave seemed to me one I couldn't ignore.'

'Leave Heaven alone!' David demanded.

The black-gloved man examined the blade. 'It doesn't seem to me that you can dictate what I do.' He smiled pleasantly; it was a grim sight. 'I have a job to do, and I don't care to disappoint my client. I'm renowned for delivering exactly what I'm paid for.' He turned and moved the blade so that it reflected the dim light of the stars. The snowflakes evaded the blade. 'And now I'm going to take your girl with me.'

The raggedy man stumbled forwards. He looked even more dilapidated than he had done a few hours ago, and he was giving off a sweet stench. The skin was peeling off his face, and he had wrapped filthy bandages around parts of it.

'I'll tell you both what we're planning to do,' said the man who was now calling himself Mr Heep.

David looked around for something that he could use as a weapon. A stick, a stone, anything at all. He could feel an impotent rage blazing up inside him, an anger that in the face of his paralysing helplessness felt like a burning knot in his stomach.

'There has been a misunderstanding,' said Mr Heep smoothly. 'We were just looking for a plain, ordinary heart, as we have done so many, many times before. I've been involved in this trade on and off for more than twenty years, and it's still highly lucrative. You should know that my client, like so many of them, is interested in pursuing long-term business relationships.' He smiled a sickly sweet smile. 'And this just happens to be my business.' He gave the trembling raggedy man a patronising look. 'Oh, what am I talking about? It's *our* business. We've often stolen hearts. But nobody has ever survived it before.' He clicked his tongue, evidently signalling to the raggedy man. 'Nobody can survive if their heart has been taken.'

Sarah Jane nodded sadly. She was standing there immobile, either undecided or unable to do anything.

'Miss Mirrlees is the only person to have got it into her head to run away from us.' Mr Heep took another step closer to her.

Heaven recoiled.

'She ran away because she has a second heart. One that our client would dearly love to have in his possession. That's why we're here.'

'A second heart?'

David was baffled, and could tell that Heaven felt

exactly the same. What did Mr Heep mean? What did he know about what had happened to Heaven? The gloved man didn't look as if he was about to explain.

'You're going to kill her.' It was a statement.

'These things happen,' Mr Heep remarked laconically. 'In our trade, death is a constant companion.'

The raggedy man shuffled closer. Earth was caked under his yellowed fingernails, which looked long and blunt. His breath stank of rot and decay.

'You're coming with us,' Mr Heep said, turning to Heaven. 'I don't know whether my client is planning to return to you the heart he already has. To tell you the truth, the generosity of my client has never interested me. I imagine he won't. But he's extremely keen to find out what the situation is with this other one.'

'You're mad.' David was wondering how much Mr Heep really knew about everything that was going on around him. It looked rather as if neither he nor his mysterious client knew exactly what to do with Heaven. His sole task had evidently been to snatch the girl alive.

'Totally mad,' Heaven burst out.

'Oh no, my dear, I'm not in the slightest bit mad.'

The raggedy man was circling David and Heaven.

He groaned softly to himself whenever he moved. An oozing rash covered his hands. He had twisted them into claws and was moving them slowly before his face.

David glimpsed a movement to one side and looked at Sarah Jane. Had she just winked at him?

The black-gloved man was smiling at David now. 'You don't matter,' he said. 'I can let you live, or I can slice you open from top to toe. You can leave the cemetery, or you can lie in a puddle of your own entrails, gazing up at the stars, wondering when the last spark of life will leave your body. Your fate lies in your own hands. The fate of your girlfriend lies in mine.'

'Like hell it does!' David spat at him. He bent down, grabbed the lantern from the grave and flung it at Mr Heep, who ducked too late to avoid it. The heavy lamp hit him on the shoulder, and he emitted a low groan of pain.

'You won't be able to save her,' the man snapped angrily, clutching his arm. 'No – you can find out just how sharp this knife really is. It looks as if you've already made your decision.'

David grabbed Heaven and pushed her behind him. The man was unmoved. Something in his shoulder cracked loudly; he moved his arm backwards and it seemed to heal instantly.

Sarah Jane was standing on the grave, looking miserable. 'I can't help you,' she whispered. 'I'm just a ghost, and I have no power over the living.'

Mr Heep grinned. 'You're on your own.' The blade flashed in the moonlight. 'There's not a soul who can help you.'

Then the raggedy man took a step towards Heaven.

Mr Heep snapped: 'Time to die, my boy.'

Heaven screamed. At top volume.

And as quick as lightning, Sarah Jane descended upon the raggedy man like a curse. David had no idea what she was doing, but she flew at him and knocked him roughly to the ground. The raggedy man snapped and snarled like a mad thing, lashing out wildly. His decaying face with its dead eyes was distorted with pain. The light that Sarah Jane gave off shone into his eyes and mouth, causing his rotting skin to split apart.

Mr Heep was visibly taken aback.

'Run,' hissed Sarah Jane, who was now not much more than a silhouette. 'Quick – run!'

The raggedy man seemed to have lost all control of his body, and was now flinging himself angrily at Mr Heep. His fingers were curled up into claws, and he was moving like a puppet on a string. Mr Heep gave an angry shout, glared at David and Heaven, and was then pulled to the ground by his sidekick.

'Is that Sarah Jane?' Heaven asked.

But David didn't want to know the answer. He had stopped thinking about what was true and false. He grabbed Heaven's hand and pulled her along with him. The black-gloved man looked wildly at them as he tried to defend himself against the raggedy man's attack. There was the flash of a silvery blade, and the air was filled with the sound of it slicing through bandages and severing tendons. The raggedy man screamed, like a predator suddenly finding himself the prey of another, even larger, predator.

'Come on!' David yelled, yanking Heaven along behind him.

A glance over his shoulder told him that Mr Heep was still lying on the ground, slicing away at the raggedy man, who was still trying to fight him off.

It wouldn't take long for the inevitable to happen, thought David, and then Mr Heep would be after them, and he would be so angry that they would be able to see the red in his eyes.

'Faster!' Now it was Heaven who was setting the pace.

David ran. His breath was burning in his throat. He glanced sideways. Heaven didn't seem to find it hard to run fast. So long as she was in the cold fresh air, there was nothing to sap her strength. Her footsteps were even and rhythmic, a song with a beat that drove her forwards.

They rounded a bend and raced back down the same path they had come along. Stone angels and sculptures with half-broken faces watched them as they fled. They raced across grass and gravestones, through a little wood where branches lashed against their faces, past a stream and a cross with a dying wooden faun nailed to it.

David eventually lost his bearings. He didn't recognise anything around him. There were overgrown thorny hedges; the gravestones were squat and weather-beaten.

'Damn, damn, damn!' David stopped in front of an expanse of bushes, thrust his arms in, and wrenched them apart. Heaven slipped into the gap, and he followed her through the hedge.

'How on earth did they know where my parents' grave was?' She was breathing quickly but evenly.

'They were in Richmond. They know your address – so they can find out anything they like.'

'But how do they know my name?' said Heaven. 'How the hell did they know about Richmond?'

David was panting heavily. 'Forget it,' he said. 'Later, OK?'

She nodded.

They made their way awkwardly through another hedge and emerged in a clearing surrounded by trees. Mausoleums stood sentinel around one part of it, their entrances yawning blackly at David and Heaven.

'Egyptian Avenue,' said Heaven.

It was a whole world of alleyways and streets, a village of graves and tombs and palace-like resting places. They'd run straight into a city of the dead.

'What about the tombs?' David said, looking hastily around. 'We could hide in one of them.'

Heaven shook her head. Her dark eyes were wide. 'What if we meet another ghost? It might not be as friendly as Sarah Jane.'

'These graves are ancient. If Sarah Jane is right, then there won't be any ghosts here because there's no one to remember them.'

'What if there are?'

'Then they can't hurt us. We're still alive.' He shrugged. 'Well, they might give us a fright.'

He remembered what Sarah Jane had done to the raggedy man, and hastily cast the thought aside.

Heaven was listening intently in the darkness. The

air was full of sounds. A strange bird was calling and the undergrowth was rustling in the wind, but there was nothing to suggest that their pursuers were getting closer. The snow was falling more heavily. A snowflake landed on Heaven's cheek where it lay there like a tear, unmelted. 'If we hide in a grave and they find us, then we've got no chance of escaping,' she said. 'It's a dead end. A trap.'

'We have to risk it.' David raised his head. 'He's coming.'

Now they could both hear the footsteps, a loud rustling in the bushes that they had come from. The urge to hide was overwhelming.

'Shit!' said David. 'Who the hell is this guy?'

For a moment, they stood there motionless in the night. It was David who finally decided. 'Come on!' He took her hand and pulled her across to an iron gate that wasn't properly locked. The old padlock that held the chain around the bars had completely rusted away. They had simply to twist the lock apart.

David quietly opened the gate so that first Heaven and then he could slip through. Once inside, he pulled the gate behind him and re-attached the chain.

'With a bit of luck, he won't notice,' he whispered.

Heaven didn't reply, but reached for David's hand again.

In the mausoleum, which was well over a hundred years old, it smelled of damp earth and undergrowth. The air was cold, and felt as if it hadn't been breathed in since forever. They cautiously picked their way across small stone steps. They were so rotten and broken in parts that David and Heaven had to be careful not to stumble.

At the end of the passageway, a small hole had been let into the roof, allowing the silvery light of the moon to come floating in. Individual snowflakes were falling to the ground.

The low walls were covered in figures of Egyptian gods, elaborate pictures and hieroglyphs that had long since faded. This kind of decoration had evidently been the done thing for wealthy people in the days of Queen Victoria.

David stopped for a moment beneath the hole and looked up at the sky. He was still breathing heavily, though now it had nothing to do with running fast. He could feel the familiar sensation of anxiety. The walls closing in on him. The noise of the door shutting behind him and the rattle of the key in the lock.

'Are you OK?' asked Heaven.

David shook his head, but managed a grin. 'I'll be fine.'

He could almost have laughed. My God, how clichéd was that? *I'll be fine?* They only said that in bad Hollywood thrillers when the wounded hero is lying on the ground trying to get his oh-so-helpless female companion to run away without losing face. *You go without me, you have to do this for me, baby, I'll manage, I'll find a way, everything will be fine...*

David's remark earned a smile from Heaven, and he wondered whether she'd thought the same thing.

Cautiously they carried on, step by step, down into the depths. This time David felt as if Heaven were pulling him along, rather than the other way round.

So much for the big Hollywood hero, he thought.

'He's there!' Heaven suddenly whispered.

They both paused. David listened intently. He could hear the footsteps outside; this reminded him of the past, too. The noises of the outside world had always sounded much louder through the shut blinds, as if life were trying with all its might to force its way into their tightly sealed house.

David could feel himself breathing faster and faster. He could almost feel the heavy stone above him. He could feel the burden that had been so infinitely oppressive for so many years.

No, there was nothing that could help him. He shut his eyes, just briefly.

It's nothing, no, I'll be fine…

'Keep going,' he whispered.

Onwards they went, deeper and deeper into the mausoleum. They followed the stairs, which ended in a chamber. From between huge columns, the figures of Egyptian deities were watching over the dead who lay behind the wooden door to the actual tomb.

The door, old and stained, was fastened to the stone wall with heavy hinges.

David opened it cautiously, horribly aware that this tomb could be their undoing. If their hiding place was discovered, they were trapped.

'Crap idea,' Heaven murmured.

'Could be.'

David looked into the chamber that lay behind the door. Somehow, they had to trick the guy. There had to be some way out. There was always a way out; it was just a matter of plucking up the courage to take it.

The silhouette of a sarcophagus was peeling away from the blackness of the chamber. Something was moving in the shadows.

'There's something there,' Heaven murmured.

'Rats, maybe.'

'Oh, great.'

David gave a start. Something was tugging at his trouser leg. Little claws were trying to make out who dared to venture into the darkness.

David fumbled in his pocket for a lighter and flicked it on. He felt a sudden bite on his leg and instinctively kicked out at the thing that had bitten him.

A rat, he thought, trying to calm himself down. *Just a rat.*

Then he saw it.

'What the hell's that?'

It was moving, lurking in the flickering cigarette lighter. The creature was as big as a cat, but it didn't look like a cat. Its eyes were white and reflected the feeble light when it hit them. Then David noticed that it had a long tail, hairless and bare. And the muzzle was too pointy to be a cat's. David was forced to admit that the creature looked like a cross between a cat and a rat, like something that had never seen daylight and never ought to see it either.

The creature snarled angrily and before David could react, it sprang at him again. Its little teeth snapped at his fingers.

Horrified, David hit out. As the thing hit the ground, he gave it a kick and sent it flying over to the sarcophagus.

Almost immediately a rustling sound came from all around them in the darkness.

'Shit!' cursed David when he saw what he had awoken.

The tomb was full of rat-cats.

They were squatting in the corners, curled up together on the ground, and draped all over the huge coffin in the middle of the room. Mangy rat-cats were waking up everywhere, staring at Heaven and David with their white eyes.

Heaven didn't wait to see what happened next. 'Get out!' Again, she was pulling David along behind her as she banged the door before the rat-cats could follow them.

Panting, she leant against the door and looked at him. David was still holding his lighter. The flame was reflected in her eyes. Then they heard a rusty sound, the rattle of a chain falling to the ground.

Mr Heep had tracked them down.

He was here.

'We have to hide somewhere,' she whispered in a panic. 'What about over there?' She pointed to the columns and figures in the walls.

David listened intently. Footsteps were echoing in the dark corridor, coming closer, quickly, far too quickly for him to react. It was either the door with the rat-cats behind it, or the columns, the stone figures, the people with animal heads.

Heaven grabbed his arm and dragged him to the side, opposite the door to the tomb. The flame from the lighter was flickering wildly.

'What are you doing?' he whispered.

They could hear the footsteps approaching from outside.

'Come on.' She pushed him behind a sculpture with large breasts and a crocodile's head and squeezed in with him. They hid in the gap between the figure and the wall, barely breathing. Then Heaven took the lighter from him and threw it over towards the door.

David heard it clattering against the timber. It provoked a low growling sound from inside the chamber, then fell to the ground. And David realised what Heaven was doing.

Everything went quiet again. Quiet as the grave. David could feel Heaven's hair softly brushing against his face. He was enveloped in her scent of cinnamon and lemon.

The footsteps were coming closer, accompanied by the searching beam of a torch.

Heaven pressed herself closer to him and then, before their pursuer arrived, her cold lips touched his. She was closer to him than she had ever been, and kissed him as if there would be no 'later', no tomorrow.

As the beam of torchlight searched the chamber they were both hidden in themselves and the kiss that had become a world of its own, a world that neither of them had been looking for but had found all the same.

Then they returned to the dark reality of the grave, and heard the man stopping by the wooden door, bending down to follow the trail.

He saw the lighter on the ground.

David could feel Mr Heep smiling his most friendly smile. Then he opened the door and quietly went in. 'Come out, come out, wherever you are,' he breathed.

There was a soft snarling. The beam of light flashed wildly on the ceiling and walls of the tomb.

David darted out of his hiding place, through the chamber to the door, and flung himself at it with all his might. It shut with a loud bang, the catch clicked into place, and Heaven was already sliding the bolt across.

At the same time they heard a hideous snarling

sound from many throats. David didn't wait to see what happened next. 'Let's go.'

He and Heaven ran outside. He could still taste her kiss on his mouth, deep and fleeting as a dream. They stumbled up the steps, gasping for breath.

It was snowing properly outside now. Large snowflakes were whirling and dancing in the wind.

David paused, looked at Heaven. Muffled cries of anger and pain could be heard coming from the tomb.

'That way,' Heaven commanded. She had found her bearings again, and set off in front. David followed her, and soon they reached one of the main paths. They raced down it as quickly as they could. Shreds of cloud were pushing their way in front of the moon, creating shadows where there shouldn't have been any. The snow was falling on their hair and faces, but they paid no attention, just kept on running in order to leave the subterranean chamber far behind them and, with it, the gloved man and the rat-cats who were doing God knows what to him.

As they finally reached the cemetery wall, they saw a glowing silhouette.

'Sarah Jane,' David gasped.

The ghost was sitting on a bench under a tree. 'The raggedy man won't be bothering you any longer.'

They ran over to her.

'What did you do to him?' asked David.

'He's one of us,' she replied in a voice that sounded like ice. 'He's a ghost; he's dead. But someone gave him back his body so he could wander around in it. Mr Heep is what used to be called a bodysnatcher. He digs up corpses for his own purposes.' She shrugged her shoulders as best as a ghost could. 'Maybe he promised him a new heart.'

'You mean to say he woke up a dead body to use him as a kind of sniffer dog?'

She nodded. 'Dead people can smell a living heart from miles off.' Sarah Jane watched the snowflakes falling through her. 'I took control of his body, but Mr Heep knew how to defend himself. That blade did a very thorough job.'

'What about his spirit?'

'Homeless, until his remains are buried in the ground.'

'That's terrible,' Heaven whispered, shocked.

'That's the life that dead people lead,' Sarah Jane replied. Her gaze fell on the rip in David's trouser leg. Three claw marks were clearly visible.

'We went into one of the old mausoleums,' said Heaven, 'over in Egyptian Avenue.'

Sarah Jane gave an understanding nod. 'Sometimes an animal gets lost in a tomb and can't find its way back out. This animal can then get together with the other animals that live down there. Their offspring tend to look ghastly. They live in permanent darkness, eating insects and mould and whatever creatures were down there before them. They never see daylight, and are constantly hungry.'

'Mr Heep was attacked by them.'

'You were lucky.'

'Yeah, I know,' said David softly.

Sarah Jane stood up. 'You ought to go now. Highgate is still a place of the dead.' She touched David's hand, then Heaven's. 'You simply don't belong here.' She smiled sadly. 'But before you go, there's just one thing I'd like to ask of you.' The gaze which gave no reflection lay calmly on Heaven and David. 'Once this is all over,' she said, looking pleadingly at Heaven, 'might it be possible to have my name on the gravestone?'

Heaven promised. 'We won't forget you,' she said to the ghost.

David touched the silhouette of a hand and simply said her name. 'Sarah Jane.'

Then they turned and set off into the night.

They didn't look back once: looking back is something that living people must never do when leaving the realm of the dead. Nobody had ever told Heaven and David that, but they knew it all the same.

CHAPTER 11

They didn't talk. Too much had happened. Neither of them imagined they were safe just because they'd left the cemetery.

They hurried to the nearest bus stop. There they were lucky, and got straight on a bus to St Pancras station. David retrieved the bag of clothes from the locker and then he and Heaven caught another bus to Trafalgar Square.

Large snowflakes were whirling in the wind when they got off, covering the whole city in enchanted whiteness. The big fountain with its stone lions was lit up on all sides, as was Nelson's Column.

He gave Heaven a couple of watchful glances out of the corner of his eye. He was thinking about what they had found out from Sarah Jane and Mr Heep, and then he thought about the kiss and started trying to say something, but Heaven remained silent and didn't return his gaze. She just stared at the road ahead of her, completely immersed in her own thoughts; it looked as though she had forgotten that she wasn't alone.

They were on the way to Seven Dials when Heaven quite suddenly changed direction in the middle of the square.

A tramp was sitting propped up against a phone box. He was wrapped in a sleeping bag and filthy blankets, and it was impossible to tell whether he was asleep or just staring into space. Without looking at David, Heaven went up to him, scrabbling around in her pockets as she did so.

'Excuse me,' she said politely.

The man squinted at her. 'Whaddya want, me beauty?'

She pointed to the bottle beside him. 'Is that new?'

''Aven't touched it.'

'The cap looks OK,' said Heaven.

David wondered what on earth she was doing.

The man looked suspicious. 'D'ya want a bit?' It was impossible to see what kind of concoction the bottle was harbouring, as it was wrapped in brown paper.

'Ten pounds for the bottle,' said Heaven, holding out a note.

'Is everything OK?' David finally found his voice.

She ignored him. The tramp looked suspicious.

Heaven said impatiently: 'I'll give you ten pounds for the booze.' She repeated her offer. 'Ten pounds.' She waved the note around in front of his nose.

That was all the persuading he needed. Bottle and note changed hands.

'Nice girlfriend you've got,' the man said to David. 'But a young girl like that shouldn't be on the booze.'

'I know,' replied David.

Heaven, however, had set off again.

David raced after her. She unscrewed the bottle, put it to her lips and took a large swig.

'Hey!' David cried. She didn't turn round, but headed straight for one of the stone lions.

'What's all this crap about?'

She stopped in front of one of the stone lions and took another swig. She pulled a disgusted face. 'Christ, this stuff is truly revolting,' she said, before taking a third swig.

David had caught up with her. 'Why are you doing that?'

'Have you ever danced on the lions?'

He recalled the photos of her and her friends that he'd seen on the internet.

'No.'

'I have.'

'Hmm.'

'You know what the best thing about it was?'

'I have a feeling you're going to tell me.' He knew that he sounded impatient, and that she didn't like it.

'I was so bloody normal when I did it.' She laughed out loud. 'I was just a schoolgirl with friends, like everyone else.' She looked at him and David saw that she was crying. 'Look at me now, for God's sake. My life is a complete shambles. My father kept it secret from me that my mother disappeared without trace when I was born. Instead of telling me himself, he gets a ghost to do it – the ghost of the woman he buried instead of my mother. I've got no heart. Who knows how long I can go on living like this? And something tells me that Mr Heep's going to reappear, probably as Mr Creakle.' She moved closer to the lion and stared it in the eyes. Then she screamed with all her might. She just stood there, screaming so loudly that the night itself trembled. It was a deep, guttural scream full of anger and despair, fear and uncertainty. 'I've had enough!' she screamed. Then she flung the bottle at the lion's head with all her might, as if it were to blame for everything. 'I've had enough, you hear me?' Cheap booze was running down the lion's muzzle. She spat on the ground, coughed, wiped her mouth with her sleeve. 'Is that really so hard? Just being normal…'

David came up behind her, put his arms round her, and tried to hold her tight. But when he felt her stiffen, he let go.

'I can't go on like this,' she whispered.

'Heaven,' he said. Nothing else.

'I want my life back.'

'We'll find a way,' he promised.

'Do you really think so?'

'Yes.' *Sometimes*, David thought, *you just have to lie at moments like this.*

Heaven turned and stared at the lions. 'I'm sorry,' she whispered.

Then she set off again. David followed her.

Together they climbed the steps, leaving the National Gallery to their left, and walked along Charing Cross Road. Silently they made their way down the streets that were now white with snow.

The quiet that snow always brings had settled on the city, a luminous blanket. The night sky was still missing over this part of London. David thought about the stories that Sarah Jane had told them, and about what had happened on the day that Heaven was born and her mother disappeared.

He looked at her out of the corner of his eye and resisted the temptation to take her in his arms. He knew that she didn't want it, not now. The kiss in the tomb, so quick and unexpected, had unsettled them both. But all the same – it was still there, and nothing could undo it. It just wasn't the right moment to talk about it. That was that. And that was fine by him.

Charing Cross Road was practically deserted. Just a few cars were battling their way through the fresh snow. There were hardly any tracks in the white powder; a few on the road and none on the pavement. David felt a fraction of the tension that had imprisoned him all day fall away from him.

Five minutes later, they reached the bookshop. It stood there peacefully in the street, a faint light visible beyond the windows. David felt as if he hadn't been there for years; so much had happened in the past few hours.

He put his key in the lock and quietly opened the door. Inside, they were greeted by the soft glow of a reading lamp. Miss Trodwood was asleep in the armchair in the middle of the shop. An open book lay on her lap.

David recognised it immediately. Dickens, of course. *Great Expectations*.

'She's been waiting for us,' Heaven whispered.

'She normally goes to bed at eight on the dot,' David murmured. He went quietly over to the armchair. The old lady's reading glasses were perched crookedly on her nose and her head was slightly to one side. She was breathing peacefully and *Great Expectations*, which had slipped halfway down her stomach, was rising and falling to the rhythm of her dreams. Her left hand was on the page that she had presumably been reading; the other hand was on the arm of the chair.

David was just about to carefully remove her glasses before they fell off. But at that very moment Miss Trodwood opened her eyes and instinctively slapped David's fingers. As she did so, her thoughts returned to sleepless reality.

'David!' she exclaimed, both relieved and reproachful. 'And Heaven.' She sighed. 'Where on earth have you been?' Then she looked at them and said: 'Oh God, look at the state of you!'

Only then did David realise how filthy they were.

'What have you been doing?' There was no trace of sleepiness about her now. 'You look as if you've seen a ghost.'

Neither of them replied.

Miss Trodwood narrowed her eyes. When she did that, it seemed as if she could see straight through you. 'You *haven't* seen a ghost, have you?'

'Well,' David began, 'now you come to mention it…'

'Yes,' said Heaven, completing his sentence.

'Kind of.'

'It was a she,' Heaven continued. 'She said her name was Sarah Jane.'

And David added: 'Long story.'

Miss Trodwood snapped her book shut and put it on the table. 'You're not going to get me into trouble?' She looked at them both sternly. 'You've not been taking drugs, have you?'

They both shook their heads vigorously.

'But you say you saw a ghost.'

Now they were nodding.

'A real ghost, like Oscar Wilde saw?'

What else could they do but nod again? 'Crazy, crazy,' Miss Trodwood murmured.

'Were you waiting up for us?' asked Heaven.

'No,' Miss Trodwood replied firmly. 'I've just been on my feet longer than normal, that's all.'

'Hmm.'

'Could Heaven…?'

Miss Trodwood pre-empted his question. 'Of course she can spend the night here. She needs our help, doesn't she?' Turning to Heaven, she added: 'We've talked about the whole business.' And with mock reproach, she said: 'How on earth could you imagine that I'd mind, David?' She winked at Heaven and hauled herself out of the armchair. 'But your story, ghost or no ghost, and however long and strange it may be, will have to wait until tomorrow. I'm an old lady and I need my sleep. I've been up long enough. You're back and you're fine, and that's all I needed to know.'

'I...'

'Why haven't you got a mobile?'

David answered truthfully: 'I don't like mobiles.'

Heaven laughed, and David understood why. After all the weird and dangerous situations they'd just been in, it felt good to be told off by Miss Trodwood about something as banal as a mobile phone. And it was nice to know that she'd been worried.

'And now,' she said, 'please excuse me. I'll be insufferably grumpy tomorrow if I don't go straight to bed.' She went over to lock the door. 'Oh, this ridiculous weather,' she said as she peered through the window. 'Snow in November.' Then she added:

'Doesn't look as if anyone's following you.' The look on her face clearly told them that she wasn't blind and deaf and had a very good idea of the trouble they had got themselves into. 'Good night, Heaven, David.' She went to the staircase. But she had one final warning to impart. 'And I'll have no funny business up there.'

David and Heaven exchanged looks.

'No, absolutely not.' David sounded as if he were choking on his words, but Heaven had herself under more control.

'Promise.'

'Good.' Smiling smugly, Miss Trodwood disappeared behind the curtain. 'I'm going to be dead tomorrow morning if I don't get a couple of hours' sleep.' Her voice was getting further and further away, and the stairs creaked with every step. Then came the sound of a door shutting further up. Then a toilet flushed, and the house fell silent.

David was still standing by the armchair, looking at the book that Miss Trodwood had left on the table.

'So she likes Dickens?' asked Heaven.

'Are you surprised?'

Heaven yawned involuntarily.

'Let's go up,' David said. He grinned. 'But…'

She started to laugh, and it occurred to David that

she laughed nowhere near often enough. '…no funny business up there,' she finished.

Heaven was still giggling as they went upstairs. For a moment, it seemed as if there wasn't a thing in the world that could spoil her good mood – but David immediately noticed that she had fallen silent again, and that she was breathing heavily. The air on the stairs was simply too warm and stuffy for her.

Upstairs, she disappeared into the bathroom, emerging half an hour later. She was wearing an old T-shirt and boxer shorts belonging to David – the same things she'd worn the previous night – and looked exhausted.

'I couldn't find any pyjamas on the boat,' said David.

'I'd rather wear your stuff,' she replied.

David had already opened the window. Icy air was streaming into the room, and a couple of stray snowflakes landed on the furniture.

'Cold enough?' asked David. He was still wearing his jacket and scarf.

She nodded. 'Can I ask you something?'

'Fire away.'

'I'd actually like you to do something for me.' She was standing in front of him. 'Can you stay with me?'

He just nodded.

'Despite the cold?'

He demonstratively pulled his collar up.

Heaven slipped into bed.

David took off his jacket and went into the bathroom. When he returned, he pulled a thick jumper on top of his T-shirt, then climbed under the covers with her.

'I'd love to see some stars now,' Heaven whispered. 'Like on the rooftops. I feel so free up there, regardless of what's happened during the day. Removed from the world I live in.'

David understood all too well what she meant. 'You feel as if you're flying, even though you're not.'

They both stared at the same snowflake. It floated through the window and landed on the floorboards, where it didn't melt.

'Do you want to talk?' David whispered.

'No.' She stared out of the window. 'At any rate, not about what happened today. Not now.'

'That's fine.' David looked up at the ceiling. He finally asked softly: 'Do you know *Great Expectations*?'

'Of course I do.'

'Miss Trodwood likes it,' said David, gazing outside. 'She reads it over and over again. She even told me to read it. She says there's no book that prepares you better for real life.' David was suddenly aware that he wanted to tell Heaven all about his life. Talking about his benefactress seemed a good way to start.

'You really like her, don't you?'

David nodded.

'Do you know her story?' she whispered.

'Miss Trodwood…' He turned on his side, propped himself up on his elbow, and looked at Heaven. 'She's lived in this house on her own for ages. She told me, just once, how she came to live here. The last day of her life, she called it.'

'That sounds sad.'

'I think she only told me about it because she knew that my life had gone spiralling out of control.'

Heaven put her head on one side, but didn't ask anything.

'I was in a bad way when I came here.'

She nodded, holding his gaze.

'I felt pissed off, alone, unhappy, angry, guilty – all at the same time.' He disliked remembering this time, even though it hadn't been all that long ago. 'I did a few things that I'm not exactly proud of.'

'And?'

'Miss Trodwood took me aside one day. I hadn't

been with her for long, and I'd just been sorting out the new releases. She offered me a cup of tea, then she told me her story.'

'I'm intrigued.'

'At first, I didn't understand why she was telling me. She was brought up by an aunt, somewhere in the countryside around Dover. She didn't say a word about her parents.' He paused. 'It actually sounded like in the book, like in *Great Expectations*. There's this little girl, brought up to be so desirable and adorable that everyone has to fall in love with her. The girl grows up in the countryside in a big house, all alone and isolated, with lots of mirrors and even more books in an old library that nobody uses but her. The years go by. The strange aunt dies at some point; the girl turns into a woman and goes to London. There she attracts countless lovers, and breaks all their hearts. She can't change, because she isn't aware that she needs to change. All she's doing is what she's been taught to do. She has learnt how to live a life without love.' He stopped, saw the night twinkling in Heaven's eyes. 'But then something happens,' he continued. 'She meets someone who would do anything for her. They plan to get married once she's opened the shop. But he doesn't turn up for the opening.'

'Did she tell you his name?'

'Not his real one. She just called him Pip.'

Heaven was listening intently.

'All the guests were invited, everything was running like clockwork. But then came the news that Pip was dead. He'd been killed by a car on the Edgware Road.'

'How did I guess that this story was going to have an unhappy end?'

'That evening, after the formal opening, Miss Trodwood swore to herself that she was going to spend the rest of her life here.'

'She told you all that?'

'Yes.'

'Did she love him?'

'She didn't tell me that.'

'What a strange story.'

'Then she gave me the book.'

'*Great Expectations.*'

'Yes. She told me that Dickens recognised real life. I should read it and I'd get to understand people that way.' David paused again. Even now, he wasn't sure that he'd properly understood Miss Trodwood. 'I had to watch out, she said. Life was unpredictable. And nobody can play a false role for ever. The mask always slips at some point. And when it's slipped, you have to be able to look in the mirror and deal with what you see there. It's that straightforward, she said. I always needed to keep that in mind.'

'Did it help you?'

He shrugged. 'Well, it did at least explain why she was always a bit weird around men.'

'Why did she take you in?'

'Who knows? Maybe she wants to put something right in her own life. Or maybe she just wants to help. Maybe she was just lonely too.'

Heaven nodded. 'I can understand where she's coming from.'

'Because of your parents?'

'Yes.'

David remembered what she had said. 'Do you believe what Sarah Jane told us?'

'Yes.'

David was silent. Then he said: 'Me too.'

'I thought we weren't going to talk about that.' She sounded harsh, brittle.

'Sorry.'

'It's OK.'

He turned over onto his back. Now Heaven had propped herself up on her elbows and was looking searchingly at him. 'How about you?'

He could tell that she wanted to see the other postcards. The ones he hadn't yet shown her.

He took a deep breath. 'Apart from what you already know?' His breath was a faint trace of mist in front of his face.

She nodded.

'You know about my mother. But what somehow made it even worse was my father. The way he dealt with it. The demands he made of me.'

She was looking at him intently.

'He works at the docks.' That was a start, at least. 'He's a big man who likes repairing things. That's the only thing he's interested in. Maybe he was interested in my mother too, once upon a time, before she got ill. But when she started having panic attacks and then stopped going out of the house, all he was interested in was how best to stop the neighbours finding out that something was wrong. I think he'd have done anything to avoid making us the centre of attention.'

'What about your sister?'

David shut his eyes very briefly.

'Sorry,' she said quickly.

He shook his head. 'No, it's fine.' And it was. 'The truth is, I left her in the lurch.' He bit his bottom lip.

'She spends all day sitting there, in that house with the blinds down, glued to the damned telly, that's what she does every day. And I just left her there.'

'Didn't you ever try?'

He hesitated. 'Once.'

'What happened?'

'She hung up on me.'

Heaven's hand found his.

David didn't stop her. 'She copes with it better than I did. And she gets on with my father. Maybe it's because she's a girl. She can be the way she is. Maybe she's a kind of substitute for the wife who's changed so much. But I…'

'You were never the son he wanted you to be.'

'I was never the boy he'd wanted me to be, just like he'd presumably never imagined living his life behind shut doors. He wanted a kid who liked doing the stuff that he liked doing. A boy who liked repairing things, who wanted to spend his time in front of the telly watching football with him.'

'And that's not you.'

'He wanted it to be me. Later on, I sometimes wondered whether it was part of this façade he'd constructed of an intact world: a smiling wife waiting for him with his supper on the table, a daughter fetching him a beer, and a son watching Manchester United matches with him.'

He remembered how often he'd rowed with his father, wars of words which he had almost completely forgotten as he hadn't looked at those particular postcards since turning his back on Cardiff. He shut his eyes, trying to drive away the images. 'You know, it's not easy to put into words the actual reason that I finally ran away. It wasn't just the stuff with my mother. And not just about my father. I just didn't belong there. There was just no place for me in that world.'

'And Miss Trodwood?'

'She showed me that you can find your own place in life.'

'You talk about your parents as if they were strangers. And you talk about Miss Trodwood as if she were your mother.'

'Strange, isn't it?' What else could he say?

'You both found what you were looking for. It's nice here,' Heaven said. She squeezed his hand. 'So homely.'

David could feel her slender fingers in his. He had come to connect the burningly cold touch with Heaven, along with the scent of cinnamon and lemons.

'The world is so strange,' he said.

She sighed softly. 'We don't even understand ourselves.'

He turned to face her. 'The business in Highgate… all that stuff about the day you were born …' He didn't finish his sentence.

It was Heaven who said: '…that's exactly how it was.'

'I…'

She put an icy cold finger to his lips. 'David,' she said. 'I don't want to talk about it.'

'OK.'

She shook her head. 'No, it isn't OK. We ought to talk about it. But I can't. Not yet. I'm frightened. About everything. But particularly about the business with my heart. I don't know what to do. Let's talk about it tomorrow, OK? We'll think about it tomorrow.' She shut her eyes, her lids flickering agitatedly in the half-light. 'I'm not feeling great, David. The cold helps, but what's happening to me really isn't OK. And I don't feel any better for knowing that there's some mysterious "client" out there who's likely to set hitman number two onto me.' She laughed unhappily and looked at him. 'What a crappy situation.'

He put his arm around her. 'When my sister and

I were little, I used to tell her stories before we went to sleep.' The cold in the room wasn't so bad when he looked into her eyes. 'She'd give me a sentence, and I'd try to turn it into something.'

'Tell it to me.'

'What?'

'The story that you told your sister.'

'That's not how it works. You give me a sentence.'

She didn't have to think for long. 'Once upon a time there was a girl who lived on a boat.'

'That's the first sentence?'

She nodded. 'Yes, sounds good, doesn't it?'

'Sounds good.'

'Can you think of a story for it?'

He held her tightly. 'Yes,' he said, 'yes, I can think of a story for it.' And so he began. The story that came tumbling out, as if it had just been waiting for the right moment, began one gloomy day in December, high up on the rooftops of a big city. It was the story of a princess who had come sailing from far away to this cold land, a fabulously beautiful girl who lost her heart to a thief. A penniless beggar helped her try to find it again. They had all kinds of adventures – and as he talked and talked, Heaven finally fell asleep.

David told half the story. Then he paused and

looked at Heaven as she slept. He wondered how the story might end; he didn't yet know (he'd never known how the stories would end when he began them – but who did?). But as she'd fallen asleep, he didn't have to worry about it.

He lay there watching her sleep, trying to think about nothing. He felt warm despite the cold.

As she dreamt, Heaven frowned and kept screwing up her nose anxiously. Her hand moved to and fro on the covers. Her breath, as cold as the icy air streaming through the window, made David shiver. He didn't know how long he spent just watching her. At some point, his eyes shut too. He dreamt of frost patterns and heartbeats, somehow knowing that he would continue to do so until daybreak.

CHAPTER 12

The noise of the traffic woke David before the sun had completely risen, but Heaven was still asleep. He got up and went for a pee. He stared at his reflection. 'You look like I feel,' he said. Unimpressed, his reflection stared back at him. It was pale, as if it belonged to a ghost. Its hair was standing on end, and it had dark circles under its eyes.

David changed his clothes and pulled on his Converse, and clambered through the open window and onto the roof.

He immediately felt liberated.

Smoke was billowing out of the chimneypots around him. The sun was coming up on the horizon in some far distant place that was much warmer than here. It lit up the clouds and gave life its colour back.

David climbed right up to the ridge and sat himself down by the chimney, one of his favourite places. Two rooftops further along, a chimney sweep was going about his business. David gave him a wave.

He yawned; it had been a short night. He imagined Heaven cuddled up in bed.

He gazed across the rooftops, guessing that down there in the impenetrable labyrinth of streets and alleyways, a man was on the hunt again; a man who was known by different names in different parts of the city. He couldn't imagine for a moment that the rat-cats had finished him off in Highgate. That guy was indestructible.

David could see down almost as far as the river. The snow had largely eased off, and just a few flakes were floating through the air. They twinkled in the sunlight, tiny speckles in a meaningless world.

David rubbed his eyes sleepily. He should have brought a coffee up with him. But he hadn't wanted to make any noise. And if he'd gone down into the shop, he'd probably have bumped into Miss Trodwood, who would have engaged him in conversation. But he didn't feel like conversation: he felt like coffee.

Now he was sitting on the roof wishing for coffee and relieved to have avoided conversation.

But what about Heaven?

David had no idea how to help her. She had trembled several times in the night. David had timidly touched the place where her heart would normally be.

Nothing. No heart, no beat. The place was cold, even through the thin fabric of David's ancient T-shirt. He had left his hand lying gently on her body and had felt her breathing. Heaven hadn't noticed anything. Her eyelids had occasionally flickered, as if secrets were trying to escape from beneath them. She had tossed and turned in her sleep; he didn't know if she'd been dreaming. Only towards morning had she become calmer. She had sometimes murmured words in her sleep, sonorous and unclear, like letters in dark ink.

It had been icy cold in the room, but that hadn't bothered him. It had felt good. When he'd spent the night at Kelly's, he'd always felt cold even though he'd woken up in a warm room.

'David?'

He whirled round.

Heaven was standing behind him. She had pulled a green jacket on over the T-shirt and David's trousers. The trousers flapped around her legs, baring her ankles. She was wearing a pair of undone Converse that she'd presumably found under the bed.

'How did you sleep?' he asked.

'I was awake while you were asleep.'

David felt caught out.

'Then I went back to sleep before the sun came up.'

'Did I talk in my sleep?'

'You ground your teeth.'

'Oh.'

She smiled. 'Oh yeah, you said all sorts of strange stuff too. But no words. More like…babble.' She sat down beside him. 'I never imagined you'd babble.'

David laughed. 'Me neither,' he said.

Their shoulders were touching. Her hair was touching his neck, tickling him. The November sun wasn't very strong, but it felt to David as if it would melt the snowflakes.

'London's so beautiful,' Heaven said softly. She gazed across the rooftops.

'Sometimes it's really quiet up here. The noises sound muffled, as if they don't want to climb up this far. Mostly in the mornings when the streets start to wake up.'

She hugged her knees. 'Do you often come up here?'

'I like being alone. Sometimes.'

'Now?'

He shook his head. 'No, I don't want to be alone now.' He smiled at her.

'How did you imagine your life being when you left Cardiff?' she asked bluntly.

'Better.' He was surprised by the speed of his reply.

'Nicer?'

'Isn't that the same?'

She shrugged. 'I don't know.'

'I wanted to be free.' He was struggling to explain. 'I wanted to live.' He gave her a sidelong look. 'I don't know exactly what I expected.' David shook his head. 'Sounds pretty naive, doesn't it?'

'You thought that happiness would find you, without you having to look for it.'

He shot back: 'And hasn't it?' He immediately wished he'd kept his mouth shut.

She looked down, embarrassed. 'There was someone – last year, last summer.' She was speaking slowly, her breath forming little clouds. 'No one really special. He chatted me up in a club.' She laughed, slightly too loudly. 'I knew he was a prick. But that didn't matter somehow. Just for a moment, I thought I'd finally found happiness. For a couple of days, I wasn't alone.' She shrugged. 'Ah well, that was that.' She made a dismissive gesture. 'It was over before it started. No big deal.'

David stared at a crow perched in the gutter of the house opposite, searching for food. It suddenly spread out its great wings and rose into the air, sailing out towards Charing Cross.

'Why are you telling me this?' he asked.

Heaven didn't reply. Then, after a pause that was neither long nor short, she said: 'Because you told me about your social worker.'

'I only mentioned her, she isn't important.'

She nodded and scanned the clouds above the rooftops, searching for words. 'It's just that I…'

'What?'

'It bothered me.'

'What – me telling you about her?'

'No. It bothered me that she existed at all.'

David felt every word hit home.

Heaven stood up and looked at him. 'Maybe it bothers you that I met that guy last year?' She was sounding a bit snappy now. Her wild hair was dancing in the wind.

David opened his mouth and shut it again. No, he mustn't reply. He could sense it was better not to.

Heaven held his gaze and finally said: 'It's like in that book again. *Great Expectations*.'

'What do you mean?'

'We all have such great expectations of our lives. But it could all be so simple.' She smiled hesitantly.

Then she winked at him and stretched. 'How about some breakfast before the shop opens?'

'Sounds good.' David got up. 'Then we need to start finding some answers.'

The fractions of seconds were quietly rearranging themselves into something new, crystal-clear, and wonderful.

But neither of them really knew whether this was the moment when everything would change. And as they didn't really know, and as all humans in that situation normally tend to do something to distract themselves completely from all such thoughts, and as the great expectations that people have of their lives can also act like nasty little stumbling blocks: because of this, and because of so many other things, they left the rooftop and went back inside, never guessing that once death has scented its prey, it lies in wait like an animal.

CHAPTER 13

After a quick breakfast, they went down to the shop and David asked for the day off. Miss Trodwood, of course, couldn't resist giving him an earwigging about the perils and recklessness of such behaviour. But she gave in, and so Heaven and David left the shop that morning and headed straight for a local café in Old Compton Street: the Doctorow Coffee & Internet Base. David had no desire to turn up at Mike's with Heaven. The two of them belonged to two completely different worlds, and that's how he wanted it to stay.

He looked at the faces of passers-by in the street. They looked remote and withdrawn. It struck him, as it often did, that most people were grumpy; grumpiness seemed to be the default setting for city dwellers. At least he and Heaven didn't have to go on the Underground, though.

Heaven had been watching him. 'You're still on the lookout.'

'You never know what's coming,' he replied.

'Do you think that guy with the gloves is still alive?'

'He mentioned a client.' This was the thing that David found most worrying of all the things that the multi-named man had said. 'And if Mr Scrooge – or whatever he's calling himself – is out of the loop, then there's bound to be someone else to pick up where he left off. You said so yourself yesterday.' He gazed anxiously up and down Shaftesbury Avenue. 'No, I don't feel safe.'

They crossed the busy road, where exhaust gases floated around like so many ghosts set free in the atmosphere – each one a wraith-like filigree, scarcely visible to the naked eye.

Magic, David thought, *really does have many different faces.*

Heaven had fallen silent.

'What's up?' he asked her.

She shrugged, but David could see how tense she was. It was her eyes: they were huge and staring, her eyelids were flickering, and she was looking alternately at the ground then up again for no apparent reason.

'I'm frightened.'

He stopped and looked at her in consternation.

'I feel so empty, David.' She rolled her eyes and

sighed resignedly. 'God, I've not got a clue what's wrong with me. It all feels wrong, do you know what I mean? All of it.' She touched her chest. 'As if it can't carry on like this for much longer.'

David frowned. 'Then we need to talk about what happened yesterday.'

She pulled a face. 'If we absolutely have to,' she said with a crooked smile that David returned.

'We do,' he said.

She nodded. 'I know.' The pale November sun gave her olive skin a golden hue, but her eyes looked darker than ever.

He set off again, reminding himself of the conversation with Sarah Jane. 'How about starting with what happened to your mother?' he said.

'She's dead.' It was a snarl. 'No doubt about it.'

David nodded. He could understand Heaven's anger and her feeling that she had been lied to throughout her entire life. But they couldn't carry on acting as if they'd never found out. And particularly not if it might help them to work out what was going on. 'But there wasn't a body,' he said cautiously. 'She simply disappeared after her death.'

'She was fascinated by the sky when she was alive,' Heaven whispered.

David took a deep breath. 'You know what happened on the day that you were born, don't you?'

'Well…' She fell silent again.

'Heaven?' David persisted.

'They just came up with stupid rhymes at my primary school,' she finally said. 'My father kept all my mother's books for me and as soon as I could read, I devoured them all. Freema, Freema, silly star dreamer – that's what they used to call me.'

David laughed. 'Children. Don't you love 'em?'

Heaven grinned, but only briefly. 'We saw the film about the twenty-fifth of November for the first time when we were in Year Four,' she continued. 'And Mrs Doomsday, or so we called our Geography teacher, just had to go and tell everyone that I was born on that very day.'

David nodded. He too remembered that film; it was a standard part of the curriculum in British schools when they were discussing the missing sky. For on that twenty-fifth of November, the empty sky above London had changed once more, two years after the comet had appeared. The numerous telescopes, cameras and satellites that had spent days and years pointing at the empty space had captured every last second of the event. A piece of sky had returned, suddenly and without warning; a little patch of sky directly above Kensington. Nobody could say what had happened. It just happened, and had made the gaping hole above the city slightly less empty.

Ever since Sarah Jane had told them about the disappearance of Heaven's mother, a question had been floating around David's mind. But he had kept on pushing it away because it wasn't the time or place to ask it. Neither last night in his room beneath the stars, nor that morning up on the roof.

But there was a right time for everything, and David knew that this time had come, here and now, as they turned into Greek Street.

'What time were you born, Heaven?' he asked.

She looked at him. Looked away again. Looked at him. And he knew that she, too, had been forcing herself not to ask. 'I don't know exactly,' she whispered.

'We need to find out,' David said firmly. 'We'll have to ask someone. Mr Mickey, perhaps, or your guardian...' A thought crossed his mind. 'Or have you got your birth certificate?'

Heaven shook her head helplessly. 'No,' she said. 'Would you know where to start looking for yours?'

David clenched his teeth and looked around him. There was a phone box on the corner. 'Can't be that hard,' he murmured, pulling Heaven along behind him. He stuffed in some coins, rang Directory Enquiries, and asked to be put through to the Westminster Register Office. 'Here,' he said, passing Heaven the receiver. 'They must know.'

Heaven spoke slowly, rolling her eyes every now and then. She covered the mouthpiece with her hand. 'It might take a while,' she whispered.

David had to feed the phone with coins twice more, increasingly convinced that they were wasting their time. They would presumably have to go to the Register Office in person, with Heaven's ID.

But then her expression hardened.

'Heaven?'

No response.

David took the receiver from her hand, hung it up, and put his hand on her shoulder. She looked as if she were struggling to breathe, even though it was as freezing cold in the phone box as it was outside.

'What did they say?'

Heaven staggered against him, and David took her in his arms. 'I was born at 3.22 AM,' she said.

David nodded slowly. The sky had returned to

Kensington at 3.22 AM on that twenty-fifth of November.

Above the door was a garish neon sign that read: *The Doctorow Coffee & Internet Base*.

The building that now housed the café had once been a little cinema. The façade was reminiscent of a theatre of the type that older Londoners remembered from the films that were shown during the war and in the austere years that followed it.

Entry was via a revolving door. Once inside, visitors were hit by the smell of days long gone by: cigarettes, popcorn and toffee.

On the walls were posters of old films: *Ladykillers, Noblesse Oblige, Blackmail, The 39 Steps, The Lady Vanishes.*

Along with the former ticket office in the foyer, a large cardboard cutout poster advertised a film art exhibition that was currently showing.

'They've always got art projects on the go,' said David. 'Pretty wacky stuff.'

'Do you often come here?'

'No,' he replied. 'I don't really come here at all. I just look at the posters when I'm passing, that's all.'

The café itself was in the old room where the films had been screened. The rows of seats had largely been preserved. Spaces had been made between the red velvet seats to accommodate round tables. On many of them were bright screens that flickered in the dim lamplight.

The canvas screen on the wall was showing the current art project, a wildly flickering mixture of images: scraps of old black and white films cut with sequences from modern films to do with alien worlds and the internet. Joan Barry met Keanu Reeves, and Cary Grant watched warriors leaping through the air clad in shiny black leather. Flashes of colour burst onto the carpet of images; *Tron* characters raged through scenes from *Sabotage*.

The sound that accompanied it wasn't from the films that flashed up like the crazed negatives of once forgotten dreams. Instead there was classical music, Nancy Sinatra, Petula Clark and The Beatles.

'What do you reckon?' said David.

Heaven laughed cautiously. 'Not sure yet.'

The film *Logan's Run* came into David's mind, but he quickly suppressed the thought.

Heaven was walking purposefully ahead of him. He followed her.

There weren't many people around the café at this time of day. Just a few students whose lectures probably didn't start until later, and people with jobs who were killing time before work. Most of the few visitors had their own laptops and were immersed in whatever they were doing.

Hardly anyone was watching the images on the screen. The music was a pleasant carpet that could take them to whatever world they wanted.

'A PC each?' asked David.

Heaven just nodded. She looked around curiously, observing the other people.

'It's warm in here, isn't it?' David frowned.

'I'll just have to keep going out,' she said. 'Don't worry if I disappear for a while. I'll come back.'

David found a PC and Heaven sat herself down at one right behind him at the next table. There was a counter with coffee, tea and little cakes. Self-service. David fetched Heaven a Darjeeling and himself an Earl Grey.

Then they plunged into the abyss of virtual reality. Head over heels, with both hands on the keyboard and mouse.

David tried multiple search terms. Murder, London and heart. Then he waited to see which rambling paths would open themselves up to him. A second later there appeared links to several thousand sources that included his search terms. He sat up and began to work his way through the links one at a time.

OK. The search was on.

He restricted his search terms and found new links. He typed in one year, then another, kept amending his search criteria, widened them or exchanged them for others. The number of references grew smaller, larger, smaller again. A constant toing and froing.

He sipped his tea.

Heaven was likewise staring fixedly at her screen. Her fingers were clicking and tapping away at the keyboard. Her eyes were bright, keen and alert, as she scanned the text and images, trying to tease out what they so desperately wanted to know.

David pulled himself together as he realised that he had been staring at her for goodness knows how long. He clicked his way through articles, mystery sites and the mass of online forums. He finally tracked down something that looked worthwhile. His fingers raced across the keyboard. Transfixed, he read what came up on the screen.

Only then did he notice that Heaven was starting to breathe more heavily. She was wheezing, albeit softly, rubbing her eyes, and gasping for air. She quickly downed her tea. She pushed the mouse across the table and her finger pressed 'return'.

'Are you OK?' It was a superfluous question.

Heaven shook her head. 'I'm just going outside,' she said quietly. Her eyes were glassy. 'Back soon,' she whispered. When she stood up she put a hand on his shoulder, and David noticed that she was propping herself up on him. She shut her eyes briefly and took a deep breath, then quickly made her way towards the door.

David saw her stopping by the counter and being handed a sheaf of paper. She had printed off several pages to read outside.

David gazed after her, concerned, until she was out of sight. Then he turned back to the screen.

She was OK, or halfway OK at any rate. They had no time to lose.

He was soon immersed in his task again, and it wasn't long before he felt as if he were lost in a dense forest of data. He left the well trodden paths and set off to explore the dark, untrodden regions. You never knew where they might take you.

Then he found something. His eyes narrowed as he skimmed the text. He could feel the excitement grabbing him by the throat as his heart began to pound so hard that he felt almost dizzy.

Could it be true?

He followed the new path and reached places with hazy images of gruesome murders, blood and stolen hearts, conveyed only in brief accounts.

Heaven came back into the café holding the sheets of paper, and sat back down at her PC. She glanced at David.

'It really is warm in here,' he said.

'I'm fine now,' she murmured. 'Fine.' Then she quickly typed something and nervously scrolled down the pages. After some ten minutes she went back outside with a couple of print-outs before returning to search for more sites while she sipped her tea, twiddled with her hair and stared, transfixed, at the screen. She seemed agitated, like someone on the trail of some kind of treasure.

Martial arts clips were exploding on the screen on the wall. Warriors were flying through the air, turning into black-and-white besuited heroes, solving different problems with brollies, charm and bowler hats. The deluge of images cascaded over the café-goers like hungry scraps of dreams wrenched from other people's memories.

David ignored them. He was completely caught up in the story that was revealing itself to him. The images just made him feel more wound up.

He finally paused, rubbed his eyes, and took a deep breath. Heaven was at her seat. The print-outs were piling up around her.

'Come on, I've got something to show you.' He had found out enough. Enough, at any rate, to start to speculate. Too much to keep to himself.

She came and leant over his shoulder. He could feel her quick breathing. Even David was starting to find the warm air slightly unpleasant. 'I've been looking for events that are similar to ours,' he said. 'Here in London.'

'And?'

'Look here,' he said, clicking on the first site he had found. It was a long text in a tiny font with several coarse-grained images that had been taken from old newspapers and turned into bad digital copy. 'Seven years ago, a twenty-five-year-old man who worked for the Inland Revenue was found dead close to Trinity Church Square. His bloody body was found between the rubbish bins of a nearby rental property. The heart was missing; it had been cut out with surgical precision. The other organs were still in his body.'

Heaven turned pale. She stared transfixed at the screen, where there was nothing to be seen apart from the rubbish bins and a typical town house.

'Well, then I searched for related pages, and found a whole series of similar cases.'

He listed the home pages of the papers and magazines: *The Independent, The Sun, Esquire, The Times*, and so on. As he talked, he clicked on all the links so that a succession of pictures and text flickered across the screen: newspaper headlines, article headers, sensational one-liners that promised more than the text delivered.

'It happens a lot, and always in London,' he said. 'The first one was in Valentine Place, near the South Bank. That was more than twenty years ago.' He gave the date.

'That must have been more or less when my parents met,' Heaven said uncertainly.

David looked at her and nodded. 'A woman who worked for a consultancy firm went down to the archive in the basement,' he continued. 'After a while, she hadn't come back so they went to look for her. The work-experience boy who found her body was taken to hospital suffering from shock. Someone had cut out the woman's heart; her blood was caked on the files and the books. The police were completely baffled. The evidence suggested that the victim had tried to fight off her attacker, and that he had been exceptionally violent and ruthless.' He opened up a page that showed the complete newspaper article. 'Then here, three years later.' He pointed to a street plan that was loading onto the screen. 'A student received a phone call from her boyfriend. She told her flatmate that she was going to meet him in the café round the corner. She left their flat in Fairclough Street.' He pulled a meaningful expression. 'It's basically the same story.' A short pause. 'After a while, her boyfriend rang her flat. She hadn't arrived at the café. He and her flatmate finally found her body outside in the courtyard. Someone had taken her heart and had thrown her body into a rubbish bin. The police didn't find any useful clues there either. But whoever was responsible for this horrible crime had carried it out with total surgical precision. So it had to be someone who knew anatomy.'

'A doctor?'

'Can you imagine Mr Scrooge in *ER*?'

'A baddy in *Torchwood*, more like.'

'I reckon so too.'

They scanned the screen anxiously.

'Organ trafficking was ruled out, because it was

only the heart that was missing. The other organs hadn't even been touched. Scotland Yard assumed a serial killer was at work, but the trail always ran cold because such a long time went by without any further killings.'

'David, that's terrible.' Heaven put her hand on his shoulder. He could feel that she was trembling.

'Here's the next case,' said David, hurrying on. 'A business school professor just into his sixties went out jogging on his lunch break and disappeared. He was found in Haggerston Park. The murderer didn't even bother to hide his body. It was lying in the middle of a field where anyone could see it. His heart was missing, too – and just his heart, same as with all the others.'

'Do you reckon the same person did it?'

'Hang on, there's more.' David recounted the next case, three years later. 'An angler was washed up on the shore of the Thames at Rotherhithe. Without a heart.' He clicked on the relevant article. A photo showed part of the riverside, cordoned off with plastic tape. A group of reporters was standing by the cordon.

Heaven put her hand to her mouth. She didn't need to see what she didn't want to imagine.

'A young couple were found in St Crispin Close

near Hampstead Heath station. Their throats had been slit, and the man was missing his heart. The bodies were found in a doorway.' He turned to Heaven. 'It happens regularly, every three to five years. And it started more than twenty years ago. The papers reported the incidents, but nobody saw any link between them. For some reason the media never put them in the spotlight.'

'Are there any other similarities?'

'Just the hearts,' David replied tersely. 'All the victims had their hearts cut out with surgical precision. When he's finished, he just dumps the bodies.' David sighed. 'Otherwise, the victims don't seem to have anything in common. They're different ages, have different jobs, different social backgrounds.'

'But why would someone do something like this?'

'I don't know,' said David. 'But there's an article about strange happenings in Bankston Gardens. I came across it because of the dates, the dates when the murderer struck.' He shook his head. 'I thought at first that I must be down a blind alley, but there are bits that maybe do fit together after all.'

He opened up the web page and clicked on a link.

Heaven read what it said.

Silence.

Baffled, she repeated: 'Desecration of cemeteries?'

David nodded quickly. 'Remember what Sarah Jane said? The man with the gloves, she said, was a sort of bodysnatcher.'

David clicked his way around the site. It was a kind of cesspit of grotesque and twisted items on the murky secrets of the city, but there was only one that interested him.

'There have been repeated cases of vandalism in recent years in various London graveyards. But the ones reported here are really weird.'

Heaven pulled a chair over from the next table and sat down.

'It's not full-moon parties or vampire hunting or anything like that. This here is something completely different.' He enlarged the newspaper article so that Heaven could see the headline: *The Return of the Bodysnatcher?*

In the middle of the nineteenth century, bodysnatching had been a very lucrative business in London's streets, alleyways and dark courtyards. Professional bodysnatchers stole bodies from graves and morgues and then sold them to hospitals and freelance doctors who could then hone their skills on dead bodies. Medical researchers would pay large sums for a fresh corpse, which often led to people being snatched and killed so their bodies could be sold.

'Someone,' said David, 'carried on stealing bodies from graves. It happens every couple of years.'

'What?'

'They were dug up,' he replied, 'and then disappeared. It was always people who had only just died. The bodies were stolen from the graves, then turned up again in completely different parts of town.'

'What do you mean, they turned up again?'

'They were just found lying around. As if someone had used them for something and then dumped them. As if they'd got up and started walking around under their own steam, and then been switched off.'

'Let me guess,' said Heaven. 'At the same time, there would be a murder. Am I right?'

David nodded. 'The dates match perfectly. It's terrifying.'

'It can't be…' She didn't finish her sentence.

He nodded. 'Oh yes it can. Whenever someone has had a heart stolen, there has always been an incident in a graveyard beforehand. The stolen body has always been found almost a day later.'

'Shit!' she gasped.

'Shit's the word. Remember how stinky the

raggedy man was. And don't forget what Sarah Jane did to him.'

Heaven was wheezing now. 'I have to get out of here,' she gasped. 'Let's go. Please.'

David jumped up, quickly put a handful of coins on the table, and helped her outside. Behind them, the screen was playing the climactic scene from *The Man Who Knew Too Much*.

Enough was enough.

The air outside was clear and freezing cold. Snowflakes were whirling around again, dancing along the street. David paid them no heed; he had more than enough on his plate.

'Let's walk for a bit,' Heaven said.

'Which direction?'

'Any.'

They set off westwards.

'I found something out too,' she said.

David dug his hands into his pockets. Up until now, they hadn't mentioned what Heaven had learned from the Register Office, but David knew that this was what she had been looking up on the internet.

'What were you looking for?' he asked.

'For people who vanish into thin air after their deaths. For holes in the sky. For lost hearts.'

'And?' He looked at the small black-clad figure next to him. Snowflakes were settling on her dark hair, twinkling like little stars.

She shrugged. 'What do you think those search terms gave me?'

'A fairy tale?' he guessed.

She nodded. 'Bingo.'

'What do you mean?'

'That's what I mean. Someone wrote it. The only problem is that it's disappeared, just like my heart.'

'Does it make me sound thick if I say that I haven't got a clue what you're talking about?' he asked, raising an eyebrow.

She laughed. 'Pretty thick. But I'll tell you anyway.' She turned serious again. 'OK, the first thing I found was a name. It kept coming up, mostly just in marginal notes, but this name was the only thing that all the links had in common. Then there was a lot about an old book that seems to have been about this topic. The author was the Earl of Rochester, and the book was *The Fallen Fairy's Heart*.'

David looked at her, surprised. 'I only know about fallen angels, not about fallen fairies.'

'Same here.'

'So what's in the book? Your fairy tale?'

'That's precisely the problem. The book doesn't exist any more.'

David frowned. Since he'd known Miss Trodwood, he'd also known that books didn't just disappear. It was just a case of tracking them down. 'There must still be a copy somewhere.'

She shook her head vigorously. 'There's no information about where exactly it appeared. No online bookseller has ever had it in their catalogue. The only reference I found to it is in the British Library.' Her eyes lit up. 'They did have a copy, many years ago. And it had a dedication: A true story, made up for Claire.'

'Claire?'

'Exactly. Claire.'

'Who's Claire?'

'Presumably it says in the book.'

'Which is untraceable.' He groaned.

'I carried on searching for Claire and the Earl of Rochester,' she said. 'John Wilmot, Earl of Rochester, lived in the seventeenth century and was renowned for his dissolute, positively immoral poetry.'

David gave her a sidelong glance. 'Immoral poems? *Very* revealing!'

'You did ask,' she said, an amused twinkle lighting up her eyes. 'But anyway, it's something else that's of interest.' She paused briefly. 'He was a bit of a playboy and a renowned ladykiller, rather a flamboyant personality. He was in the second Anglo-Dutch war where he did all kinds of brilliantly heroic things, but then fell into disfavour with Charles II. He kidnapped the heiress of some rich family, Elizabeth Malet, whom he later married. After their wedding, everything finally went quiet for him. But then, two years before his death, he travelled across Spain and Portugal. On one of the islands, so the story goes, he met a fabulously beautiful woman.'

'What about his wife?'

'She knew nothing about it. Or she was OK with it. I don't know.'

'Strange times.'

Heaven continued, 'In his letters, he called the Spanish woman Lady Claire.'

'And what does that have to do with us?'

'Lady Claire vanished one day. Without trace.' Heaven's eyes met his. It wasn't hard to see that she was thinking of her mother. 'The Earl was inconsolable. He wrote about it in letters that he never sent. He was pining away for her.'

David raised his hand. 'Tell me that the letters at least do exist.'

She sighed. 'There aren't any originals, so far as I could discover. This Earl of Rochester was a strange guy. Lots of documents relating to his life have gone missing too.'

'Including the letters?'

'There are just sources that keep on referring to further sources. Authors who wrote about this stuff after he died, and who refer to sources that they had never seen themselves, though had presumably heard about. Totally reliable witnesses, needless to say.'

'That's how myths arise,' said David.

She nodded. 'But anyway – I've come across something and, again, it fits with what we're looking for. He apparently called Lady Claire his heavenly heart.'

David stopped.

'Heavenly heart?'

'Yes.'

'Might be a false trail, mightn't it? Maybe he was a romantic?'

'No, I don't think so. He was more of a down-to-earth type. Just think of the lewd poems.'

'So, not a romantic. Do you think he meant it literally?'

She shrugged. 'No idea, but there's more. After I'd found out which places he'd been to, I carried on searching.' She looked around. 'I remembered a poem I read once, several years ago. It's in one of the books about the sky that my mother left me.'

A noisy group of pensioners was heading towards them, possibly on a coach trip to London, two days return for only thirty pounds. A couple of them were brandishing guidebooks; the men were wearing flat caps, and one of them was swinging his umbrella in a raffish sort of way. They were harmless, but David suddenly found them threatening, and he remembered how his mother must always have felt when she went outside.

'We need to go this way,' he said casually, changing direction.

'Fine.'

They walked on, David now paying attention to where they were walking.

Heaven continued to talk. 'My mother's book is about an island somewhere in the Mediterranean that's covered by day – only by day – by a blanket of cloud that blacks out the sunlight. But as soon as night falls, the clouds disappear and the stars shine in the sky. The sky, so it says in the poem, simply disappears in the daytime. It is no longer there.'

'There's no problem with the night sky?'

'A problem with the day sky, more like. And then there's something else.' She gave him a meaningful look. 'The daytime sky above the island only disappeared for a short while. For four months, to be precise. It wasn't of any particular significance to historians. The peasants and fishermen on the island reported it to the authorities on the mainland, and asked them to send someone who could help them with it.'

'And did anyone help them?'

'No idea. At any rate, there are no official reports about what might have happened.'

David could sense what was coming next. 'Does the Earl of Rochester have anything to do with this?'

'He was there,' said Heaven.

'On that actual island?'

'The Earl of Rochester met Lady Claire on the island, according to some sources. She disappeared at around the same time as the clouds went away and the missing daytime sky returned.'

David thought about River Mirrlees and what they had discovered just a few hours previously. At the very moment that River died and Heaven was born, a bit of sky returned over Kensington.

And he knew he ought to have been sceptical. He'd

normally have said that it was impossible, complete nonsense. But instead, it was crystal-clear to him that it had really happened. And so long as this reality involved Heaven, David was willing to accept it.

'The Earl of Rochester wrote the story of Lady Claire after she died,' said Heaven. 'But later on, he evidently went off the idea of anyone finding out about it. Rumour has it that he made sure the book was destroyed. He apparently spent his last couple of years travelling across Europe, destroying any copies that he came across.'

'Why?'

'Don't know. Maybe he knew what the missing sky was all about.'

David regarded the bustle of people in Piccadilly Circus. He struck off in a different direction, northwards into Great Windmill Street, which was quieter than Shaftesbury Avenue. 'Did he really manage to destroy all the copies of his book?'

She nodded. 'At least that's what all the sources say.'

David stopped. His eyes were bright. 'Miss Trodwood!' He clicked his fingers as if that were the answer to all their problems. 'She can track down any book. We have to ask her.'

'How long would it take her?'

David pondered. 'It depends,' he said hesitantly. Miss Trodwood had her own, very particular methods of sniffing out lost books. She used her old-fashioned phone and sometimes, very rarely, she went off on the train – never on a plane.

The advantage to this method was that she always found what she was looking for. The disadvantage was that it normally took a while.

He told Heaven this.

She stopped, and David could see the despair in her face. 'If that's the case, we could have spared ourselves the effort, couldn't we?' she said. 'All these links to serial killers, bodysnatchers, weird earls and missing Mediterranean beauties – it's all a load of crap!' She sniffed. 'It's been a complete waste of time. We don't know any more than we did. We haven't got the faintest idea how to find my heart.' She looked as if she wanted to kick something, but the only thing near to her was a kindly-looking elderly lady with a brown and white beagle that was looking up at her with faithful eyes, wagging its tail eagerly. Heaven looked at the beagle for a moment, then groaned. 'God, I've had enough, David.'

David was thinking madly. He didn't want to give

up, not now, not when they'd got this far. He could sense that they were getting warmer, but Heaven was right to say that what they had found out thus far wasn't going to help them. The book seemed to be the key. It surely had to be possible to get hold of the damn thing.

'What about Mr Merryweather?' he suddenly said. 'He knows every story. And he sometimes has them, too.'

Heaven looked up. 'Do you think?' There was a trace of hope in her voice.

David nodded and stared up at the rooftops. That was the quickest way to Kensington.

Heaven nodded, but then hesitated for a moment. 'David, I've not got much time left,' she whispered. 'Whatever it is that's keeping me alive, it's not going to carry on forever.'

David put his arm round her shoulder. 'I know.' What else was there to say? 'Let's go and see Merryweather. We have to at least try.' His eyes said: *We've got nothing to lose.* And Heaven, who held his gaze silently, whispered wordlessly, desperately, with eyes that were as dark as night: *Apart from ourselves.*

Then he pulled her along through the first house entrance and up a long staircase, up and up, and then they ran like the wind across the crooked, twisty rooftops of the city, free from people and as cold as snow and ice.

It was like flying, and it was like dreaming. And it was theirs alone.

THIRD INTERLUDE
THE VISIT

All was quiet in the big house in Richmond. Mr Mickey was in the spacious kitchen, drinking black tea. Mickey Jones had spent much of the past few hours thinking about Heaven.

She had been a quiet child, and Jonathan Mirrlees had loved her. Once she was older, nobody had been able to tie her down. She had roamed around town, but as there had been no problems at school, Jonathan hadn't minded. She might have had no mother, but Jonathan had always been full of confidence.

'She has to find her own way, Mickey,' he had always said.

Mr Jones still missed Heaven's father. He had been a good friend, and he had trusted Mickey to look after Heaven when he was away.

'You take care of her,' he said every time he packed his suitcase and left the house. 'I'm relying on you.'

But he couldn't have known what he was asking of Mr Mickey.

Mr Jones looked at the time. He was expecting a visitor.

The cat that he had let in an hour ago was sitting calmly in her place beneath the window, licking her paws.

Mickey recalled the many tests, all of which proved negative. Heaven had never asked any questions, she had simply put up with them, fearful at first, then just irritated. They were routine checks on her heart, and after all, they never lasted very long.

But then her father had died. Mickey could well remember the day he had collected her from school and taken her home.

She had gone up to her room, silently and with a fixed expression. She had spent six hours there, refusing to talk to anyone. During that time, she had covered her walls with lines and notes. A melody that she had called the Music of the Spheres. Only then did she cry. Nobody knew why she had written the notes on the wall. She had never talked to Mr Mickey about it.

Mr Jones was listening intently. Something had moved outside. The cat jumped up in a fright and ran out of the kitchen.

Mickey went into the corridor. Shadows crouched in the corners even by day. Further back, the cat was sitting there, hissing at him.

'What is it, princess?' he said.

The cat didn't reply. The light was reflected in her green eyes. She turned and fled in the opposite direction.

'Hmm,' grumbled Mr Mickey. He looked at the time again.

Then he made his way down the corridor to the hall. Two figures were unpeeling themselves from the shadows near to the staircase.

'You wanted to talk to me?' said Mr Drood.

The raggedy man didn't say a word.

Mr Mickey looked at them both. 'Yes,' he replied.

CHAPTER 14

David led Heaven to Kensington across the high paths and gangways, the gutters and skylights, the ladders, the bridges of iron and steel. They were alone up there, and the world, ticking away like a strange clock, was so far beneath them that nobody noticed they were there.

They ran as if their lives depended on it. They jumped over abysses and ran on, not looking back even once. Kensington Gardens flew past them to their right; the dome of the Royal Albert Hall shimmered in the dull grey daylight; Big Ben struck the hour for the eleventh time that day; and the Thames lay there silently beneath them.

They stopped on the rooftop of a house in Reston Place.

'What's up?' asked Heaven.

David was suddenly thinking of so many things that he couldn't find the words for them. He saw the city stretching out on all sides as far as the horizon.

Then he moved towards Heaven, reached for her hand, grabbed it, and kissed her.

She returned the kiss hard; it was as if she had spent the whole of the last few hours waiting for it to happen. She nestled against him, gently stroking his hair.

'Sometimes,' Heaven said as their kiss ended, 'life can be so straightforward.' She laughed so brightly, it was if all great expectations had been blown away by the wind.

For a while, they stood there together up on the roof, just looking at the city. This was life, and they were right in the middle of it. It was like music, but louder.

Then they hastened onwards. David remembered Kelly, and how complicated it had all been. And he looked at Heaven, struck by how different everything could be.

They finally reached Kensington – or, to be more precise, 18 Phillimore Place.

They found a skylight, and David helped Heaven through it. Then they ran downstairs until they reached the door of Mr Merryweather's apartment.

David rang the bell. He could hear shuffling footsteps coming to the door. Then a key was turned, a latch clicked, and the door was opened. Mr

Merryweather was blinking at them.

'Mr David Pettyfer?' he asked in astonishment. 'With his delightful girlfriend. What on earth brings you here?'

'We need your help,' said Heaven.

'Ah, when a young lady asks for help,' he declared sonorously, 'then one can't refuse.' He winked at David. 'Not if one is a real gentleman, isn't that right?' He laughed good-naturedly. 'It's draughty out on the stairs.' With these words, Mr Merryweather ushered them into the parlour.

Soft light was falling into the room through the half-open blinds, making striped patterns on the shelves and books. It smelled of cold tobacco and old books, of printing ink and the old newspapers which lay on the table with teapots and cups and cake leftovers piled up on them, just as on the night before last. The high shelves stood against the walls which were decorated with lurid patterned wallpaper and wooden panelling.

'Have you been reading it?' asked David, pointing to the book that lay open on the armchair.

'*The Bride of Lammermoor*?' Mr Merryweather smiled happily. 'Oh yes. It's been fun, reading to her from the old book.' He motioned to one of the picture frames holding his wife's photo. 'Life has suddenly come back to life.' Today he was wearing a brown cord suit, and looked like something from a P. G. Wodehouse novel. As he filled the kettle in the kitchen next to the parlour, David told him about the strange things that had been happening. He did of course try to make his version of events rather more vague. After all, Mr Merryweather didn't need to know everything. All the same, he listened quietly.

As he poured the tea, Heaven asked him to open the window a crack so that she could sit by it. Classical music was coming from the radio on the shelf above the gas oven.

'Gilbert and Sullivan,' Mr Merryweather said, seeing David's questioning look.

'Oh,' he said.

Heaven found a chair right by the window.

'I'm quite happy for us to stay in the kitchen,' said Mr Merryweather. 'I like kitchens. The best conversations of my life have always been in kitchens. Kitchens are magical places.' He put two cups of steaming tea in front of David and Heaven, then came straight to the point. 'The story you've told me sounds quite incredible,' he said – although he seemed not to be all that surprised. 'But what can I do for you?'

'It's a book,' said David.

'A missing book, to be precise,' Heaven added.

Mr Merryweather pricked up his ears. 'They're the best kind,' he said slowly. 'So long as they can still be tracked down.'

'*The Fallen Fairy's Heart*. It's by one Earl of Rochester.'

Mr Merryweather nodded thoughtfully. 'The title rings a bell,' he murmured. He frowned, hesitated, then his expression cleared. 'Yes, I have even read it. It was many years ago, but I can still remember it.'

David's eyes lit up. 'Where is it? Here in your apartment? Can we borrow it?' he asked.

Mr Merryweather smiled good-naturedly. 'Ah, I may have read it, but I don't have a copy. It's very rare. Hmm, maybe I should order it from Miss Trodwood, who knows?' He looked at them closely. 'It's a fairy tale, nothing more. Like the fairy tales that Oscar Wilde wrote. Very adult, so to speak.'

David glanced at Heaven. '*The Fallen Fairy's Heart*,' he said. 'Is the book actually about fairies?'

'Well.' Mr Merryweather brushed a speck of dust from his spotless cords. 'The image that the Earl of Rochester has of them is rather different from the image of fairies that most English people have.' He cleared his throat and sipped his tea. 'Oh, what am I talking about? *Rather* different? Actually the Earl's story turns everything that we've ever heard about fairies on its head.' He shook his head. 'If I remember rightly, the story is about a young nobleman from Wales who meets a woman while he's on a journey that takes him right across Europe. It's really a story just like so many others. It starts with the young man and his desires, and ends tragically.' He felt around in his jacket pocket for his pipe. 'And as in all fairy stories, the heroine is fabulously beautiful. A Spaniard, if I remember rightly. He falls in love with her and takes her back to Wales. But then she becomes ill. She's called Hope, but there is no hope.'

'A Spanish girl called Hope?' David persisted.

'Poetic licence. That's what Rochester called her.'

David mulled this over.

'Whatever her name,' Mr Merryweather continued, 'he summoned the very best doctors, but none of them could help. She finally asked him to take her back to where he found her. They travelled all the way back, and the journey only strengthened their love.' He picked up a heavy old lighter and and slowly lit his pipe. 'As love grows, writes Rochester, so too does pain.' The old man raised a finger. 'Loving, you see, means fearing loss. That's what Rochester was ultimately concerned with.' He looked around at the picture frames that were all over the apartment. 'Lose your heart to someone, and at some point it will break. That's the way things go.' He looked at them both. 'You're still young, and you don't worry about what might happen. Your whole lives are ahead of you. But sooner or later the day will come when one of you has to leave the other behind. That's the day when the other's heart will break, and they realise that it would have been better never to have loved.'

Heaven reached for David's hand and held it tightly. He was thinking about what she'd said about the boy she'd met in the club.

'So, the Earl of Rochester wasn't exactly a bundle of laughs.' Mr Merryweather puffed pale smoke into the air and coughed. 'And his writing is anything other than joyful. But let's get back to the story. The nobleman takes Lady Hope to this Spanish island. It's rugged, away from all the shipping routes, but people have heard of it because it's said that its daytime sky has disappeared.' He looked at them both closely. 'Like here in London, but different.'

They nodded. Another song was playing on the radio.

'Korngold,' the old man said, lost in thought. '*The Sea Hawk.*'

'Oh,' David replied.

Mr Merryweather waited a moment before continuing with the Earl's story. 'The beautiful woman, whom Rochester called Lady Hope, finally told him that she had to leave him. In tears, she told him that she was once a little piece of the bright sky, yes, a piece of sky that fell to earth during a storm from its place high above the earth, thanks to the evil hand of fate. And since everything that falls to earth has to take on a form of some sort, the beautiful sky that came plunging down took on the form of a human.'

Heaven took a deep breath. Her hand was trembling.

'The sky,' Mr Merryweather declared, 'turned into a wonderfully beautiful woman called Hope. That's what it says in Rochester.' He coughed again. 'The nobleman, of course, doesn't know what to make of it. But he can't see any trace of a lie in her eyes; there's no way she could be telling him an untruth. So he listens to what she has to say, and finds out the secret that she's been harbouring. She tells him that there are others of her kind in the world. She tells him that humans have a name for the creatures whose hearts go back up to the sky when they die.'

'Fairies,' Heaven whispered. Her lips could scarcely utter the word. It captured her like a dark dream, like a truth that wishes to remain unspoken.

'Yes. Was there ever a child who didn't believe in them? The magical creatures of old. Fairies, faeries, fays. Call them what you like.'

'Rochester really meant it, didn't he?' said David.

'Of course he did. The Earl wasn't a joking kind of man.' He shook his head vigorously and scratched his whiskers. 'But let me finish the story before I forget what I want to say.' He picked up the thread again. 'The nobleman now realises that the creatures normally called fairies are actually nothing but lost bits of sky that have fallen to earth and will return home one day.'

Heaven jumped up, raced to the window, pulled it further up, and took a couple of quick breaths. Mr Merryweather looked from her to David, but made no comment.

David sat where he was. He was remembering what they had found out about River Mirrlees, and about when Heaven had been born. It all fitted. He looked at her leaning out of the window, desperately gasping for air, and everything inside him was screaming at him to go over to her. But he didn't. He knew that she needed to be left alone at that moment.

'In Rochester's story,' Mr Merryweather continued, 'she needs the nobleman's help. Lady Hope asks him to kill her for the sake of their love.'

Heaven turned round. Her olive skin was grey; her eyes sunken.

'How does it end?' she asked. No, she didn't ask: she was almost shouting. 'Tell me, how does it end?'

Mr Merryweather didn't turn a hair. Heaven's behaviour, however rude, didn't seem to bother him.

'Lady Hope goes back home. The pair of them, she and the nobleman, renounce their love and get the sky in return. At the end, you see, she promises him that her heart will rise up after her death, high up to where her family lives, and that the sky, missing for so long, will return.'

'When my mother died,' Heaven said, her voice cracking, 'a bit of the night sky returned.'

David thought about that twenty-fifth of November when River Mirrlees disappeared and Jonathan passed off Sarah Jane's body as his wife's.

Heaven took a deep, shuddering breath. 'But it wasn't the whole sky that returned – just a bit of it.' The wind was rattling the shutters and sweeping through the kitchen. 'Why?' She answered her own question. 'Because I'm here. Because part of my mother's heart carried on living inside me. She passed it on to me and it's grown with me for all these years. That's why I'm still alive.'

Her eyes sought David's, and they held one another's gaze for a moment.

Mr Merryweather looked at her quizzically. 'If that's true, then your mother was a fairy.' Not a trace of humour. 'To judge by Rochester's story, at any rate, that would indeed have to be the case.'

'So what am I?' Heaven asked in despair. 'What's this emptiness, this coldness inside me? It's not me – it's never been me!'

David could feel his mind racing. All the jigsaw pieces that they had picked up thus far were whirling around in his head.

'That's why they're after you,' he whispered. 'They don't want you – they want what's keeping you alive.' He hesitated. 'They want the heart your mother gave you. That's what Mr Heep meant.'

'But why?'

Mr Merryweather shrugged. 'I really don't know. But I can finish the story.'

David and Heaven nodded. They did so automatically, too perturbed to reply.

'So, they both arrived on the island,' Mr

Merryweather said. 'The nobleman and Lady Hope danced together one last time. Then he gave her a cup of poisoned wine. She drank it, then died in his arms. The nobleman was grief-stricken. And as her life ebbed away, the body he was holding in his arms simply dissolved into a shimmering dream and was carried away on the wind.' He blew two smoke rings. 'And Hope? She really did go up into the sky. The clouds dispersed and the hole in the heavens was replaced by the daytime sky.' He gave an exaggeratedly long, loud sigh. 'That's the end of the story. That was the best Rochester could come up with.'

The music on the radio faded away and was replaced by the BBC news jingle.

How mad could the world really be?

Had River Mirrlees been a bit of sky that had plunged down into London and turned into a woman? A woman who had fallen in love and had borne the child of a human? Had River Mirrlees really been a fairy who had returned home to the sky after her daughter's birth?

David rubbed his eyes, exhausted.

It all sounded plausible, and yet...

Heaven was still leaning against the kitchen window, desperately breathing in the icy air that was streaming in from outside. 'What could anyone want with this heart?'

This was the question that nobody could answer. That was the mystery that had yet to be solved.

David strained to put together the picture that the individual jigsaw pieces might make. It was still too fuzzy to really see anything. Lost in thought, at first David didn't notice Heaven jump with fright.

Then he did. Something was panicking her. Her frenzied movements wrenched him from his reverie.

'What is it?'

But she wasn't listening. Heaven raced from the window to the shelf above the gas stove and turned up the volume. Her hands were trembling as she did so.

A crackling voice was saying: '…no clues as to the motive for this brutal crime. Investigations have just begun. The inhabitants of Richmond are shocked. Everyone has been left horrified by this bloody deed.' Short pause. Then: 'That was Marcus Wallace reporting for BBC Radio One.'

Heaven reached her hand out towards the radio, but didn't have the strength to switch it off. Exhausted, she let her arm fall.

'A murder in Richmond,' she stammered. Her eyes were full of the utmost despair.

David knew what she was afraid of.

'Could we use your phone?' he asked Mr Merryweather. He was already holding the receiver.

Mr Merryweather nodded wordlessly.

David gestured to Heaven. She took the receiver and dialled the number.

It rang once.

Twice.

Heaven drummed her fingers impatiently on the table.

A third time.

Then – at last! – someone answered.

But it wasn't Mr Mickey. It was an unfamiliar voice.

'Who are you?' asked the voice. Neither friendly nor unfriendly.

Heaven gave a false name. 'Harriet Jones.'

'Are you a relative?'

She didn't reply.

'Hello?' the voice persisted. 'Are you still there?'

'Can I speak to Mr Jones?'

Pause.

A crackling line.

'I'm sorry to tell you,' the voice said, 'that Mr Jones was the victim of a violent crime a couple of hours ago.' The voice was so businesslike and cool that it hurt.

'Might I ask you to answer a few questions for me?'

Heaven didn't reply. She was staring into space. Her lips were trembling and her eyes had filled with tears.

'Was Mr Jones a relation?'

'Something like that,' she stammered.

'Do you know anyone named Julian?'

Her eyes widened. 'Julian? Why do you want to know?'

'Please answer the question.'

She was silent.

'Where are you calling from?'

Heaven hung up. The receiver fell to the ground.

'Mr Mickey. He's dead.' She tottered and clutched at the table. 'What does Julian have to do with it?' she stammered. 'I don't get it. Julian and Eve, they didn't even know where my parents' house was.' She looked wildly at David. 'What's happened? What on earth has happened?'

She bent and picked up the receiver. Evidently panicking, she dialled another number.

Another ringing tone, but not for long this time. Someone picked up.

'Julian?' Heaven cried down the phone before the person could say a word. 'Julian, what's happened?

What the hell's happened?'

'Oh my God, Heaven, it's you.' He sounded hoarse. David could hear him clearly although he was standing slightly away from Heaven.

'What's going on? Why—?'

'Eve's disappeared,' Julian interrupted Heaven roughly. His words fell into the silence like rocks. 'The houseboat had been turned completely upside down when I came back. There was a card on the floor. With a name on it: Mr Drood. And a phone number. Christ, Heaven, I think they've got Eve. Do you know anyone called Mr Drood?'

'Julian…'

'I called the number on the card. A policeman answered. He was on about a murder in Richmond. Heaven, please tell me you're nothing to do with it.'

Heaven looked helplessly at David.

'They killed Mr Mickey.' She bit her lip 'He's dead, Julian. Dead!' She shut her eyes, but couldn't stop the tears from falling.

'Shit – and what's happened to Eve?' The voice at the other end of the line had risen to a screech.

David went over and gently took the receiver from Heaven's hand. 'Julian, we don't know what's happened.'

'David?'

'Yes.' He swallowed, thought, quickly, quickly, quickly. 'Where are you?'

'On the boat.'

'Stay where you are. We'll come to you.' Then he put the phone down.

'They've killed Mr Mickey,' sobbed Heaven.

David tried to take her in his arms, but she pushed him away and paced manically up and down the apartment. 'What on earth am I supposed to do? They've got Eve.' She ran her fingers wildly through her hair. 'Oh my God, they're going to kill Eve, David, what on earth is happening?' Her words were falling over themselves. 'What's wrong with me? Why do I cause trouble for everyone I come across?' She laughed hysterically and started sobbing again. 'Trouble! That's what Mr Mickey would call it! If he could call it anything!'

'Heaven. Calm down. Please,' said David. 'We need to go to the houseboat. We've got to help Julian.'

But Heaven seemed not to hear him. She kept on pacing around the kitchen table, her hair all over the place, tears pouring down her cheeks.

David hesitated for a moment, then blocked her path, took her in his arms, and held her tight.

She tried to fight him off, beating his chest with her bare hands and screaming at him, but he didn't let her go. He held onto her in silence until she had quietened down and her tears had at last run dry.

Mr Merryweather, who had been watching in shocked silence, just said: 'I'll let Miss Trodwood know, if you like.'

Then they set off for Marylebone.

FOURTH INTERLUDE
SCROOGED

The black-gloved man who called himself Mr Drood or Mr Heep or Mr Scrooge or Mr Quilp held the knife in front of him, observing the reflection of his own eyes in the blade.

He twisted and turned the knife as if he were dancing with it.

The young woman sobbing on the ground looked up at him, trembling from head to toe.

The raggedy man, who had only been working for him for a few hours, didn't take his dead eyes off her. His presence alone stopped her from trying to escape. For this reason, she hadn't been tied up. The idea of what the raggedy man might do to her not only prevented her from running away, but stopped her from even thinking of it.

Mr Drood was satisfied. He was exactly where he had wanted to be.

He phoned his client. It was a good conversation.

'She won't give me the slip for a second time,' Mr Drood promised softly. His knife was dancing around in front of the young woman's face.

'When can you get here?' asked the crackly voice at the other end of the phone. It sounded as impatient as ever.

'Not long now.' Mr Drood knew that everything was running to schedule. Dusk wasn't falling yet.

'You're not going to disappoint me?' asked the voice.

'Have I ever disappointed you?'

Mr Drood received no answer. 'Mr Scrooge,' the voice said softly, 'you surely know how much depends on you bringing me what I need.'

'Of course.'

'In that case, I can be reassured.'

'Yes, you can.'

'Do I have your word?'

'You have my word.'

There was a pause. 'Then I will see you soon.'

'I'll bring you the girl.' Mr Drood, who was always Mr Scrooge for this particular client, didn't so much as blink when a light flashed in the blade, briefly dazzling him.

'Nobody is to lay a finger on the girl,' the voice said

firmly. 'Things are a bit different this time.'

'As you have already mentioned.'

The voice on the telephone said: 'Don't let me down.' That was the end of the conversation.

Mr Drood seemed composed. He listened to the dialling tone for a moment, then threw the phone away into a corner. He would not be needing it again.

The woman, who was trying not to look at him or the raggedy man, let out a whimper. Mr Drood ignored her. He went over to the window and looked outside, where trees lined the waterfront.

In less than two hours' time, they would all be at the London Eye. It would all end there. He relished the view from the window. He liked this area. The snowflakes were falling more heavily, whirling through the air.

Mr Drood smiled.

Before long, London would witness a miracle. And the girl named Heaven would die.

CHAPTER 15

The city was like ice: smooth and shimmering on the surface but cold and treacherous beneath. Snowflakes were whirling through the air, faster and heavier than before. The cars were driving more erratically; the pedestrians hurried more bad-temperedly in and out of the shops; the doves hid themselves away in their nests high up under the eaves.

And this was precisely where David and Heaven were running. Heaven was, as always, faster than David, and he cursed his skiddy Converse, which turned everything into an ice rink.

On the way to the rooftops, they had passed a fast food place, and had silently watched, as if paralysed, an image of Mr Mickey on television. It was an old picture that someone had taken one summer. Heaven had quickly looked away as it flashed up on the screen. Since then, she had said very little and had just looked silently ahead of her. Her lips were pressed tightly together, and she seemed completely composed – but in a brittle, unnatural kind of way, as if one touch would destroy the whole facade.

David knew that feeling.

There was nothing of her past left. Everything that had been, had disappeared, leaving only memories that you wanted to run away from as though from a wild animal, hour after hour, day after day, until you had run far enough not to hear the vile creature snorting behind you.

David could well imagine what Heaven's beast looked like: its eyes were the windows of the house in Richmond; warm lights were aglow behind them, telling stories of days gone by. In the beast's guttural whispering she could hear the gentle words of comfort that Mr Mickey had used when she had refused to go to the cemetery. In the scratching of its claws was time that blazed like a fire and clawed away at skin, heart and mind.

Decisiveness. This was what was in Heaven's eyes now. The only thing she could do was run to Little Venice. Julian was still there, and Eve was alive. Two people whom Heaven didn't want to lose were not yet lost.

'It might be a trap.'

'I'll go on my own if need be.' She had sounded uncompromising.

'Wouldn't you just!'

Those were the last words they had exchanged.

They had then clattered up the stairs of 18 Phillimore Place and clambered through the skylight onto the roof in order to use the paths high above the city, far from the hustle and bustle of people beginning to leave their offices and shops and wending their way into the labyrinth of London, heading for rail and Tube stations.

A new block of houses loomed up ahead of them, its roof much lower than the one they were running along. David thought the gap looked too wide to jump across safely.

Heaven didn't hesitate for a second. She lengthened her stride, then took off. For a moment she flew through the air, a black arrow heading straight for its target, unstoppable. She landed on the next rooftop like a cat, and carried on running.

David clenched his teeth. All the warning lights were flashing in his brain, but he didn't think about plunging downwards, about slippery metal and freezing downdraughts. He would normally have found something to help him; a rod, a bent aerial or something similar. But he had no time for this, not least as Heaven was racing ahead.

He jumped, felt the current of the abyss, felt it clutching at his legs and dragging them down. The moment seemed to last for hours, but then he felt the impact. He tumbled, rolled across the rooftop like a Man United goalkeeper, struggled up and back onto his feet. Every muscle was hurting.

He took a deep breath.

Heaven stopped briefly. 'We have to carry on,' she said. 'Please.'

David nodded. *Just don't think about what might be happening in the meantime, on the boat in Little Venice.* David pictured Mr Mickey as he had met him on that one occasion. David had been suspicious; he had thought that the butler was playing his own particular game. In truth, he had only been thinking of Heaven. David was convinced of it now. It had cost him his life.

He set off, ignoring the pain that was shooting across his back, and ran on. He could hear Heaven's regular breathing beside him in the cold. Her reserves seemed never-ending.

They reached the next roof crossing, higher this time. He drew himself up and leapt. Used his momentum to carry him across. It was easier this time.

On they went.

David saw random moments of his life flickering in his mind like clips from silent movies. The stuffy room. The shut blinds. The screech in his mother's voice. The rows with his father, who refused to accept the truth. Geraldine sitting in front of the TV day in, day out, without a life. The stories he told her to take her mind off it. The decision to leave Cardiff because the broken fragments of a life that lay there just tore at his flesh and could never be put back together again.

Everyone is running away from their own beast. But it's even harder to deal with it on your own.

David thought about fairies and sky, about hearts and kisses – and he could feel the beast losing ground.

At Oxford Circus, they left the rooftops. Here, the snow was dangerously slushy. They went the rest of the way on the Bakerloo Line. The Underground took them to Warwick Avenue.

Little Venice looked as if it had undergone a metamorphosis. The brick-built houses were casting longer shadows than yesterday; all the bridges and narrow towpaths with their deserted benches, dusted with fresh snow, looked like living silhouettes reaching out into the gathering night. There was even less going on than there had been the day before; there weren't even any joggers around. The smell of the green water reminded David of Cardiff – but not of the sea – it was the musty smell of the old bathroom that was never aired.

'It's gone!'

David immediately saw what Heaven meant. Julian's and Eve's boat was still in the same place as yesterday, but Heaven's boat was missing.

David touched her shoulder. 'Be careful,' he said.

Heaven just looked at him. 'Says who?' she replied. She tried to grin, but it just looked ghostly.

They crossed the little curved footbridge and walked towards the landing stage.

Inside the boat, all was quiet. There was a light on in the cabin, but there was no sound. All they could hear was the soft splashing of the cold water against the boat's solid body, and the distant traffic on Wellington Road and St John's Wood Road.

David could feel the boat rocking beneath his feet. The mandalas on the wall weren't looking very happy now, and the stone Buddha squatting on the roof remained silent and serious. The plastic wrappers of the shrubs were flapping around the stone tubs; the ash had long since been swept up from the open fireplace. A white layer of fluffy snow was resting on everything.

They were now leaving footsteps behind them. David knocked on the little door, hesitantly at first, then more insistently. They heard someone approaching. A key was turned in a latch, and Julian opened the door.

'Heaven!' The round face with its skinny goatee and dense sideburns looked pale, aside from a couple of red patches. His matted dreadlocks swayed with his every movement, and his eyes were glittering feverishly. 'At last!'

He hugged her.

A gust of unpleasantly warm air wafted towards her and she screwed up her eyes, as if someone were throwing fine sand into her face.

Julian was wearing a brightly coloured T-shirt with a cannabis motif, paired with grubby combat trousers and sandals.

David peered past Heaven and Julian to the inside of the houseboat. It looked like a jungle and smelled like one too: of earth, damp and heat. Huge palm trees stood everywhere, and dense foliage festooned the shelves. Even though it was November, flowers with red blooms were flourishing in the clay pots jammed among the old books and records.

No wonder it was so warm in here.

They entered and took in the devastation inside.

'Oh God,' said Heaven in horror. 'Oh my God, Julian, what have they done with Eve?'

Julian rummaged in his trouser pocket and pulled out the business card he'd spoken of. It was grey, made of coarse paper, and the text was no-frills.

The card bore a single name: Mr Drood. Beneath it, someone had written a number in neat, curved handwriting. It was a number that Heaven recognised only too well. It was her home phone number in Richmond.

'What's going on?' Heaven looked around wildly.

David, too, stared at the chaos in the cabin: upturned easels, tubes of brightly coloured paint on the floor, slashed half-finished canvases. In amongst the painting equipment were smashed stars with cracked stones in the middle, pages of sketches, paintings and drawings, and several tools whose function he couldn't make out at first glance.

He could, however, clearly see that there had been some sort of struggle. 'Come on, Julian! What happened?' he asked.

Julian bolted the door. He looked around in a panic, as if he already feared that someone was inside.

He slipped the key into his stitched-on trouser pocket, ran both hands through his hair, then dropped them helplessly. 'You have to help me.'

David undid his jacket, and Heaven undid her coat. It was unbelievably warm in here. David didn't know how long Heaven would be able to cope with this kind of temperature.

And it could be a trap. He'd said as much to Heaven when they'd set off – and, if he was honest, that's what it looked like.

Every fibre of his being was telling him to run; he could feel the familiar old anxiety starting to overwhelm him, making it hard for him to breathe. He looked across at the windows, but the tiny portholes didn't help. And was he imagining it, or was it as stuffy in here as in the house in Cardiff? David suddenly felt as if he were suffocating, and he knew that he had to get Heaven out of there straightaway.

But he didn't move a muscle.

'You have to help me.' David could hear the panic and the fear and the darkness in Julian's voice, and he knew that they couldn't leave him on his own. He was waving the business card around. 'They've got Eve.'

'Who?'

'Who do you think? Mr Drood and the other man.'

David glanced around the little cabin again. There was a door at the far end, presumably leading to a kitchen or to the bunks, but definitely not to the outside. 'What other man?' he asked.

'Looked like a piece of crap.'

'The raggedy man?' asked Heaven.

Julian nodded. 'Yeah, you could call him that.' His left eye was twitching, as if it had a life of its own. 'That's what he looked like.'

David almost cursed out loud. How the hell did Julian know about the raggedy man? Hadn't he said on the phone that he'd only found the card?

Heaven's breathing was becoming more laboured, and David didn't know how long she would cope with the hot air. She didn't seem to have noticed that there was anything amiss; didn't seem to notice that Julian was avoiding their eyes. Instead, she looked as if she were about to faint at any moment. If she moved, even just a tiny bit, she tottered, clinging on to tables and chairs.

'They wanted you to come here,' Julian said in a tone that could only be described as apologetic. 'There was nothing I could do. He threatened to kill Eve, and he almost did kill her.'

Julian gazed vacantly into the room.

David finally jumped into action. With one bound, he was at the door, trying the handle.

'Is this the only way out?' he asked.

Julian nodded. 'When I got home, they were already here.'

David cursed. His stomach lurched. Damn it – he'd known all along! But had there been any alternative?

'You utter bas—'

Heaven staggered, so suddenly that it surprised Julian too. 'What's wrong with her?'

David had already leapt to catch her.

'I'm fine,' Heaven gasped. She tried to look cheerful, but completely failed. 'It's…' Her voice turned into groaning and gasping, as a door further back in the cabin opened and Mr Drood emerged from the darkness of the next room.

David was no more surprised than Heaven. The cry for help, the boat, the unbearable heat, the shut door…the trap had been all too obvious.

Heaven turned her head.

'At last,' Mr Drood said in a tone that was simultaneously agreeable and languidly cold. 'We meet again at last.'

He looked just the way he'd looked when they first met him. Of average appearance, nondescript, apart from a couple of features that didn't quite fit: his eyes, which glittered with murderous desire; the knife, which was curving through the air; and the deep scratches on his face, some of which had taken on a deep blue hue.

Mr Drood had escaped from the rat-cats, just as they had assumed – but not without cuts and bruises, from which David briefly derived an absurd, childish feeling of pride.

'Glad you could make it,' Mr Drood said pleasantly, gliding across the room without any visible haste. 'I hadn't expected you so soon. The traffic in London is so unpredictable these days.'

David clenched his fists.

The trap had been so simple – and that's why it had been so effective. It hadn't given them any alternative.

Mr Drood kills Mr Mickey. He leaves Richmond and sets off for Little Venice. He forces his way into the houseboat, kidnaps Eve, and forces Julian to ring Richmond. Then he waits. He knows that Heaven will be ringing the house.

With a bit of luck, someone will mention Julian. And when the police go looking for the murderer, they'll suspect anyone who's behaving strangely. And Julian will be behaving strangely because he's anxious and hasn't got a clue what's going on. Heaven will in turn call Julian and will come to Little Venice because she's worried about him, about him and Eve.

There was just one question remaining.

'How did you find the boat?' David hissed from between clenched teeth.

Mr Drood smiled a fatherly smile. 'Mr Mickey told me. Before he had to die.'

Heaven just murmured: 'Mr Mickey knew where I lived.'

'Oh yes, he knew all the time. He was always concerned about you, my girl. He promised your father he'd look after you.'

'He would never have betrayed me.'

Mr Drood examined the blade in his hand. 'You must be aware that every living creature, every animal and every human, can take a certain degree of pain. Believe me, finding out where the threshold is is an art in itself.' He moved into the cabin. 'With some people, it just takes wild threats; with others, you have to…' He gave the blade a long look. 'Mr Mickey, as you call him, was courageous.' He paused, then carried on speaking softly. 'Following our phone call, he thought I might be the one to help him. It was so easy to deceive him.' He grinned. 'Though it did take a bit longer to get him to talk.' He shook his head. 'Tut, tut, tut. And he knew all along how it was going to end.'

'You bastard!' hissed David.

Icy tears came to Heaven's eyes. She staggered, held on to the back of an armchair. Gathering all her remaining strength together, she clenched her fists. 'Why did you kill him?' Her eyelids were fluttering like butterflies that weren't going to see another summer. She began to tremble violently.

David knew that she had to get out into the fresh air there and then. He looked around madly for something that he could use as a weapon.

'Why?' Heaven gasped for a final time. Her knuckles were white from clutching the chair.

'I was unfortunately compelled to show the two of you just how serious my intentions are.' Mr Drood looked at Heaven as if he himself played no part in all this. 'Drastic methods are permitted at times like this, I believe.'

'Eve's in there,' Julian whispered, pointing to the back room. 'I'm so sorry. I didn't want to lie to you. But…Eve…the other man's in there with her.' He swallowed whatever was in his throat and making it difficult for him to speak. 'He's in there with her and…' He didn't finish his sentence.

Mr Drood nodded. 'She's so terrified that she can't

even scream.' He sucked in his breath between his teeth, making a whistling sound as he did so. 'But I think there have been enough deaths for today. My assistant is with her. If she doesn't do anything to him, he won't do anything to her.' Looking at Julian, he added: 'That's presumably in your best interests, too?'

Julian swore. 'He was going to kill her,' he repeated. 'And she…'

Mr Drood was the very embodiment of composure. 'Threats form the basis of my negotiations. That's just the way it is.'

Heaven was visibly struggling to keep her cool. 'Leave it, Julian.' She used the last of her strength to say these few miserable words, then succumbed to a coughing fit. 'I'd have bumped into this bastard sooner or later, regardless.' She glared at Mr Drood. Her throat was making a rattling sound that didn't sound good.

'It's rather warm in here, isn't it?' Mr Drood was still wearing his black gloves. They made a squeaking noise, like skin being overstretched, whenever he moved his fingers. 'These tropical temperatures don't necessarily suit everyone.'

His knife blade flashed, and David noticed that the handle was made of a pale, shimmering substance.

Ivory, perhaps – or maybe something else, something that David didn't want to think about.

'It isn't the heat that's bothering me,' hissed Heaven.

'Oh really?'

'If you think that I—'

Mr Drood interrupted her. 'You don't like the heat,' he said, as if it were just a matter of course. He turned to David. 'Our Heaven has, you see, a heart that belongs to the night sky.' He raised his eyes theatrically to the ceiling. 'It's so cold up there. So cold. Hearts that are meant to live up there can't bear any kind of heat.' Mr Drood pulled a mock sympathetic face. 'Such a pity that it really is extraordinarily warm in this boat.' He grinned smugly. 'What a coincidence, eh?'

All the colour suddenly drained from Heaven's face. David grasped her and she looked at him. Her eyes were filled with fear, like tears behind glass. She struggled to stand one final time, then collapsed.

David caught her, held her tightly. Then he went down on his knees and laid her gently on the ground.

Think, think, think, he told himself.

The trap had been so simple. Mightn't there be an equally simple way out of it?

'What are you going to do to her?' He stood up and glared at the gloved man.

'Her cold heart,' replied Mr Drood. 'That's what I'm after.'

'What do you want it for?'

'I don't want it.'

'What, then?'

Mr Drood shook his head regretfully. 'This,' he said, in the calmest possible manner, 'isn't some film that you're watching in peace and quiet in some old cinema in Oxford Circus.' He gave a snort of laughter. 'Why should I tell you what I'm planning to do? Nobody would gain anything from that. Nobody.' He gestured to Heaven, who was lying on the floor by David, breathing with such difficulty that he started to worry that she might suffocate. 'Not her, either.' He took a step towards David. 'I'm taking her with me, and you can't stop me.'

David could see his knife dancing in the dim light. The silver blade was curved like a claw.

'Bear in mind,' Mr Drood breathed patronisingly, 'that I always get what I want.'

David spotted a bag of golf clubs leaning against the cupboard. He glanced at Julian, who seemed to understand what he meant.

'I will leave the pair of you now. The girl is coming with me.'

'No!' David said emphatically.

'If you get in my way, then sweet Eve will die.'

Julian clenched his fists. Despair was etched on his face.

Then everything happened very quickly. A scream cut through the silence. A loud banging came from the next room, then Eve came plunging through the door. She stumbled and crashed right into the middle of a large palm tree, which swayed menacingly, and then she screamed again as the raggedy man appeared behind her in the doorway.

The raggedy man was bigger than the creature they'd fought off at Highgate Cemetery. He looked… fresher. David didn't want to begin to imagine which grave Mr Drood had dug this one up from.

Now, David thought. *Now!*

The next seconds were a series of snapshots, wobbly and out of focus. Julian took a step towards Mr Drood, who fixed him with an alert stare. David seized the moment, darted to the cupboard and pulled a golf club out of the bag. He didn't hesitate – despite thinking all the time about what could go wrong. He could fall over. The club could get stuck in the bag. All sorts of things. But none of them happened. He grabbed the club and whirled around.

Eve was creeping backwards along the floor away from the raggedy man, who was pursuing her with all the calm of a dead person. Julian had meanwhile flung himself at Mr Drood. His T-shirt stood out like a flash of lightning against Mr Drood's black silhouette.

Heaven was unconscious now. Her eyelids were flickering and her fingers were trembling wildly.

David raised the golf club above his head, preparing to strike. He just had to hit Mr Drood's head and it would all be over. He'd worry about the raggedy man later. He put all his strength into the blow.

And then he saw the blade.

Or, rather, he just saw its silvery light as it pressed, razor-sharp, against Julian's throat.

The raggedy man had reached Eve and had grabbed her. David couldn't see exactly what he was doing to her, but it had silenced her. She was cowering on the floor, whimpering to herself, staring with tear-stained eyes at Julian, who had stopped moving.

'So you're going to play the hero, are you?' hissed Mr Drood, looking straight at David. 'You're going to risk me slitting his throat?'

David was silent. His pulse was racing. Mr Drood

stood up with a slow gliding movement, the blade still pressed against Julian's throat. 'You want to be a hero like our Julian here?' he asked again.

'Leave him alone! He's got nothing to do with it!'

A note of anger flared up in Mr Drood's voice. 'All he had to do was make a phone call. Not such a difficult thing to do.' He turned impatiently to Julian. 'But instead of just waiting to see how it would all end, he had nothing better to do than play at being Action Man!'

David could see that Julian was trembling. Trembling with anger, helplessness, impotence.

David was still holding the club. He gazed quickly at Heaven, Eve, the raggedy man. The cold handle of the golf club suddenly felt incredibly heavy.

'Didn't I say that nothing would happen to you if you did everything I told you?' Mr Drood's voice was quiet and clear.

Julian nodded dumbly. His lips were sore and cracked.

'See!' Mr Drood turned to David. 'They lie to you, no matter what you promise them. That's how people are.'

'Let him go!'

Mr Drood ignored David. Instead, he turned back

to Julian and whispered in his ear: 'You're a hero, aren't you? You'd do anything to save your girlfriend.'

Julian looked pleadingly at David. *I'm sorry*, his eyes were saying: *I'm so very sorry*. They were wide, like deep lakes with a life floating around in them that David had until then only seen in fragments.

'Are you a hero?' Mr Drood raised his voice.

'No,' Julian croaked.

'No?'

'I'm not a hero.'

Mr Drood shook his head sadly. 'But what you just did was heroic.' He grinned. 'Stupid and unsuccessful, but heroic all the same.' He winked at David. 'Wasn't it, David?'

Julian was breathing shallowly. His eyes were rolling in their sockets.

Mr Drood bent over him. 'You know what happens to heroes.' It wasn't a question, but he asked it anyway. 'Everyone knows what happens to heroes.'

Julian didn't move.

'You tell me.'

Sweat was running down his face.

'Go on, tell me!'

Julian spat in his face.

'Heroes,' Mr Drood said calmly, wiping his face,

'mostly die heroic deaths.' He suddenly stuck the knife into Julian's stomach as if in passing. It all happened so quickly that neither David nor Eve nor Julian himself realised. There wasn't even any sound; just Julian's incredulous gasp and the look on his face when he finally understood.

'True heroes,' said Mr Drood, releasing his victim, 'never think of the consequences.'

Julian slumped to the ground clutching his wound. Blood was pouring out from between his fingers. He groaned, incapable of speaking.

'What about you, David? Do you want to be a hero too?' asked Mr Drood. 'For her?' The silvery blade, now covered with red flecks, made elegant curves in the air.

David didn't have to think for long. He struck.

He could feel the handle of the golf club in his hand as he focussed only on hitting his target.

But then Mr Drood did something that David hadn't banked on.

He simply reached out and grasped the golf club firmly at its lower end. With a sudden movement, he wrenched it out of David's hand. He knew what he was doing. He was an expert.

David yelled with surprise and rage.

Then he felt two arms wrapping themselves around him from behind, as if death itself were embracing him. The raggedy man stank; it was the sweet smell of decay.

'You bastard!' David cursed, kicked out, to no avail.

Heaven was lying lifeless on the ground. Eve was screaming somewhere, screaming desperately. Red was seeping out onto the rug, now wet, that Julian was lying on.

Mr Drood came up to David and stopped in front of him. David could feel Mr Drood's breath, faintly pepperminty, on his face.

Then he grabbed his throat. David choked. The hand in black leather was holding him like a vice. David could feel his breath faltering. Everything began to flicker before his eyes.

'Soon, very soon,' he heard a sharp voice much too close to his ear. 'Soon it will be night!'

Mr Drood laughed, but only with his voice.

Then the gloves pressed hard, and fingers as bitter as death closed around David's throat, tighter and tighter. Everything around him went black. All hope vanished, and the music in his head became a muffled sound that accompanied him as he slid into oblivion.

Silence, at first. Deafness, underwater sounds.

Noises that were taking on sharp edges.

When David came to, Heaven had gone. But he didn't realise that at first. He could feel the air in his nose and mouth, and drew it in as if every breath were his last. He could feel the boat gently rocking on the water; he could smell the wooden floor that his face was pressed against; he wasn't sure where all these images were coming from, but he did know that he hadn't died.

'David!'

His name.

Yes.

David opened his eyes and looked into a face that he recognised.

'Eve?' He coughed. His throat was dry.

'He's bleeding to death.' Her voice was shrill and wobbly. 'Oh my God, he's going to die.' She couldn't keep still. One moment, she was kneeling beside him; seconds later, once she was sure that he was OK, she had gone again.

'Where's Heaven?' That was the first question that occurred to him. He looked around at the cabin and everything came back to him. How long had he been lying there on the ground? He struggled to sit up.

'Julian's bleeding to death!' Eve cried.

David shook off the rest of his stupor.

The facts came back to him like a thump in the stomach. His hands instinctively reached for his throat, which was painful where Mr Drood had choked him.

A song came to mind. 'The Stowaway'. By Yamit Mamo.

The stranger with the haunting face
Here then gone without a trace.

The song reminded him of Heaven, but he couldn't remember why.

Eve was suddenly kneeling beside him again. 'David!' She grabbed his shoulder. 'Are you listening to me? Julian's bleeding to death!' she yelled. 'He's dying!' Then she slapped him in the face, presumably to try to make him come to his senses. 'You've got no time. *We've* got no time!'

David turned his head and saw what she meant.

'Shit!' he said. Images pounced on him like hungry animals hunting for prey. Adrenaline was bringing him back to life, forcing him to stand up.

He tried mentally to organise the flood of images. Snapshots, ripped and blurred: Julian lying on his back. Blood, almost black, around him, everywhere on the floor. A bit of clothing that he was pressing against his wound. Open eyes. Silent mouth.

'Where's the phone?' David asked instinctively. He was once again back in reality, looking around the chaos of the cabin.

Eve, who seemed to be paralysed, looked at him as if he'd just asked the most ridiculous question in the universe.

'The phone?' He was shouting now.

She was sobbing; her whole body was trembling. Then she stretched out her hand and pointed. 'There.'

David raced over to the ancient radio-sized mobile and dialled 999. His fingers flew across the buttons. He involuntarily drew breath when he looked at Julian. It occurred to him that he'd been spared that fate. But why? Why had Mr Drood spared him?

Christ, why wasn't anyone answering? This was 999, not a call centre!

His thoughts jumped back to Heaven, who was no longer there. They weren't clear thoughts; more like feelings and undertones that scratched at his soul like a blunt knife on metal.

A clicking sound.

An emergency services phone operator, bored and perfunctory. As he told her what had happened and gave her the information she needed – stab wound, deep, stomach injury, yes, presumably very serious, lots of blood, dark, almost black, just a T-shirt pressed to the wound, yes, for God's sake, send someone, and do it quickly! No, for crying out loud, I'm not a doctor, no idea what you mean – he surveyed the scene as if he weren't really there.

Julian was pale. He was breathing wildly. Dark blood was still seeping from between his fingers. The T-shirt was sodden. There was a sweet smell in the small cabin.

Eve was sobbing her heart out. She was kneeling next to Julian, yelling at him, stroking his hair, touching his bloody T-shirt and dropping it again as if it had burnt her. Her face was covered in scratches that were presumably the work of the raggedy man.

David didn't follow the operator's instruction to stay on the line, but cut her off. A moment later, he was kneeling next to Eve. 'Where's Heaven?' He battled to keep his voice even.

Eve looked up. 'They took her with them. She was unconscious.'

'What about you?'

She was fighting back the tears again. 'I was with Julian.'

David felt anger blaze up inside him. Why hadn't

she tried to stop the others from taking Heaven? She could have… He stopped. No, it wasn't Eve's fault. It wasn't anyone's fault, of course it wasn't, he had to pull himself together, to keep his head.

What now?

David stood up, paced around the room, then stood still for a moment. Then he screamed loudly, shrilly, angrily into the silence, kicking desperately at anything in the way: a flower pot, a chair, a lamp. He grabbed a pile of newspapers from the floor and hurled them around the room. They fell to the ground like so many swatted moths. He screamed again, yelled, felt as if pieces were being torn from his body.

Get a grip! This won't help her.

He knew that, but couldn't do anything about it. It was as if he had gone mad. One single thought was flashing up in his mind in huge letters: *SHE HAS GONE! They've taken Heaven somewhere. They're going to kill her. They're going to cut out her heart, and nobody will ever know.*

He raced to the little porthole and peered outside.

'What am I supposed to do? Help me!' Eve had paid no attention to his angry outburst. She was just staring at Julian and at the growing lake of blood.

This was what finally brought David round. For at

that moment he realised that Eve felt just as he did. The man she loved was lying on the floor, bleeding to death, and she hadn't got a clue what to do about it.

'OK, he needs to stay awake,' David said. He bent over Julian. Dull eyes stared back at him. David wasn't sure whether Julian even recognised him. His eyelids were fluttering agitatedly. 'Julian? You mustn't go to sleep!' David emphasised every word. 'Do you hear me? Keep your eyes open, stay awake.' He thought he could remember hearing people say that in films. If someone was injured, then they mustn't under any circumstances lose consciousness. He had to stay awake until the paramedics arrived.

But there weren't any paramedics, for God's sake.

And there was so much blood.

'Help's on the way,' David said.

He laid a gentle hand on Julian's shoulder. His whole body was positively on fire. 'You're not going to die,' he promised. 'You're too cool for that. Believe me.'

Julian didn't nod. He shut his eyes. His breathing was irregular.

'Damn it!' said David.

'How long are they going to be?' Eve had briefly gone over to the window, but returned immediately.

David looked at her. 'How am I supposed to know?' He could feel himself losing control again. No, no, no, he had to stay calm. Julian's life depended on it.

A thought was forming in his mind, a vague thought that was anything but reassuring. The police would be coming along with the paramedics. After all, he had reported a stab wound. The police would start asking questions – indeed a whole host of questions once they'd seen the mess in here.

And the very last thing David wanted at that moment was to attract the attention of the police.

His mind was racing. 'First-aid kit?' he asked Eve. She shook her head.

David looked at the T-shirt that Eve was pressing to the wound. It was drenched in blood. He needed a bit of material, a towel, a bandage, anything.

David's eyes flashed around the houseboat. A cupboard door was open. David didn't lose a second. He ran to the cupboard, pulled out two clean T-shirts, ripped them up as he hastened back to Julian, and pressed the strips of fabric against the wound. Then he said to Eve: 'You have to keep pressing – try to stop the blood until they get here. I've got to go.'

She nodded dumbly.

'I have to find Heaven.' He felt the burning lump in

his throat as he said: 'Otherwise they'll kill her too. They want her heart.'

Eve was still crying, but silently now. 'Her boat's just this side of Camden Lock,' she said in a high voice. 'Julian took it there.'

David wiped a tear from her face. 'He'll make it. Believe me, he'll pull through.'

A siren was wailing in the distance.

Eve looked up. A faint trace of hope ghosted across her face.

'They're coming,' said David. He grasped her shoulders and said her name. 'Eve!' He looked into her eyes as calmly as he could. 'Eve!' Their eyes met, just for a matter of seconds. 'Everything will be fine.' He was aware that she and Julian had only been dragged into it all because of Heaven and him. 'I'm sorry,' he said. 'I'm so very sorry. Truly.'

Eve nodded feebly. 'It'll all be OK, won't it?' Each word sounded as if she had to struggle to spell it out.

'Yes,' David replied, although of course he didn't have the faintest idea whether anything would ever be OK again. But all the same. Sometimes you have to promise things. Sometimes lies help you to see life as it really is.

The sirens were getting louder. There was more

than just one. David took a last quick look at Eve and Julian. The new bandage wasn't saturated yet.

'Find Heaven,' said Eve. She nodded to him.

'Good luck,' he whispered. 'See you soon.'

Another promise that might be a lie.

The lurid, blazing, howling sirens were practically upon them, and David slipped away from the boat. He felt mean for leaving Eve alone, but there wasn't any choice. There was nothing more that he could do here. And if the police found him on the boat, then he'd spend the night in a police station, being asked questions that he couldn't answer. They would arrest him, and nobody would ever believe what he had to say.

He ran out of the cabin, and after the unbearable heat inside, the snowy world outside felt colder than ever. It had long since started to get dark. He could see footprints leading from the quay in the direction of Bloomfield Road, but they vanished much too soon where the broad tracks of car tyres had imprinted themselves in the snow.

They had evidently dragged Heaven off into a car and then had set off in the direction of the Edgware Road. The trail would run cold there; they could be anywhere in the city.

David could feel his knees trembling. Behind him, he could hear two vehicles racing up from Warwick Avenue and stopping by the houseboat with a loud squealing of brakes. The sirens were then switched off.

David pressed himself against the wall of a house, smelling the ivy that was creeping up it. He felt something flapping, and gasped for breath. Right next to him was a bird. It stared at him intently with its dark button eyes; its feathers were brightly coloured. Far too exotic for this time of year. There were sometimes animals in the city that looked like this bird. They looked as if they had escaped from a zoo.

There was a babble of voices, and David imagined a scene of the kind he had seen on television. Fast-moving paramedics, inquisitive policemen, black and yellow plastic tape to seal off the area. And he desperately hoped that what he'd said to Eve wouldn't turn out to be a lie.

A moment later he ventured out of the shadows and went across to the Edgware Road, where the car tracks ended. He stood there for a while, staring at the traffic. The headlights of the cars glowed through the whirling snowflakes. Darkness had already descended now – or very nearly.

He set off again at last. He ran down the Edgware

Road and then turned into Marylebone Road. He ran and ran, as if running would solve everything. The cold burned his throat; snowflakes landed in his hair. He ran and ran, on and on.

There were cars and people everywhere. Every street led into another street. London suddenly felt like a terrible Moloch, huge and hungry, like something that would eat humans alive. The city before him was dark, even darker than ever before, because David had lost something – the light of his life.

He tried to keep calm, but didn't entirely succeed. He shut his eyes, took some deep breaths. Where could they have taken Heaven?

He thought again about the song they had heard in the taxi. 'The Stowaway'. Barely two nights ago. He thought about Heaven: her smile, her dark eyes. Words popped into his mind; things that he had experienced. Stories that he had been told. They shaped themselves into a vague sketch made up of suppositions that one could cling on to when standing on the edge of an abyss.

Mr Drood was just a henchman; he'd said so himself. The actual client was someone else. But who? Where had Mr Drood taken Heaven? OK, so he wanted her heart – but if he'd been able to take her heart in the way that he took her other one, he'd have done it on the houseboat.

But he hadn't done it on the houseboat.

And that meant…

What?

That he couldn't just cut it out of her body in the way he had done before? Was that why she was still alive? Did Mr Drood have to take her to some special place to have her heart taken out? And if so, what kind of place? A hospital?

David groaned. He had no idea. He wasn't going to find her. Not with these vague conjectures. He needed help.

But where was he going to find help? Who could he ask?

Richmond, his brain was telling him. Mr Mickey was dead, but he had asked David to pass a message on to Heaven if she was in trouble. She was to go to Canary Wharf.

Canary Wharf.

David had a vague idea who he might encounter there. And this idea seemed to be the best one he'd had all day.

Canary Wharf was the home of high finance and the boardrooms of all the big companies. And if he was on the right track, he would find Heaven's father's firm there along with Heaven's guardian, Mr Sims, who might be an arrogant Mr Moneybags, but who would be bound to pull out all the stops to find his ward. And, of course, he had the necessary loose change to do so.

David didn't lose another moment. He raced off into the gathering night to the part of London where there was no sky.

CHAPTER 16

Nobody in the Portland Place internet café batted an eyelid when a tattered figure in a grubby jacket came racing in. Panting and wild-haired, he flung himself at one of the PCs like a madman.

London was full of strange characters; one more or less wasn't going to bother anyone.

David didn't look around either. He didn't want to waste a second.

Come on! His fingers flew agitatedly across the keyboard – then the results of his search appeared on the screen.

David scanned the facts that he already partly knew: Juno Sims, director of Sims Enterprises, formerly Mirrlees and Sims Waist Company. Market leader in traditional British fabrics.

Blah, blah, blah.

The address! He clicked on 'Contact'.

At last.

The head office was at One Canada Square. David

knew the building. It was a gleaming, flashing block that looked like a steel and glass obelisk and was better known as Canary Wharf Tower. A monument that towered above the houses of the old city like an alien object.

David threw some money onto the counter and raced back out onto the street.

Without a single thought for his aversion to the Underground, he had taken the Jubilee line to Canary Wharf station, the glassy monster where all those people scurried about busily as if hopelessly lost. It took him a good half hour to reach his destination, and that half hour felt like a hundred years.

Now, though, he was finally standing amidst the modern buildings and blocks of flats crowded together on the Isle of Dogs. The high-rise buildings were brightly lit, as if to show the whole world that they weren't as cold and empty as everyone in London had been saying for years. It was a sea of glass and steel, marble and granite stretching out over the tongue of land on the Thames that had once housed a collection of docks and warehouses, dry docks and shipyards. Then it had been an exotic place, where ships had unloaded their cargoes from the furthest reaches of the Empire; where the big freighters bringing fruit and vegetables from the Canary Islands to England had dropped anchor, giving fodder for countless swashbuckling tales recounted in the area's pubs and drinking dens.

That was all long ago.

And then, about eight years before the night sky high above London disappeared, the city fathers and the obstinate Prime Minister who never laughed had started transforming the former docks into the soulless landscape that it had been ever since. Only the evocative street names borne by the immense, sunless chasms between the buildings bore witness to an exotic past that had once been a playground for dreams of faraway places.

Like a lot of Londoners, David had never been here before. Those who worked here avoided the place out of hours because it was cold and empty and dark. At the weekends, so it was said, there wasn't a soul around; not even the stray dogs to whom the peninsula owed its ancient name chose to roam around this man-made wasteland.

David dashed through the streets without paying any attention to their sonorous names: the West India Docks and the East India Docks, the Royal Victoria Dock and the King George V Dock.

City slickers hurried past him with their laptop cases, some of them walking even faster than he was. Posh cars were gliding down the smoothly tarred roads, and everything was covered with snow, which seemed perhaps the strangest thing of all to David. It was like a winter fairy tale in an area where fairy tales had long since died out.

David didn't need to figure out which way to go. He couldn't miss the massive tower. It loomed up like a mausoleum above the surrounding medley of post-modernism and megalomania.

He thought about Heaven and about what she might be going through. How could he have let this happen? Fragments of the unbelievable story were swirling round his head, throwing up new questions. River Mirrlees hadn't been human, and she had left Heaven something after her death that would bring her daughter only unhappiness. Had she known how things would turn out? He couldn't imagine she had.

David found himself looking up at the sky. Strangely enough, the Isle of Dogs was in an area where the night sky had returned. From here, you could see the stars and everything else besides. The rumour that the night was darker there than anywhere else in London came from the fact that Canary Wharf, despite all the windows and the plethora of glass and open space, rarely seemed to be truly light.

He finally reached Canary Wharf Tower, the obelisk-like building stretching more than two hundred and thirty-five metres up into the sky. Everything about its construction was symmetrical. There was nothing uneven, nothing imperfect.

David felt as if everyone was bound to be staring at him as the doors to the entrance lobby opened. Everything was gleaming and shimmering; everything looked and smelled clean. He was greeted by a blast of warm air. The people darting around all wore the same grim expression. They looked grey and dangerous, all terribly important. By the row of silvery sparkling lifts were large boards with the names of the companies that were based there.

It took David two minutes to spot the Sims Enterprises logo. The firm was on the twentieth and twenty-first floors.

David glanced over his shoulder. The porter and two security men were watching him. They had an unflinching look to them, and their uniforms probably cost more than all of David's possessions put together.

David didn't have to think for long. OK, he couldn't be doing with any trouble, and they had noticed him anyway. He turned back and went over to the porter to sign himself in.

He was going to see Mr Juno Sims of Sims Enterprises. No, he wasn't there on business. More like a purely private matter of the utmost importance.

The porter made a quick phone call, nodded grumpily, and let David through. They were allowing him to go up.

David gave the security men a long look, then went across to the lifts. The lift button was smooth and cold. He waited impatiently.

Then the doors slid open and discharged a stream of highly important-looking business people who ignored him.

David entered the lift. It smelled of carpeted floors, artificial fragrance and mirrored walls. Synthetic music was purring from a loudspeaker that was presumably hidden somewhere up in the ceiling.

David looked at himself in one of the mirrors. There were dark shadows under his eyes, and he was deathly pale. But at least the blood on his black jacket had dried. And in any case, making the best possible impression wasn't exactly high on his agenda.

He just hoped that what Mr Mickey had said in Richmond would turn out to be right. But then he remembered what money could do.

He was upstairs in under a minute. The lift doors opened and David found himself facing a swanky reception desk. A secretary who looked as if she had come from a mail-order catalogue (Competent Model – you won't be disappointed!) looked him up and down.

'You're the young man who would like to see Mr Sims?' She sounded testy, even though David hadn't said a word. According to her name badge, she went by the name of Mrs Willenbrock.

'It's important,' he said.

'It's always important,' Mrs Willenbrock replied tartly, baring her immaculate teeth with a smile that looked more like a threat.

David had evidently chosen the wrong word. He tried again. 'It'd be nice if...'

Mrs Willenbrock looked ostentatiously at the gold watch on her wrist, evidently intending David to see it. David found himself wondering whether it was included in the secretary package. 'Be brief. What's this all about?'

'Tell him that Freema Mirrlees sent me.'

Mrs Willenbrock peered at him over her sharp-cornered reading glasses like a bird of prey. Her forehead was completely smooth, which made her face look curiously expressionless. 'Freema Mirrlees sent *you*?'

'Yes.'

She stared at him for a moment in silence. 'Mr Sims isn't here,' she finally said. This was presumably as much help as she was willing to give.

David took a step forward. He could feel the anger beginning to bubble up inside him, red and loud. This stupid cow didn't have a clue what was at stake. But even if he told her that Heaven was in mortal danger, she'd presumably still sit there with no expression on her Botoxed face.

'When?' he said in a menacingly calm voice. 'When can I see Mr Sims?'

Mrs Willenbrock took a long look at her computer screen, scrolling slowly through his appointments. 'In three weeks' time,' she finally said.

David lost it. 'Didn't you hear me, for Christ's sake? It's important!' He kicked the reception desk so hard that the silly cow's coffee slopped over.

'You...!' she burst out. She didn't get any further.

'Just shut up, or I'll—' He paused, leant over the reception desk and hit the flatscreen monitor with his fist. 'I have to see him – can't you understand that?'

Mrs Willenbrock thought again. 'He's out on urgent business,' she gasped. 'He went down to the car park five minutes ago. If you hurry, you might see his car.'

David glared at her. 'Call him!' he yelled, grabbing her by the arm and shaking her.

Her face was still completely expressionless, but David could see the panic in her eyes.

He left her and ran back to the lift, waiting for a torturous minute for the doors to open. He jumped in and went down all twenty-one floors. The doors finally opened and he sprinted through the entrance lobby, dodging the two security guys who were standing, feet apart, in his path, and raced through the doors and outside. The security men were now gawping at him.

David glanced left and right.

Over there!

A black limousine was pulling out of the underground garage. David didn't have the faintest idea whether it was Mr Sims' car, but it didn't matter. There was only one way to find out.

He threw himself in front of the car.

Angry hooting cut through the snowy silence, but the expensive brakes stopped the wheels, just as the manufacturer had promised.

The car stopped in front of David. A chauffeur lowered the window. 'Get off the road, you dosser!' he barked.

David got to his feet. 'Is this Mr Juno Sims' car?' he asked breathlessly.

'Piss off, kiddo!'

'It's important! Tell him it's about Freema.' He tried to catch a glimpse of the inside of the car, to no avail. A blacked-out glass partition separated the back seat from the driver.

David heard shouts coming from behind him. He glanced hastily over his shoulder. *Damn!* The two security men were running through the glass door, their hands reaching for their belts. David rolled his eyes. Wannabe sheriffs were all he needed.

'It's about Freema Mirrlees,' he yelled, leaning slightly towards the door, ignoring the apoplectic chauffeur. This was the only chance that the passenger in the back seat might hear something. 'Freema's in trouble,' he yelled. 'You have to help her…'

The glass partition was lowered with a whirring sound. A sparse-haired man was sitting in the back, looking curiously at David. His lean face looked hard, but he had the brightest blue eyes that David had ever seen. It was hard to tell how old he was, but he was clearly the same man who David had seen on the internet video. 'Freema Mirrlees?' he asked. His voice sounded as British as the Ten O'Clock News theme music.

David nodded. 'Are you Mr Sims?'

'Did Freema send you?'

'Yes.'

'Get in, young man.'

The door opened.

'Thanks.'

The security men stopped by the car, unsure of what to do. The chauffeur made an angry gesture and they exchanged looks, evidently disappointed not to have had a go at David.

David sank back into the expensive leather seat and a moment later the car was purring away so smoothly that he hardly noticed it. He couldn't hear the engine; his panting was the only sound that broke the silence.

Mr Sims, who was wearing a dark suit, leant forward and took two glasses from the mini-bar directly in front of his seat.

'A drink?'

'Water, thanks!' said David, still out of breath.

Mr Sims reached for a bottle, opened it, poured water into a glass, and handed it to David.

'My name is Juno Sims,' he said, shaking David's hand. 'I've been trying to get in touch with Freema for a while now. Especially because I heard the news about Mr Jones. I'm very concerned, I must say.'

It took David a moment to realise that Heaven's guardian was talking about Mr Mickey in Richmond.

'David,' David merely replied.

'No surname?' said Mr Sims.

'No.'

The car glided through the streets between the high-rise buildings. David took a sip of water. His throat felt like cardboard.

'Why are you here?' Mr Sims eyed him sharply.

David hesitated. Mr Sims didn't look as if he would believe him for a minute, even if he had substantial facts to back up his story. He was just the type of man who was persuaded only by money and figures. But he had to try, even if in vain.

'Forget about wherever you were going,' David said quickly. 'Freema's been abducted.'

Mr Sims raised an eyebrow.

David took another sip, then told him about Mr Drood, the houseboat, the attack. He left the raggedy man out, along with what had happened to Heaven on the roof.

Mr Sims listened silently as the limousine pushed its way through the traffic in Whitechapel. It seemed to David, though, as if he had turned distinctly paler.

'Freema is rich,' he said thoughtfully once David had finished. 'Richer, perhaps, than she knows. Her father and I made Sims Enterprises what it is today. Did you know that the girl is worth millions? That shouldn't be underestimated in an era of economic crisis.'

David stared at him. What was the guy on about? Hadn't he been listening?

'Freema's been abducted, for God's sake!' he yelled. 'And you're worrying about her money? Didn't you just say she was worth millions? Then do something! Find her! It's nothing to do with money, is it?'

Mr Sims looked at his reflection in the window. 'No, strictly speaking, it isn't. You're quite right.' He reached for his Blackberry and dialled a number. Waited.

The radio newsreader was just announcing that a corpse that had recently been stolen from St Paul's graveyard had been found on a park bench at the foot of Westminster Bridge.

David immediately thought of the raggedy man.

The phone was ringing.

Then someone answered and said something. Mr Sims just nodded and looked at David earnestly. Then he finished the call and said: 'That was Mr Scrooge. I think he knows you.'

David stared at him. He felt as if he'd had an electric shock.

'Mr Scrooge or Mr Drood or Mr Heep,' Mr Sims continued. 'He loves changing his name.' Mr Sims smiled benevolently. 'You're surprised, aren't you? Well, you can get out now, or you can carry on listening. It's up to you. Nobody's going to force you to do anything.'

'Tell me,' David simply said. 'I'm listening.'

What choice did he have?

'You love Freema?' It wasn't even a proper question.

'That's nothing to do with you,' David replied shortly.

Mr Sims nodded, satisfied. 'So you do.'

'What do you want from me?' David looked outside.

The tower with its illuminated spires glided by to their right. They were heading across Tower Bridge towards Southwark.

'I want you to listen to me.'

'That's it?'

'It's more than you think,' he replied, sipping his water.

'Do I have any choice?'

'As I said, you can get out.' The bright blue eyes sparkled. 'Whenever you like.'

''S'OK,' David growled.

Mr Sims put his glass back in the bar. 'I'm sure you have all sorts of questions for me.'

Indeed he did. 'You know Mr Scrooge?'

'Yes.'

'So you're the client he was talking about.'

'That wasn't a question, was it?'

'No.'

'Mr Scrooge works for me. I've known him for a long time. Him and his many names.' He leant across to David and whispered: 'But what do names matter?'

What the hell was all this about? Small talk? 'You stole her heart,' said David.

'Yes.' Mr Sims turned serious. 'I, unfortunately, don't have one of my own,' he said. 'That's why I need the services of Mr Drood. Every three to four years he sets off on the hunt for a healthy heart.' He leant forwards.

David stared at him. 'You...bastard.'

'Don't judge what you don't know,' Mr Sims replied mildly.

'You've killed people.'

'Yes.'

'Don't you feel any remorse?'

'Would that change anything?' Mr Sims shook his head. 'No,' he answered his own question. 'It wouldn't. I feel no remorse for anything that I've done.'

'Did you kill Jonathan Mirrlees? Were you behind his accident?'

'No!' He sounded indignant. 'Jonathan was a good friend. The best!'

David could feel his whole body tensing up. He turned his glass to and fro in his hand, absurdly enough thinking about Kelly. Then about what Mr Merryweather had said to them. Was this the day when he would be forced to realise that it would have been better never to have loved? Was this the day that he was going to lose Heaven?

The lights of Tower Bridge disappeared behind them.

'But Mr Mickey – you had him killed. Heaven loved him.'

Mr Sims nodded. 'Yes, I'm afraid that's true,' he

said sadly. 'But he could have made it easier for himself. All he had to do was keep hold of you in Richmond yesterday; I'd have taken it from there. Everything would have worked out nicely.' He sighed. 'But Mr Jones made a mistake. He let you go.' He rubbed the bridge of his nose, which was long and thin. 'Jones had this fixed idea from Jonathan. He thought that nobody should be allowed to tie Freema down.'

'You're utterly evil.' David couldn't think of another word for it.

'Who isn't? But I'm trying to do a bit of good.'

David laughed bitterly. As if giving money to a couple of welfare programmes could compensate for taking other people's lives.

'Why?' he asked. 'Why all this?'

Mr Sims regarded the brightly lit city. 'Have you ever looked up at the stars and asked yourself what wonders might be hidden up there?' His bright eyes began to glitter. 'There are worlds so full of beauty that it almost kills you to have to remember them.' A deep sadness had entered his voice. 'Do you know how it feels to leave your home?'

David didn't reply.

'Imagine a world that you can't imagine,' said Mr Sims. 'A place where poets live, and every day brings some new miracle, full of beauty.' His blue eyes lit up dreamily, only to be dulled by the intrusion of dark memories. 'A world like this can be destroyed too. It's always the same. In their striving for power and their rage to destroy all that is beautiful, many creatures are very similar to humans.' He made a dismissive gesture. 'But none of that really matters. No: the only thing that matters is that the place I once called home was destroyed in a war. You'd see it if it were still there. You could have seen it with a decent telescope when it was still full of light.' He sighed. 'Everything that once lived there was turned to stone and hurled out into the infinite reaches of the galaxy.' His eyes sought David's. 'I was so young when I was driven out. I was hurt.' His eyes were now fixed on that place that had long since ceased to exist. 'A gigantic lump of stone, in full flight. Yes, just imagine it. I approached the earth in a blaze of light. I plummeted downwards.' He frowned, suddenly looking ancient. 'I was falling, I can still remember that, and I tried desperately to cling on to a scrap of sky. I could feel pain, something was tearing in the sky, and it plunged to earth with me.'

'You were the comet?' David wondered whether it could possibly be true.

'I was the comet.'

'Quite a difference: you then, you now!'

Mr Sims gave him an impatient look. 'I woke up over in Hammersmith,' he said. 'In this body. As a human who was no longer young, but wasn't yet old.' He laughed, as if he'd made a splendid joke. 'Everything that falls to earth, you have to understand, turns into something living.'

David remembered the shooting star that had plummeted down over Bloomsbury. For a moment he had imagined seeing it turn into a bird that had spread its wings and flown off in the direction of Marylebone. Could it be that his eyes hadn't been deceiving him at all? 'You're really telling me that you were a comet?'

'Is that so absurd?' He was being completely serious. 'I dragged a piece of the night sky down with me. I didn't do it on purpose; it just happened.'

This was the part of the story that David thought he might already be vaguely aware of. He couldn't help thinking of the exotic bird in the ivy. And the shooting stars that appeared over London every once in a while.

'I guessed that the night sky must also be wandering round London in a new form. But how was I supposed to find it?'

'Why should you have needed to find it?'

'The night sky that fell to earth had a heart. And I felt weak because my heart was missing, and no living creature can exist without a heart.' His face clouded over. 'So I took a human heart. It belonged to a young man who was on his way home with his girlfriend. I killed them, ripped his heart out with my bare hands, and made it my own.'

David didn't want to hear any more.

'Only then did I begin to live. I created an existence for myself. Comets are highly skilled liars. And London is a place where anything is possible. Getting a false ID has never been a problem; nor has making up whatever CV I like. Oh, everything is so easy here. I started to work. Took someone else's identity.'

'You're not Juno Sims?'

He shook his head. 'Juno Sims died a long time ago. And I brought him back to life. It's the same old story. So in a way I am Juno Sims.'

'But why?'

'Why?' He laughed. 'Because I wanted to live. Life, David, is such a wonderful thing. It helped me to accept that this world would be my home from now on. There are so many crazy things here that I didn't know about. Seasons, sushi, butterflies, *EastEnders*, *Torchwood*.'

David was speechless.

The car turned into St Thomas street.

'I lived my life like the other people around me. I'd given up searching for the fairy.'

'Which fairy?'

He laughed. 'When a piece of sky falls to earth, it turns into a fairy. Everyone knows that. All sorts of things that fall to earth from up above turn into magical creatures. But not all of them can return.'

David thought about the magical creatures that he knew from books and films: vampires, werewolves, demons, fairy tale figures – could they really have quite different origins from those that people had been imagining for centuries?

Mr Sims continued. 'But one November night, precisely that happened: a little bit of the night sky suddenly returned above London. That was the day when everything changed for me.'

David remembered Heaven's birthday, and let him carry on. He suddenly felt very sleepy. It must be the adrenaline. It was all too much. The stories about fairies and immortals, about heaven and earth.

'At that moment I knew,' Mr Sims continued, 'that the night sky that had fallen to earth because of me, had returned home. The fairy, whom I'd never found, had died.'

'How did you find out?'

'It was obvious. It was all over the papers and in the news. Of course,' he laughed contemptuously, 'nobody knew why it had happened. All they could see was that the emptiness in the sky was still there, but smaller.' He nodded pleasantly at David. 'What they saw as a problem was actually an opportunity for me. The fact that a part of the sky had returned could only mean that the fairy had left part of her heart behind somewhere on earth. And that meant…' – he paused for a moment – '…that she had had a child with a human.' He smiled, as if that were the solution to all his problems. And that's precisely what it was, David realised. It made sense; it made terrible sense. The comet had spent its whole time on earth searching for River Mirrlees the fairy, without ever tracking her down.

'I used all my contacts to find out who had died on the relevant night. And it had to be someone who had had a baby. That was all I had to go on.' He scrutinised David, as if to ensure that he was still listening. 'I discovered that a certain Jonathan Mirrlees had married a woman called River. Nobody knew where she had come from. She was a mystery and, moreover, beautiful and dark, like a fairy from the deepest night. It all fitted: River had died that particular night. There was just one thing that didn't add up: all the test results for her child, a girl, were normal. She had an ordinary heart, and that was that. Just an ordinary heart, not a heavenly one.'

'How did you know? How can you test for that kind of thing?'

'A heavenly heart is cold because the world that the sky lives in is likewise cold.'

'And her heart?'

'Was a human heart,' he said, 'full of warmth and all the other things that are in human hearts.'

'But you kept watch on her all the same.'

Juno Sims nodded. 'I wanted to be on the safe side. I quickly gained Jonathan's trust. It was a year after River's death, and lonely people are desperate for someone to trust.'

'You joined the firm.'

He laughed. 'Of course.'

David suddenly saw what had happened. Heaven had talked about tests, about an alleged heart defect when she was a child. Mr Sims must have been behind all that. He had probably bribed the doctors to say that the tests were necessary.

Mr Sims looked out of the window. 'Time passed. The faster the years flew by, the more convinced I was that River Mirrlees hadn't been a fairy after all. Her daughter was a completely ordinary girl.'

'Who told you?'

'That Freema had a heavenly heart?'

'Yes.'

'Nobody told me.' He seemed to find the idea amusing. 'I found it out two days ago by accident. Mr Drood has kept on providing me with new hearts ever since I arrived in London. He doesn't know why I need them. He doesn't know who I really am. Mr Drood isn't someone who asks questions. He's lived in this city for a long time, and if London teaches you one thing, it's that you don't ask questions if someone is paying you a lot of money to do a particular job.'

David came out in goosebumps at the thought of Heaven being in the clutches of the black-gloved man. The idea of it robbed him of all his energy, sapped his strength, made everything swim before his eyes. But one thought managed to penetrate the dense fog of fear and worry. He turned to the window and stared up into the sky, up at the gleaming emptiness, and breathed a sigh of relief. If Mr Sims was telling the truth, then Heaven was still alive. Her mother's heart was still beating inside her.

Mr Sims ignored him. 'Every three to five years,' he continued, 'Mr Drood went out hunting for me.

With the help of a corpse, he went searching for healthy hearts. Corpses are best at sniffing out this kind of thing. They can only smell fresh goods.' He looked thoughtful. 'But then...' He paused, watching dingy London Bridge station looming up on their right like a ghost in the snowstorm. 'Then the unthinkable happened.' His bright blue eyes sparkled. 'Mr Drood's walking corpse finds a new heart. They follow the girl as far as Phillimore Place and cut it out of her body, as they've done countless times before. But then the girl gets up and runs away. Without her heart.'

'So you knew you'd found her heavenly heart.'

'No.' He shrugged. 'All I knew was that I had found someone who was so unusual that they could only have fallen from the sky. But I had no idea who it was, because the girl had escaped. Then Mr Drood called her by the name that he'd picked up in town: Heaven.' He nodded meaningfully. 'And then of course I knew who it was. That's what Jonathan Mirrlees had always called his daughter.'

The car turned into Borough High Street and continued towards Waterloo.

'I sent Mr Drood and the corpse to Richmond, but Heaven didn't live there any more. She had obviously retreated into town somewhere that nobody knew about. I paid Mr Jones a visit, but he claimed not to know where Heaven was. She didn't turn up at the college the next morning either. I was running out of time. I had to find her, and not just for my own sake.'

David grimaced. 'Oh no?' he said sarcastically.

'She only has the cold heart of the heavens. The heart of a fairy, if you like. But she will die and return to the sky if she doesn't get her normal heart back.'

'So what about this human heart of hers?'

Mr Sims gestured to his chest. 'It's beating in me. Mr Drood gave it to me.'

David felt sick. For a moment, he thought he might throw up on the expensive leather upholstery. Maybe that would be the best thing. To puke on this sicko's feet.

'When I realised that she would die, I had to act quicky.' Mr Sims glanced at David. 'That's why you're here. You need to do me a favour.'

'You're not bothered about Heaven,' David said tonelessly. 'All you want is her second heart.'

Mr Sims nodded. 'Absolutely. When I get her heart, I can return to my world. I can become a part of the night sky up there above London. I'll be able to do what normally only fairies can do.'

David's head felt light, weightless, like cotton wool.

He had a vague feeling that Mr Sims had left something out of his story. The really crucial question was this:

'Why are you telling me this?'

'You want to see Heaven again? Then you'll have to come with me. And, what's more, I have a job for you. You have to do something very important.'

'Like hell I will.'

'Are you so sure?'

'Why should I do anything for you?'

He smiled and leant back. 'Because Mr Scrooge is waiting for us at our destination.' He looked David straight in the eye. 'And Mr Scrooge is the only one with the antidote.'

David's throat suddenly felt tight. 'Antidote? To what...?'

'To the poison that you've just been drinking.'

David turned the glass around in his hand, stared into it. There were remnants of white powder at the bottom.

'You...'

Mr Sims couldn't help grinning. 'That's not the poison,' he said. 'The poison doesn't leave any residue.'

David looked at him in horror.

'The white powder is a sedative.'

'I...'

The colours were becoming wilder. Everything was swimming around. David saw the partition between them and the chauffeur being lowered. He heard the man telling Mr Sims that they were nearly there. He stared out of the window and saw something incredibly large heading for him. Then his head fell backwards onto the upholstery. He shut his eyes, drifting into nothingness. The last thing he was aware of was a gentle swaying and the smell of the nearby Thames.

CHAPTER 17

David Pettyfer was standing high above the rooftops of London, higher than ever before. Far below him, on the other side of the river, Big Ben, the Houses of Parliament and Westminster Bridge looked like finely wrought structures in a miniature landscape. The whole of London appeared tiny, from Southwark to the horizon. The nothingness above stretched out across the sky like a torn tent. Its centre over the city spanned the area southwards right into Southwark and over to the fringes of the South Bank, further northwards to Spitalfields, and across to Soho.

Snowflakes were whirling madly through the air. The whole city looked as if it were caught in a snow-globe.

David pressed his hands against the thick glass surrounding him. Far below him was the black limousine that he'd been travelling in. He had no idea how he had come to be inside this pod. But here he was. The pod was large and sealed. In the middle was a large wooden bench. Warm air was was being puffed in by an air-conditioning system, accompanied by a soft humming that sounded like a hive of bees and made the floor vibrate.

David was alone.

And it didn't take him long to work out that he was trapped in one of those places from which there was little chance to escape. Down below were the Jubilee Gardens, at the western end of which the London Eye had been built several years ago. One of the biggest Ferris wheels in the world: a monster, a one hundred and thirty-five metre high technical miracle of steel and wire and glass. Thirty-two pods carrying more than twenty passengers apiece, each pod representing one of the London boroughs.

The metal struts, white and elegant, made the London Eye look like the spoked wheel of a giant bicycle. The big passenger pods, hanging from the wheel like eggs, were entirely made of glass so that people could look out in all directions.

That's where they had taken David. To judge by the height and the speed, he must have been here for at least fifteen minutes. He had woken up on the floor.

He stared through the glass. *What now?*

It wasn't the first time he'd asked himself this

question. This question and others besides. What had happened to Mr Sims, and what was this all about? A glance at Big Ben, which looked tiny from up there, was enough to reassure him on at least one count. Not much time had passed, so he couldn't have been unconscious for very long. But it was the business with the antidote that really bothered him.

The other pods were empty, so far as he could see. Bright LED lights lit up the whole of the wheel, twinkling like living creatures. Had they closed it for a night? Had Mr Sims pulled strings with some of his contacts to make sure he could do whatever he wanted?

David cursed. What on earth was going on? Why was he here? He thought about Heaven and the story that Mr Sims had dished up.

The wheel was turning. Slowly. So horribly slowly.

He clenched his fists angrily. It was precisely this slowness that made his prison so unbearable; the absolute certainty that he was trapped here until the pod made its way back to the ground.

The pod had reached the top and was already on its way down when David suddenly realised that the fourth pod behind – or rather above – him was occupied. He screwed up his eyes and stared at the three silhouettes that stood out from the deep black London night.

One of them was tall and slender. Wild hair framed the small face. And as the figure went over to the glass window, he almost let out a cry of delight.

Heaven!

She was in the pod. No doubt about it. She was up there in the brightly lit space. But she wasn't alone. Two men were with her; he could clearly make them out. Mr Sims and Mr Drood. David could see exactly what they were doing.

Heaven, at any rate, didn't look weak now. She was standing by the window, frightened but fine.

She nervously glanced from one man to the other. Then she looked down and saw David.

Her face lit up for a moment, then she looked simultaneously horrified. David could tell by the way she gave a start.

Mr Sims nodded at her. He was holding something. David thought he could see the men's breath making little clouds on the glass. They had presumably switched the climate control to cold.

Mr Sims was holding the thing up in the air. From a distance it looked like a remote control. Then there was a sudden crackling in the loudspeakers that were set into the walls. David could hear the voices of the people in the other pod, loud and clear. They were talking about fairies. And a heart. Over and over again: the heart.

'Heaven?' he cried, banging on the glass with his fists.

She didn't reply.

Instead, he saw Mr Sims move next to her by the window and point to something on David's pod – something that must be up on the roof.

Her hand went to her mouth. Mr Sims now pointed, smiling, at the remote control.

'What are you going to do to him?' Heaven's angry voice suddenly came through the loudspeaker as clearly as if she were standing next to him.

David screwed up his eyes. What had made her so furious?

Mr Sims was trying to make eye contact with David. He knew that David could hear him. And he also knew that none of them could hear David.

'Can't you imagine?' he asked Heaven.

'I'm not going to.'

'Well then,' murmured Mr Sims, 'I'd like to show you something that might make you change your mind.'

There was a bang. David jumped. What was that? It had sounded like a small explosion, directly above him. The sound of bursting metal ripped through the silence. It came from the place where the pod was connected to the big spoked wheel.

David's pod started to wobble. Metal squealed on glass, high and shrill, noises that didn't sound at all good. The pod began to sway uncertainly – something that wasn't really possible, given that it was supposed to be fixed firmly to the wheel.

'Christ, what's happening!' David yelled.

Heaven's desperate eyes met his across a hundred-metre gulf. He'd long since stopped worrying about the antidote.

'It's your choice,' said Mr Sims.

'No.' She was pleading.

'I'm sorry to have to resort to such methods.'

A second explosion jolted David's pod. Another bursting sound, this time from a different place. The pod rocked again in a way that was anything but reassuring. In front of the window, a big fat bolt fell downwards into the blackness.

David was having to hold on with both hands in order not to fall. He had no desire to see where the bolt had gone. It would drop into the Thames. It was more interesting to wonder where the bolt had been before.

'What—'

He didn't get to finish.

'Free will,' Mr Sims was intoning through the loudspeaker. 'You have to give it to me of your own free will.'

Heaven took a step away from him. She shook her head defiantly. David could see it clearly.

'No,' she said.

That was the moment that David began to understand what was going on. It occurred to him that Mr Sims seemed to be very good at coming up with plans that were both simple and effective.

Why hadn't he worked it out sooner? Mr Sims needed the cold heart of a fairy in order to return to the sky. But for some reason that David didn't understand, and which he didn't care about anyway, Heaven had to give him the heart of her own free will. That was why he had to have someone bring her to him. That's why he'd needed her alive. And that's why he needed David too.

David had been the bait.

'If you want him to live,' the voice in the loudspeaker said, 'then you'll do it.'

David banged on the glass. 'Bollocks,' he said aloud. 'Complete and utter bollocks!'

Heaven looked at him.

His lips formed one word alone: NO!

Unmistakable.

He heard Heaven's voice, crackling with static. 'He understands me.' She turned briefly to Mr Sims. 'David?' She went closer to the window and looked at him with her big eyes.

Mr Sims merely watched her.

'Why are you doing this?' she shouted at him. Then she looked across at David again and said his name, nothing else.

David was yelling with sheer anger. He wanted to run up and down to vent his rage and helplessness, but he didn't dare move in the damaged pod. The floor was slanting dangerously.

'If you kill David,' he heard Heaven saying, 'then you'll never get the heart.'

'Those two houseboat hippies, Eve and Julian – they'll be next.' That was Mr Drood, Mr Heep or Mr Scrooge or whatever he called himself.

'You bastard.'

David took two steps back. He had to think. There was always a way out. You just had to find it.

He forced himself to take a couple of deep breaths until he felt the panic diminishing slightly. Then he looked around. Up on the roof of the pod was a hatch; presumably the emergency exit. David had no idea whether he could open it, but it was worth a try. He stood on the wooden bench, stretched, grasped the lever set into the ceiling. He pulled it downwards and the trapdoor unlocked with a click.

David ignored the signs warning him against improper use of the hatch. *For Emergency Use Only*.

'Emergency,' David murmured aloud, just because he felt the need. 'Dire emergency.'

He opened the hatch slightly. Icy cold wind immediately streamed into the pod. Snowflakes blew into his face.

It was windy out there. Stormy, to be more precise.

David jumped down from the bench and moved carefully back to the glass frontage.

Heaven was still defying the two men. David estimated how far it was to the pod above him and got back onto the bench.

This time he pulled himself up by his arms, squeezed through the narrow hatch, and lay there for a moment on the roof of the pod, flat on his stomach.

The wind was powerful and vicious. One false move and he would go plunging down a good hundred metres. If he was lucky, he'd drop straight into the Thames; if he wasn't so lucky, he'd hit the tarmac. Then he wouldn't need an ambulance – he'd need a street cleaner.

It was so high up.

David remembered how much he loved the rooftops of London. Child's play compared to this. Leaving aside the fact that it was the middle of the night, which didn't make things any easier.

Over in the other pod, Mr Sims saw what he was up to. And David saw that Mr Sims had seen.

Mr Sims was first to react. He gave Mr Drood an instruction. Four pods above David, the emergency hatch opened up and Mr Drood clambered onto the roof of the elliptical contraption, jumped onto the ironwork of the wheel, and started working his way forwards. He looked grotesque with his conservative suit and his neatly parted hair, which sat ill with his predatory eyes and the curved knife that he held between his gleaming white teeth.

He was moving quickly, horribly quickly.

OK, this was going to make it harder. But what had he expected?

David looked around.

He was still lying on his stomach. It was freezing cold up there. If he waited any longer, his muscles would be too stiff for what he had in mind.

He stood up cautiously and, with both hands, grabbed a steel bar that was right in front of him.

The struts didn't give him much room to manoeuvre. Every time he moved, the capsule swayed. He glanced quickly at the large hinges that attached the pod to the big wheel. They had been wrecked, or at any rate were now supporting a load that they wouldn't be able to bear for much longer. Black packages were stuck on in several places.

Explosives.

David glanced ahead to where Mr Drood was approaching. There was only one possible route – and that was the route that meant passing Mr Drood.

He cautiously proceeded one step at a time, being careful not to look down. He used everything he had learnt on the rooftops: move with the wind and get your balance, even though it chills you and tugs at your clothes.

He worked his way along several struts, supporting himself on the huge bolts that stuck out of the metal frame every now and then. The surfaces of the wheel were smoother and more slippery than any moss-covered roof tiles that he'd ever clambered across. And then the constant slow turning motion made it hard to steady himself.

David stretched out his arms. He had to strike the right balance against the effects of the wind and the vibrations of the wheel, or he'd go plunging straight into the abyss.

He waited for a gust of wind, then balanced his way further forward.

OK, now for the next strut. He took a deep breath – but just at that moment, the wheel gave an unexpected jolt and he lost his grip.

Shit, he thought. And fell.

He milled his arms around, and in some corner of his brain he was aware that his last ever thought had been 'Shit'. Then he felt something metal against the tips of his fingers, and his fingers instinctively gripped it. His other hand reached out to grasp whatever his first hand had found.

David gasped. His breath was icy mist in the air.

He didn't want to look down, but did it all the same. His red Converse were dangling above a chasm that would certainly do him no favours. Pain was dragging at his arms, whispering to him to let go, to let himself fall, to give up.

'No!'

David's yell echoed through the night. He was swaying to and fro, dangling, trying to reach one of the struts with his foot.

Christ, where was the bloody thing?

He finally managed to hook one of his legs over. He twisted his body so that he could feel the rotation of the wheel. He groaned loudly; every single muscle in his arms and legs hurt, and the cold was just about finishing him off. But no matter. He was still alive.

OK. Onwards. He glanced quickly ahead of him. Mr Drood was getting closer. He clearly had the advantage. While David was having to climb upwards, it was all downwards for Mr Drood. All he had to do was let himself drop down bit by bit, which meant he was gaining on David far too quickly.

David clambered on. The skin on his palms was torn, and he could feel his fingers knotting up more and more on the freezing cold struts. He had no idea what he would actually do if he reached Mr Drood. All he knew was that he couldn't carry on much longer. He was pretty much finished.

This was Mr Drood's moment, and all of a sudden he was right there above him.

He had jumped the last bit, closing the final gap between them by letting himself drop down. He landed surefooted on a strut close to David – and then a black leather-clad hand grabbed David's arm and forced him up against the strut right next to him. David rammed his elbow as hard as he could into Mr Drood's stomach, simultaneously shifting his weight to one side, but to no avail. He couldn't shake off the black-gloved man.

David felt a hefty kick in his stomach. He groaned.

'Why put yourself to all this trouble, boy?' said the purring voice that David would now recognise anywhere. 'Don't you realise that we'll easily find other people who are close to her heart?' Mr Drood smiled at him.

All David could think was: *Shit, who is this guy?* and then it dawned on him that Mr Drood had just said something – which had to mean that he was no longer holding the knife between his teeth, but in his hand.

Something silver flashed before David's eyes. He dodged between the struts, leant backwards – and avoided the blade by a hair's breadth. He reached for an icy piece of steel, lost his grip, and fell. His back crashed into an iron mesh that threw him to the right, where he clung with both arms to a mast sticking out beyond the struts.

Mr Drood was looking down at him. His smile was as pleasant as ever. Then he came nearer.

David gasped for breath and glanced down.

His pod was just three metres beneath him. He had barely climbed out of it, but it felt as if he'd climbed Mount Everest.

Eighty metres further below was the Thames.

Mr Drood dropped down again. This time he hit David with his full weight. They both clattered into a couple of cables. A wave of cold air grabbed David and slammed him against a strut. He gave a yell of pain.

Mr Drood hit him hard in the face, and David tumbled backwards. Out of the corner of his eye, he could see the blade flashing. He leant back and felt something cut his throat. He instinctively put his hand up to the burning cut, letting go of the strut.

That was it. He had lost his grip. In that millisecond before he plunged into the chasm, he thought – *No, no, that can't be it, not without defeating that bastard* – and then his numb fingers found Mr Drood's waistband.

For a fraction of a second he held it tightly, pulling at it, until Mr Drood also lost his balance and fell, dragging David into the abyss with him.

David waved his arms around wildly, his hands searching for something to grab onto. In vain. *So this is how it feels to die*, he thought.

And then he thought of Heaven, more intensely than he'd ever thought of another human. He remembered her laugh, how she'd slept in his clothes in that freezing cold bedroom, how she'd talked in her sleep, how dishevelled she looked in the morning. He thought of all the moments which would be lost forever if it all ended now in the way it had to end. Everything would...

No!

He could feel something.

As he was falling.

Something grabbed hold of David, something cold and dauntless, something that wasn't the icy wind.

It felt as if something were lifting him up. It was like flying, but different. It all happened so quickly that he didn't know whether it had really happened at all.

He was floating, yes, that's how it felt, he was floating briefly – then he banged hard into some struts. Blood was pouring from his nose, but no matter. He wasn't going to die. Not yet, at any rate.

Mr Drood carried on falling, plunging into the depths, until his black glove managed to catch hold of a spar. With a degree of strength that seemed utterly inhuman, he clung on, using the momentum to drop down onto the nearest pod. Only a moment later did David realise that it was the pod with the open hatch that he had left a couple of minutes ago.

An explosion ripped through the night. Mr Drood looked confused. What was left of the fastenings holding the pod in place finally burst apart.

In slow motion, David saw Mr Drood standing on the roof of the pod, which was detaching itself from the wheel more quickly than he would ever have thought possible. It tipped to one side, then snapped off. Only once the pod started rolling, plunging downwards, still rotating even as it fell, did Mr Drood – who had long since lost his footing on the roof – start to scream. The wind swallowed his scream until there was nothing left but the impact, far below in the waters of the Thames; a fountain of dirty water, washed away like a nightmare at daybreak.

David gasped. He was clinging to the strut that the unknown force had slammed him against, trying to regain his strength. He didn't know how long he had been poised there before he finally gathered himself and clambered onwards.

His limbs were stiff; his legs and hands were trembling. Every movement of the wheel, which was still slowly turning, sent a jolt of pain through his body;

but he carried on doggedly, not stopping until he finally reached Heaven's pod.

Mr Sims, who was still calmly holding the detonator, didn't take his eyes off him. David had no idea what he was going to do next.

Somehow, Heaven had managed to climb out onto the roof of her pod, and was waiting for him. She stretched out her hand, even colder than his, and together they fell through the hatch and landed inside.

David struggled up. 'Heaven,' he gasped. 'You…' She pulled him to her, and they kissed. Everything about her was cold, but so familiar. They kissed again, deeply and firmly, as if it was their last ever.

'Was it you?' he finally asked. 'Did you…me… down there…?'

She nodded. 'Don't ask me how I did it.'

'You don't know?'

'I was terrified for you. That was all.'

His reflection was swimming in her eyes.

'That's what fairies do,' they heard Mr Sims saying. His hair was standing on end like tall grey grass. He looked much older than before.

'I'm not a fairy,' said Heaven.

'Your mother was.' Mr Sims seemed exhausted. 'And she gave part of her heart to you.'

'I'm just Heaven,' she said, adding meekly: 'Freema.'

'Everything that falls to earth turns into a magical creature,' said Mr Sims. 'That's the magic that connects all the worlds around us.' He smiled a tired smile. 'All over the world, there are holes in the sky that close up again at some point. It is just as it says in the old tales. Fairies are creatures who fell from on high and go back when dead to where they came from. But while they are on earth, they have the ability to help humans. That's the special thing about your heart.'

'I'm Heaven,' she whispered, as if her name were some kind of mantra.

David put himself between Heaven and Mr Sims. He didn't know what he was going to do next. Comets, he had learnt, liked to play tricks, and this one's shouldn't be underestimated.

'Leave us alone,' he said. 'It's all over. She won't give you what you want.'

Mr Sims looked at the detonator he was holding. 'Mr Drood is dead.' He threw the little black box onto the floor.

'What about the antidote?'

Mr Sims allowed himself a smile. 'There isn't any antidote.'

David turned pale.

'There isn't any poison,' Mr Sims, the comet, said. 'There never was any poison.'

Heaven, who seemed to understand what was going on, heaved a sigh of relief. David was too stunned to do anything. The pod carried on moving towards the ground, slowly, so slowly.

For a moment, there was silence.

'I imagine you're wondering what I'm going to do now.' Mr Sims was still completely calm as he looked down at London and said: 'So many lights. Life goes on, doesn't it?' Snow was falling like tiny dreams. 'There are stowaways everywhere, and that's what we are too.'

'What are you going to do?' asked David.

Mr Sims shrugged. 'Nothing,' he said. He sounded tired. He looked up at the sky. The deep black nothingness stretched from Kensington to Hampstead.

'You're giving up?' asked David.

He nodded. 'Yes,' he said tiredly. 'If that's what you want to call it. I give up.' His face was now lined with tiny wrinkles, and he suddenly didn't look superior and decisive, but infinitely sad.

'No,' said Heaven. She took a deep breath.

He looked at her. 'No?' he asked, raising an eyebrow.

'You don't have to give up,' she said calmly. 'You can have what you want. You can go home.' Heaven's firmness sounded like a kind of wisdom that nobody but she had ever recognised.

She moved towards Mr Sims. It only took David a moment to understand what was happening.

'What are you doing?' David could hear the panic in his voice.

She turned to him. 'Don't worry. I know what I'm doing.'

'Crap. You've got no idea. You haven't got the faintest idea.'

She shook her head. 'I can sense what I have to do. Just like before, when you were falling.' She looked at him with her dark eyes. 'This is what I have to do.' Then she shook her head. 'No: this is what I *want* to do.'

She stopped before Mr Sims and stretched out her arm. Then she put the palm of her hand on the place where her own heart was beating in his body.

Mr Sims looked at her. And if it were possible for the light of all faraway hopes to shimmer in the eyes of a comet, then that's what was happening now, high above the rooftops of London.

'If you help me,' he said, 'you'll become an

ordinary person. You'll die like an ordinary person. And you'll never be able to return to your mother.'

She nodded, her eyes swimming with tears.

'You've felt what you're capable of,' he said insistently, as if he still hoped to change her mind. 'You saved David because you wished for it. That's the magic that fairies can do. If you give me your heart, you'll lose all that.'

'I'm not a fairy.' She smiled. 'But I understand.'

A trail of glitter started to come from her hand, timidly at first, then more strongly. She moved her fingers. Crystals of ice were forming on her skin. Her breath turned to hoarfrost, and for a moment it seemed as if even her eyes were frozen lakes with miracles waiting to be discovered in their darkness.

Mr Sims opened his mouth, but no sound came out. A thin layer of ice suddenly covered his chest. It was spreading, creeping slowly up to his neck and wetting his eyes. His breath froze and something inside him started to glow dark red.

The glowing cracked the ice on Heaven's hand and arm. It crept deep inside her body, so suddenly melting all the ice that covered her that it seemed as if it must have been a dream. She was coughing out bright snowflakes which were drawn as if by a magnet towards the creature that had once been Mr Sims.

The iciness spread to the windows. Even the air conditioning was spitting out snowflakes.

Long, zigzag fissures were spreading across the window of the pod. The glass cracked like music that nobody was listening to.

David went over to Heaven and took her in his arms. She buried her face in his chest. Then the windows broke. Fine shards of glass rained down onto the floor of the pod.

Mr Sims was now transparent, like a block of ice. What had once been organs were shimmering glassily inside him. Everything within him was moving, rejoicing, because the icy air that was blowing their hair was a harbinger of his new home.

A light gust of wind caught him. And all the ice that had been Mr Juno Sims became a cloud of tiny, swirling crystals which were sucked from the pod and became one with the blustering snowstorm where they rose up, higher and higher.

Heaven detached herself from David.

'How did you do that?'

She didn't answer. There was no answer to give.

As the pod made its way back down, they could see

something glimmering in the sky. The higher it rose, the darker it became.

David could feel Heaven's hand in his. It was warm, as warm as her own heart which was now beating inside her. As real as the life that now lay ahead of her.

Just the blink of an eye away, the sky returned, and everything that had been dark and empty was restored to its former glory once again. After all those years, the night returned to London, as clear and true as it had been for so long in stories – but only in stories.

Heaven stared up at the sky like a child looking at a long-lost friend. 'We're all no more than stowaways,' she finally said, 'until we find someone who makes us see.' She laughed, then she cried. She put her arms round David's neck and he held her tight, and they both knew that this wasn't the end, but a new beginning. And as the capsule reached the ground, they stepped out into a life that finally belonged to them.

EPILOGUE

No story that begins like a fairy tale ever really ends. It carries on after the book shuts. David Pettyfer, who had travelled from Cardiff to London like a stowaway, knew how very true this could be.

He was walking with Heaven along the twisty path that wound its way up the hill through all the gravestones. Moss and ivy were buried beneath a fine coating of snow. The Egyptian-looking mausoleums with their figures and columns jutting from the walls housed memories that were still all too vivid. The wind was scraping the bare branches against the gravestones. Occasional lanterns tried to defy the shadows.

'Did you ever think it would end like this?' asked Heaven. David put his arm round her. He was thinking about what lay behind them.

Highgate Cemetery.

They had buried Mr Mickey there. Not even a week ago. Heaven talked about him every day, telling stories about him.

Julian and Eve hadn't come to the funeral because Julian was still in hospital. David took a daily detour to Barts Hospital on his way from the bookshop to Little Venice, where he now lived. It's easy to get used to new things, and that's how it was for David: it felt to him as if he had only ever lived on that little boat, stuffed full of books and odds and ends.

In the days immediately following the strange events that had come to a head on the London Eye, David and Heaven went up every evening onto the roof of 18 Phillimore Place, where it had all begun. They stood there silently, watching the night sky. It had been discovered again at long last, because things that get lost sometimes find their true home in unexpected places.

If David woke up at night, his hand would gently creep under the T-shirt of the girl lying next to him. He would leave it there, feeling her heart beating, and would be lulled back to sleep by the melodious rhythm that now governed his life.

Heaven pulled him by the hand and he followed her along the narrow pathways edged by headless angels on high plinths, pale marble virgins and sculptures of watchful lions. The path took them into a little wood. The ground was white and everything was frozen. Silence lay all around them.

Miss Trodwood had been reluctant to let David move out. But she had agreed. She had even hugged him goodbye whilst reminding him that he would have to get up earlier now that he was living in Little Venice, so as not to be late for work. She had hugged Heaven too. Then she had put on her strict face. 'Don't you go getting into any kind of trouble,' she had said. They had given Miss Trodwood their word. And they – particularly David – fully intended to keep it.

Meanwhile Mr Merryweather had asked Miss Trodwood to find him another book. Life went on as if it had never stopped – and maybe paths crossed as a result that ought to have crossed far sooner.

The newspapers and the TV were full of investigations into the mystery of why the night sky had returned to London. Tabloid magazines tried to outdo one another's headlines, but neither experts nor mystics would ever find out what had happened.

'Some things,' Mr Merryweather had said, 'just have to remain in the dark.'

David and Heaven knew what he meant. They had returned to Richmond and had organised Mr Mickey's funeral. Heaven had discovered that he had relatives whom he'd never mentioned, but who turned up to pay their respects. And David had discovered that things are never quite as you expect, and that suspicions are often mere delusions that leave you with nothing but a guilty conscience.

Heaven was going to sell the house in Richmond as soon as she could find a buyer. That was the final shackle for her to shake off.

The disappearance of Mr Juno Sims rocked the world of finance. After only a few days, though, this mystery was just another headline that nobody could be bothered to read.

'Do you think he's happy?' Heaven asked, the day after the events at the London Eye.

David, who had never much cared for Mr Juno Sims, replied: 'I hope he is. Really.' He paused for a while before adding: 'Yes, I think he is.' They both looked up to where the intact sky stretched out above a world which housed magical creatures in hidden places. Even in Cardiff, perhaps; maybe there, too.

They had reached Heaven's parents' grave. It was as simple as ever, just a gravestone sticking out of the ground. It was covered with snow; they could only read the top part.

It had two names on it.

Jonathan Mirrlees and River Mirrlees.

Heaven stood by the grave, motionless.

'Hello, you two,' she whispered. She took a step closer and touched her mother's name. 'Hello, fairy.' She knew that her mother wasn't down there beneath the earth, but was living high above London. She knew most things in life were different from how they seemed.

David knelt down next to Heaven. He gently wiped the rest of the snow from the lower part of the gravestone. There was another name, freshly carved into the stone: Sarah Jane Cavendish.

He stood up, holding Heaven's hand.

'I love you,' he said into the silence. He kissed her as he always kissed her, as if it were for the last time. 'Heaven, my Heaven.' Then he pulled her away from all the strange things that represented death, sadness, the past – and led her back into the city that had found its lost sky. The place where life was waiting for them, wild and tumultuous and full of the magic that is pure reality.